Titles by Sofie Ryan

TeLLIng TaiLs

A SECOND CHANCE CAT MYSTERY

Sofie Ryan

BERKLEY PRIME CRIME
New York

BERKLEY PRIME CRIME
Published by Berkley
An imprint of Penguin Random House LLC
375 Hudson Street, New York, New York 10014

Copyright © 2017 by Darlene Ryan
Penguin Random House supports copyright. Copyright fuels creativity, encourages
diverse voices, promotes free speech, and creates a vibrant culture. Thank you for buying
an authorized edition of this book and for complying with copyright laws by not
reproducing, scanning, or distributing any part of it in any form without permission.
You are supporting writers and allowing Penguin Random House to continue to
publish books for every reader.

BERKLEY is a registered trademark and BERKLEY PRIME CRIME and the B colophon
are trademarks of Penguin Random House LLC.

ISBN: 9781101991206

First Edition: January 2017

Printed in the United States of America
5 7 9 10 8 6 4

Cover art by Mary Ann Lasher
Cover design Katie Anderson

Acknowledgments

Getting from an idea to a finished book takes the efforts of more than just me.

Thank you to my editor, Jessica Wade. Your hard work makes every book better. Thank you as well to Kim Lionetti and the staff at Bookends Literary Agency. You make my working life so much easier.

Thanks to Jesse for the information about foghorns and to Judy for explaining how a registrar's office works. Any errors are mine, not theirs.

And thank you to Patrick and Lauren who never complain when I'm talking to imaginary people.

Chapter 1

The last thing Rose Jackson saw before she was cold-cocked with a plastic sailboat fender was the body of Jeff Cameron being dragged across his kitchen floor. At least that was what she was telling everyone from her bed at Northeastern Medical Center.

Earlier that Wednesday evening, Elvis and I had been settled in the big chair in front of the bedroom TV. We'd watched part one of the *Gotta Dance* reunion special, and when the credits had begun to scroll across the screen, I'd intended to get up, but before I knew it I was caught up in the campy drama of *Restless Days*, the popular new nighttime soap that was turning out to be the hit of the summer television season. Elvis was sprawled across my lap and I didn't want to move him. At least that's what I told myself.

I tucked my feet up underneath me and reached for the big bowl of popcorn covered in Parmesan cheese that I'd made just before *Gotta Dance* began. It was empty.

I glanced down at the floor to see if any had spilled. No. "I guess we ate it all," I said to Elvis.

The cat lifted his head, looked at me through narrowed green eyes and made a soft murp.

I made a face at him. "Okay, I ate it all."

Satisfied that had been cleared up, he dropped his head on my lap again.

Elvis was the only one with whom I could share my secret addiction to *Gotta Dance*. Since he was a small black cat with a scar across his nose and not the King of Rock and Roll, he wasn't likely to say anything about how caught up I was in the must-see-TV celebrity dance show. Because I had two left feet myself, I knew if my brother Liam found out he'd laugh himself silly, not to mention wheedle that video of me doing the bird dance in middle school from Mom.

"Part two will be on in an hour and a half," I said, setting the empty popcorn bowl on the footstool. I reached over the side of the chair and picked up the small dish of cat crackers I'd brought in for Elvis. There were three left. The cat, it seemed, had paced himself a little better than I had.

I arranged the star-shaped treats in a row on my leg. He glanced at them, then looked at the TV, where the spinning mirror ball now filled the screen again in a promo for part two of the *Gotta Dance* reunion special. Finally, he focused his green eyes on me with a seemingly—to me—quizzical expression on his furry black face.

"Matt Lauer, Kevin Sorbo, Lee Child, Christian Kane and the cute guy with the beard from that cooking show Rose made us watch," I said, ticking off the names of the show's second-half participants on the fingers of my left hand.

Elvis cocked his head to one side as though he was trying to decide which celebrity he was going to root for. After a moment he made a soft "mrrr" sound as though he'd made up his mind. I picked up a cracker and held it out to him. He took it from me, wrinkling his whiskers in a thank-you.

My phone rang then. I glanced at the screen. It was Liz. Elizabeth Emmerson Kiley French was one of my grandmother's closest friends, and since Gram had been gone on what seemed like a never-ending honeymoon, Liz had been keeping an eye on me. Among other things, that meant she asked pointed questions about my mostly nonexistent love life and showed up with takeout when she thought I wasn't eating properly.

"Hi, Liz," I said. "What's up?"

"Rose is in the hospital," she said flatly. Liz wasn't the type of person to beat around the bush.

"What happened?" I asked, sitting upright in the chair. Elvis rolled over and turned to watch my face, as if somehow he sensed something was wrong. My stomach lurched as though I'd just swung way out over deep water on a rope swing and let go. Rose—who was also close friends with my grandmother—was like family to me. The thought of anything happening to her was something I didn't want to even consider.

"She's all right," Liz said, and I pictured her gesturing with one perfectly manicured hand. "Someone hit her over the head and knocked her out. I think that hard noggin of hers is what saved her."

I swallowed down the lump in my throat. "You're sure she's okay?"

I heard her exhale. "I promise," she said softly.

Elvis put his paws on my leg, his eyes locked on my face. He adored Rose, too. Without thinking about it, I began to stroke his fur. "What happened? Where was she? I thought she was here," I said.

"Here" was my house, a two-story restored Victorian from the 1860s within walking distance of downtown North Harbor. It was divided into three apartments. Elvis and I lived in the front, main-floor unit, Rose had recently taken over the small back apartment, and Gram—when she was home—lived upstairs. On paper it didn't sound like it should work, but so far it had.

"She wasn't mugged," Liz said. "Not exactly. Remember the man who came into the shop this afternoon and wanted to have those candlesticks delivered to his wife?"

I pressed the heel of my hand against my forehead. "Tell me she didn't do what I think she did." I owned a repurpose shop, Second Chance, with an eclectic selection of merchandise, much of it given new life—a second chance—in our work space. Rose worked part-time for me.

"Oh yes, she did. She went over to that cottage to deliver those candlesticks. And I have the damn things, by the way." I could hear the click of Liz's high heels. She was probably walking in a hospital corridor, I realized. "She gave in too easy, you know," she continued. "We should have known. Rose has a stubborn streak a mile wide, and before you start on about people in glass houses throwing stones, I'm going to remind you that I am not stubborn. I'm persistent, which is a completely different thing."

"Noted," I said. I wasn't going to argue over word choice. Liz was just as stubborn as Rose was, which meant their longtime friendship got contentious at times, but this wasn't the time to point that out. "I'm on my way," I said. "You're at Northeastern?"

"The ER. Just ask at the desk," she said. "I better get back. Alfred could probably use some moral support."

"Okay, I'll be there soon," I said.

Elvis had already jumped down from the chair and started for the living room. I turned off the TV and stood up. Liz had said Rose was all right. That was what mattered.

It took me only a couple of minutes to pull on a pair of jeans and grab my purse and keys. Elvis watched me from the top of his cat tower.

"I'm just going to make sure Rose is okay and I'll be back," I told him. He bobbed his head as though he were saying that was fine with him, and for all I knew maybe he had understood every word I'd said and that was exactly what he meant.

Northeastern Medical Center is a ninety-nine-bed full-service hospital with a trauma center just off the highway exit for North Harbor. It's one of the top-rated hospitals in the state of Maine. As I drove I realized I hadn't asked Liz how Rose had gotten from the cottage on the shoreline, where I was fairly certain she'd been assaulted, to the health center. Liz had mentioned Alfred, who was Rose's "gentleman friend," but she hadn't said anything about whether Rose's children—who didn't live in North Harbor—had been called.

Knowing Rose, I was pretty certain the answer to that was no; in fact, I was surprised Rose had called anyone at all.

Liz was right about Rose's stubbornness. I'd seen that dogged streak in action enough times. I should have known that just because she seemed to acquiesce when I asked her not to deliver those candlesticks, that didn't mean I'd won the battle.

Why had someone attacked Rose if it wasn't for the two silver candlesticks she had with her? They were antiques, made by S. Kirk & Son more than a century ago. Kirk had learned the silversmith trade in Philadelphia and then opened a shop in Baltimore. His work was exquisite and in demand by collectors all over the United States and beyond. Finding them for the store had been nothing short of serendipity.

I'd gone to an auction up in Bangor and at the end of the day bid on the contents of a sealed cardboard box. It wasn't the kind of thing I ever did, but I'd been with my best friend, Jess, who had encouraged me after two other boxes had gone for twenty-five and thirty-two dollars, respectively.

"Go for it. What do you have to lose?" she'd whispered in my ear.

"I could lose thirty-two dollars," I'd hissed back at her.

"So bid less," Jess had retorted, and before I'd really thought about it, I'd raised my hand and nodded in the direction of the auctioneer. I'd ended up getting the box for twenty-seven dollars. Inside I'd found a selection of ladies' vintage gloves, which Jess had happily taken, a Brambly Hedge full-size teapot, several hand-crocheted dish towels and the badly tarnished candleholders. It was an auction jackpot. Rose had washed and blocked the dish towels and they'd sold in the shop for enough to cover the twenty-seven dollars I'd paid for the box.

"Are you going to say 'I told you so'?" I'd asked Jess as she sorted through the gloves, which had been in a white pillowcase with a crocheted lace edging.

Jess had held up one long black evening glove with a rhinestone clip at the opening edge and smiled. She owned a small shop down along the waterfront with two other women where she sold her up-cycled clothing. I could tell by the gleam in her blue eyes that she already had some ideas about what to do with her find.

"Nope," she'd said, rooting around in the pillowcase for the mate to the glove she was holding. She found it, admired the pair and then gave me a sideways glance, the smile still pulling at the corners of her mouth. "It's enough to be right. I don't need to rub it in." Then she'd put her free hand over her heart and tried to look humble. She didn't exactly get there, and I couldn't help laughing.

I'd known as soon as I saw the teapot that I could probably get more than a hundred dollars for it. I'd had no idea how valuable the candlesticks were. After I'd gotten back to Second Chance and figured out what I had, I'd taken them downstairs and asked Rose if she'd polish them.

"I'd be happy to, dear," she'd said. "They'd look lovely on that cherry table Mac has been refinishing."

"You're right," I'd said, putting one arm around her

shoulders to give her a hug. "In fact, I'm going out back right now to see how it's coming."

Behind the shop, along the back edge of the parking lot, was a garage that we'd converted into work space and storage, although we all still called the space the garage. Mac, my second-in-command, jack-of-all-trades and good friend, had been working out there, stripping a coat of brown paint from a dining room table we'd found at the curb during North Harbor's annual cleanup week in the spring.

When I'd returned to the shop, Rose had caught me just as I stepped into the store proper from the back workroom. Her gray eyes were sparkling behind her glasses. She was barely five feet tall, with short white hair, and she was a cross between a mischievous elf and Cinderella's fairy godmother, with a little doting grandmother thrown in.

"Sarah, would you take four hundred dollars for those candlesticks?" she asked.

I glanced across at the cash desk, where a man in jeans, a black T-shirt and a pair of bright red running shoes was standing, one hand resting possessively on the top of the silver candleholders.

"They haven't been polished," I said. "I haven't even logged them into our inventory yet."

"I can do the cleaning," Rose said. "And you can take a picture of them. Then Avery can do all the rest of the computer work later."

Avery was Liz's granddaughter and another of my employees. She'd been taking on some of the work of logging in new stock and doing it much faster than I could.

I hesitated.

Rose leaned her head close to mine. "Four hundred dollars," she said. "But he has to have them today."

"Why?" I asked, eyeing the man, whose head was now bent over his cell phone.

"They're a gift for his wife." Rose glanced in the man's direction, too. "So it has to be today." She patted my arm. "You know how some men are. They never do these things until the last minute." She gave me a little smile. "Not every man is as organized as Alfred."

"I think I should talk to Mr. . . . ." I looked expectantly at Rose.

"Cameron. Jeff Cameron." She handed me the man's business card. Jeff Cameron worked in client services for Helmark Associates. He looked up then, as though he'd heard his name, and smiled in our direction. "He and his wife are new in town," Rose added, as though that explained everything.

North Harbor sits on the midcoast of Maine: "Where the hills touch the sea." The town stretches from the Swift Hills in the north to the Atlantic Ocean in the south. It's full of beautiful old buildings and eclectic little businesses, as well as several award-winning restaurants. Our year-round population is about thirteen thousand people, but that number more than triples in the summer with summer residents and tourists.

Occasionally one of those seasonal visitors fell in love with the town and relocated permanently. I wondered if that was the case with Jeff Cameron and his wife. It was kind of what had happened with me. Growing up I'd spent my summers in North Harbor with my grandmother. When my radio job disappeared, it was the place that most felt like home.

We walked over to join Jeff Cameron at the counter. I offered my hand.

"Mr. Cameron, this is Sarah Grayson," Rose said before I could introduce myself. "She owns Second Chance."

"It's nice to meet you," he said. His handshake was firm but not obnoxiously strong. He was several inches taller than me—maybe five-ten or so—with blond hair and the lean, angular build of a distance runner, which explained the flame red running shoes.

"You as well," I said. I gestured at the counter. "You're interested in the candlesticks."

He nodded. "Mrs. Jackson tells me they aren't for sale yet, but I'm hoping you'll make an exception. I'll give you four hundred dollars for the pair. I recognize that they're Kirk & Son."

I hesitated. From my research I felt the pair was worth between four and four hundred and fifty dollars. And it seemed likely, I'd discovered, that they had at one time belonged to the late Purves Calhoun, though how they'd ended up in that cardboard box was anybody's guess. Given what I'd paid for the contents of the box, Jeff Cameron's offer was more than fair. But I hated to send the candlesticks out looking less than their best. I didn't like to let anything leave the shop that wouldn't reflect well on the quality of our stock.

"If tomorrow would work for you, then yes," I said. "That would give us time to clean them, and it would give you the chance to get a better look at what you're buying."

He started to shake his head before I'd even finished speaking. "I know what I'm getting. That's not a problem. But I have to have them today." He pulled a hand back through his thick hair. "Ms. Grayson, my wife's grandmother had a set of candleholders that, based on the photographs I've seen, were identical to these ones. They somehow disappeared after her death." He raised his eyebrows when he said, "disappeared."

"My wife was very close to her grandmother, and if she were still alive, today would have been her eighty-third birthday. I know Leesa is missing her and I know what those candlesticks would mean to her. I'll give you four hundred and fifty dollars."

I felt Rose's elbow dig into the small of my back. "Sarah dear, I can polish them for Mr. Cameron as soon as Charlotte gets here," she said.

I turned to look at her. She gave me a sweet smile. "It's no trouble," she added.

"Thank you, Rose," I said. I turned back to Cameron. "All right. We have a deal."

"Excellent," he said. "Could you deliver them late this afternoon?"

I shook my head. "I'm sorry. We don't deliver."

Cameron made a face and glanced at the expensive Polar sports watch on his arm. "I have a meeting in Portland this afternoon and I'm not sure when I'll be back. Can you make an exception?"

I reached behind me and caught Rose's arm before her elbow jabbed me again. "Sarah, Alfred and I could deliver Mr. Cameron's gift to his wife," Rose offered, undeterred.

I didn't bother turning around to look at her because I knew she'd be the picture of innocence. "Where are you living?" I asked Cameron.

"We're still house shopping, so for now we're renting a cottage at Windspeare Point."

I did turn to Rose then. "It's too far to walk," I said quietly, hoping my expression told her that I wasn't going to argue the point with her.

She eyed me for a long moment, then let out a soft sigh and nodded.

I faced Jeff Cameron again. "Northridge Taxi also runs a delivery service, and their drivers are bonded."

"I can take care of all that, Sarah," Rose said. She moved past me, around the back of the counter, holding her upper body straight and a bit rigid, which told me that even though she'd given in with grace, she was still annoyed with me.

The parking lot for the medical center was just ahead. I took a ticket from the machine, and the barrier arm went up. I spotted a parking space at the end of the fourth row of cars, close to the emergency room entrance. I was glad that Rose was all right. I should have remembered that she never gave in, and certainly not gracefully.

I stopped at the security desk just inside the ER doors. The lobby area had recently been renovated. The walls were now painted a warm, pale yellow, the color of late summer corn, instead of the bilious green they'd been before.

"I'm here to see Rose Jackson," I told the young man on the other side of the Plexiglas panel. He was wearing dark blue hospital scrubs and his muscular arms were tattooed from his wrists as far up as I could see.

"You're Sarah Grayson?" he asked.

I nodded, wondering how he knew my name.

"Your mother is in Observation 5." He pointed over my right shoulder. "Go through those double doors and turn right at the nurses' station."

My mother? I suddenly had a pretty good idea of why the young man had known my name. Ahead I could see Liz, standing by the nurses' desk. She had the handles of Rose's blue-and-white L.L. Bean tote bag over her arm. As always, she was beautifully dressed in a pale pink cotton sweater and cream trousers, her blond hair curled around her face.

I walked over and gave her a hug. "You told them I'm Rose's daughter?" I said.

Liz waved my comment away. "I said you were *like* a daughter to her. Is it my fault people don't listen?"

I looked at her, shaking my head.

"You keep making that face, missy, and it's going to freeze like that," she said.

"That didn't work on me when I was seven, and it's not going to work now," I said. "You lied to them. What if someone asks me for ID?"

Liz gave a snort of derision. "And what exactly are they going to ask for? Your birth certificate? I don't think so."

Liz had grown up in North Harbor and for years ran the Emmerson Foundation, her family's charitable trust. She knew everyone in town and was quick to use her influence if it could help someone she cared about. I could see the lines pulling at the corners of her mouth and eyes under her expertly applied makeup, and I knew that despite her feisty attitude she was worried about her friend.

"You're certain Rose is all right?" I asked.

Liz nodded. "She's just down there." She gestured over her shoulder. "The doctor is in with her right now. They kicked Alfred and me out."

I took a step sideways and looked down the hallway. Alfred Peterson was standing in front of a closed door about three-quarters of the way down the corridor. He was a small man with just a few tufts of gray hair and warm brown eyes. While he may have looked like the stereotypical grandpa who showed up in life insurance ads, he was in reality a computer whiz whose skills rivaled those of hackers a fraction of his age. Mr. P. smiled when he caught sight of me, and I raised a hand in greeting. I saw his shoulders relax a little. I might not have been Rose's daughter, but I felt responsible for her—for all of them.

"So she delivered those candlesticks, after all," I said to Liz. "I told her to get the taxi service to take care of it."

Liz nodded. "She tried to deliver them. You'd think at her age she wouldn't get caught up in some romantic nonsense." She patted the canvas bag hanging from her arm. "I've got the damn things right here, along with Rose's purse, and for the record I told you they were cursed."

I swiped a hand over my neck. "What happened to Rose didn't happen because of a pair of cursed candlesticks. And by the way, they aren't cursed. There's no such thing."

Liz jabbed her index finger at me. Her nails were painted a deeper pink than her sweater. "Don't tell me you never heard of karma. Those candleholders have bad karma attached to them. Purves Calhoun was a mean, coldhearted son of a bitch who mistreated his wife and kids just like his father before him, until his mother-in-law put a curse on him and he fell off the roof of the barn." She gave me a triumphant look.

"Purves Calhoun fell off the roof of his barn because he had a still in that barn and he spent too much time sampling his own product," I retorted.

"Whatever works," she said. "Purves's grandfather bought those things for his wife when she gave him a son, Purves Senior—just as much of a quarrelsome old coot as his son, by the way—after six girls, as if that was her fault," Liz scoffed. "Then Purves Senior continued that reprehensible tradition and gave them to his wife when Purves Junior was born after four beautiful daughters."

"I thought the candlesticks belonged to Purves's grandmother," I said, thinking it was kind of an odd conversation to be having while we were standing in the emergency room.

Liz shrugged. "Like father, like son. Every single thing, every pot and plate, every stick of furniture, belonged to the old man as far as he was concerned." She fished in Rose's bag and pulled out a box wrapped in blue paper and tied with a silver bow. "Here," she said, handing it to me. "They have bad juju."

"Bad juju?" I said.

Liz narrowed her blue eyes at me. "Don't make fun. There are things out there that we don't understand."

She was going on about curses and bad juju because she was worried, I realized. "Rose is going to be all right," I said, reaching over and laying my hand on her arm for a moment.

Liz nodded. "I've been telling her for years that she's hardheaded."

Mr. P. joined us then. "Sarah, I'm glad you're here," he said. The smile he gave me was a small one, and the lines on his face, like those on Liz's, seemed to be etched just a little deeper. "Rosie told me not to call you." He glanced at Liz. "So I called Elizabeth instead."

"Rose went to Windspeare Point," I said.

"I didn't know, my dear," Mr. P. said. "I assure you that if I had known, I would have stopped her." He adjusted his glasses and smoothed down the few wisps of hair he had left; then he looked back over his shoulder. The closed door he'd been standing next to was open now. "I think the doctor is finished."

"Let's go," Liz said.

"Isn't there a two-visitor limit?" I asked.

"Doesn't apply to us," she said over her shoulder without turning around.

Mr. P. patted my arm. "It's not the first rule that doesn't seem to apply to us," he said to me as we followed Liz toward Rose's room.

Rose was sitting on a hospital bed wearing a wrinkled blue-and-gray robe over an equally wrinkled green gown, her white hair standing on end all over her head. Both items of clothing dwarfed her small frame. A nurse was putting a bandage on her left wrist.

I paused in the doorway, my chest tight, the lump in my throat too big to swallow away, it seemed. Rose looked small and fragile, and it suddenly hit me like a sucker punch to the gut that this could have ended very badly.

Rose looked up and caught sight of me. She shifted her gaze to Alfred. "You promised you wouldn't worry Sarah," she chided.

"He didn't call her. I did," Liz said.

"You shouldn't have done that," Rose retorted. "You brought Sarah all the way over here for nothing."

I could see that this was about to deteriorate into one of their back-and-forth sessions. I crossed the space between Rose and me and wrapped my arms around her shoulders, dropping a kiss on the top of her head. "I didn't come over here for nothing," I said. "I came here for you."

Rose reached up with her free hand and gave my arm a squeeze. "It's all right, sweet girl. I'm just fine."

I could see a swelling about the size of a Grade A large egg on the other side of her head. "That doesn't look fine," I said. "It looks nasty."

Rose looked at the nurse, who was just taping the gauze bandage in place on her arm. "Will you please tell Sarah I'm all right?"

The nurse gave me a warm smile. "We did a CAT scan. Your mother is fine. We're just waiting for the results from some blood work, and if that's okay she can go home."

"Thank you," I said.

She picked up the tray with her supplies. "I'll be back," she said to Rose. "Push the buzzer if you need anything."

"Thank you, my dear," Rose said.

As soon as the nurse was gone, I sat down next to Rose on the edge of the bed. "You took those candlesticks to Jeff Cameron's house," I said, holding up the gift-wrapped package and trying to keep the frustration I was feeling out of my voice. "Why didn't you just call Northridge and have them delivered? You know Tim's people are reliable."

Rose made a dismissive gesture with one hand, wincing a little at the motion. "That doesn't matter right now," she said. "What I need from you is to call Michelle—and Nicolas as well."

Michelle was Michelle Andrews, my friend and a North Harbor police detective. Nicolas—Nick Elliot—was an investigator for the medical examiner's office. I'd known him all my life. His mother, Charlotte, also worked for me and, like Liz, was one of Rose's closest friends.

"Didn't whoever found you call the police?" I asked.

"Of course they did," Rose said. "I gave the patrol officer my statement, for all the good it did. He all but patted me on the head and told me to go home and bake cookies." She shifted her gaze to Liz for a moment. "Mo Theriault's grandson," she added, as though that explained everything. Liz nodded knowingly, so maybe for her it did.

Rose turned her attention back to me. "I can't get anyone here to take me seriously."

I glanced at Mr. P., who was spreading a blue cotton blanket over Rose's feet. He shook his head at my unspoken question. He didn't know what she was talking about, either.

"Take you seriously about what?" I asked, wondering if that CAT scan was wrong. Was Rose's head injury more serious than it seemed?

"The body, of course." She looked at all three of us. "Why else do you think I was hit over the head? I saw it."

"What on God's green earth are you talking about?" Liz asked, moving around the bottom of the bed to Rose's other side. "Whose body did you see?"

Rose looked at Liz, irritation evident in the set of her mouth. "Well, Jeff Cameron's, of course. He's dead."

Chapter 2

"Jeff Cameron is dead?" I said, feeling dumbfounded by the direction the conversation had taken.

Rose nodded. "Yes."

"And you know this how?" Liz asked, sitting down on the green vinyl chair by the bed. "The police didn't find any body. All they found was you and some plastic tube thing by the side of the road."

"It wasn't a plastic tube thing. It was a boat fender. And you haven't been listening to a word I've been saying, have you?" Rose cocked her head to one side as she studied her friend, and then flinched at the motion.

"I'm listening," Liz said, leaning forward in the chair. "You're just not making a hell of a lot of sense at the moment."

I covered Rose's hand with my own, which caught her attention, exactly as I'd intended. "You saw Jeff Cameron's body."

She nodded again.

"At his house."

Rose pressed her lips together for a moment. "Yes," she said. "That has to be why I was hit over the head." She held up her bandaged hand. "And before you all start in on me, I don't have a concussion, I'm not a feeble old woman and I know what I saw."

I knew that tone of voice and set of her jaw. Rose wasn't going to be swayed from what she believed she'd seen.

Liz and Mr. P. both spoke at the same time.

I held up one hand. "Hang on," I said. "Just hang on a minute."

They both stopped talking.

I put my arm around Rose's shoulders again, shifting on the noisy vinyl mattress. "Start at the beginning," I said. "Start from when I left you with Jeff Cameron."

"We don't have time."

"Yes, we do," I said. "A dead man isn't going to get any deader."

Rose nodded. "I guess you're right." She tugged at the sheet over her legs and Mr. P. immediately pulled the cotton blanket up over her. She smiled a thank-you at him. Then she sighed softly and began. "I told Mr. Cameron that I would make sure his wife got his gift. He said that he didn't want me to get in any trouble. I said that you would come around."

I raised one eyebrow but didn't say anything. Rose's cheeks grew pink, and she looked down at the nubby blanket for a moment before looking up at me again. "It wasn't a lie, Sarah," she said. "I thought I could make you change your mind if I really had to."

Liz made a small snort of skepticism, but I ignored it.

"Rosie, why didn't you tell me what you were planning?" Mr. P. asked. There was no recrimination in his voice.

Rose stretched out her hand to him. He caught it, giving it a gentle squeeze before letting go again. "I'm sorry, Alf," she said. "I probably should have; it's just that you would have tried to talk me out of it."

"Yes, I would have," he agreed.

"That's the problem," she said, looking from Mr. P. to me. "Sometimes I get tired of being treated like I'm made of glass and might break."

"After that whack on the head you took, it's pretty clear your head, at least, is made of something other than glass," Liz commented dryly. She reached forward once more and laid her hand on Rose's leg for a moment. "And I'm glad it is," she added. They exchanged smiles.

"Keep going," I nudged.

"We were working out the details of the delivery when you came in." Rose looked at Liz.

"I remember." Liz leaned back in her seat, crossing one leg over the other.

"Avery was in Augusta, remember?" Rose said to me. "With some kids who had been in her history class. Their teacher organized the trip."

After some problems at home, Avery had come to live with her grandmother and attend a progressive alternative school that had only morning classes. She worked afternoons for me. Now that it was July, she was spending more time at the shop.

I nodded. Liz raised an eyebrow but didn't say anything.

"And she may have had my phone with her."

"May have?" I asked.

"All right, she did have my phone. It ended up in her bag by mistake."

Things were getting more complicated by the moment. "And that would be because . . . ?"

"I was showing Avery a video on my phone because she only has text and calling—no data on her own phone." Rose's gaze shifted over to Liz.

"Avery has a perfectly good computer at home with Wi-Fi," Liz said. "She doesn't need data on her phone because she spends too much time with her head bent over it as it is."

Rose sighed. "You sound like you're a hundred and six when you say things like that."

Liz made a dismissive gesture with one hand. They'd had several versions of this conversation before.

"What happened after that?" I asked, reaching for the glass of water on the table next to the bed and handing it to Rose.

She took a sip before answering. "Liz wanted me to take *her* phone. I told her I'd be fine without a phone for one night and she left."

Out of the corner of my eye I saw Liz nod.

"I think Mr. Cameron may have heard us talking," Rose continued. "When I went back to the counter he said he needed to get going, so he gave me his cell number and asked if I'd call him about four thirty and he'd be able to tell me then when his wife would be home."

"So that's what you did?"

Rose nodded once more. "I had the address, and it

just seemed easier to call a taxi and go over there myself. It wasn't a lot different from having the gift delivered."

"The driver didn't wait?" I asked.

"I told him not to, so don't get on Tim's case."

I cleared my throat for a moment and looked up at the ceiling. There were no answers up there. I looked at Rose again. "I'm assuming you had a good reason for not getting the driver to wait."

"No, I had a stupid reason," she said calmly.

I'd crossed the line, I realized. "I'm sorry," I said.

She smiled and patted my hand the way she often did when she was humoring me. "I thought after I gave Mrs. Cameron her gift—her first name is Leesa, by the way—I'd walk down to Sam's, call Alfred, and see if he wanted to join me for pizza."

"Yes, I would have," Mr. P. immediately said.

"I've been wanting to try the sausage and mushroom pizza ever since Sam told me he was getting that all-natural sausage from that little place in Lisbon Falls," Rose said.

We were about to get way, way off track. "We'll get one on the weekend," I said.

"That's a lovely idea," Rose said. "We should see if Nicolas and Charlotte are free. And I could teach you how to make Caesar salad."

Mr. P. cleared his throat. They exchanged a look and Rose gave an almost imperceptible nod. "Or maybe apple-carrot salad would be a better choice?" She looked over at Liz and I saw her eyes dart, briefly, in my direction.

She was still trying to play matchmaker between

Nick and me. They all were—Rose, Liz, Charlotte, who was also Nick's mom. Even Mr. P. apparently. That was why Rose had nixed the Caesar salad; the garlic would derail any romance, at least in her mind.

I rubbed the space between my eyes with the side of my thumb. We were officially off track into the conversational bushes.

Rose caught the gesture. "Do you have a headache, dear?" she asked. "I can just press this little button and have the nurse bring you a couple of Tylenol. I'm sure she wouldn't mind."

"I'm fine," I said.

"Rosie, you were about to tell us what happened after the taxi dropped you off at Mr. Cameron's house," Mr. P. interjected.

"That's right, I was," Rose said. She studied my face for a moment and seemed satisfied with whatever she saw there. "There were no lights on in the house, but it wasn't really dark and I thought maybe Mrs. Cameron was in the backyard." She leaned around me. "They're renting the Baxter place while they look for a house to buy." She directed her words to Liz.

Liz nodded. "Screened-in gazebo," she said quietly to me.

"There was no one in the backyard," Rose continued, "so I knocked on the side door, and when there was no answer I looked through the porch window." She held up her bandaged hand. "And before anyone thinks I was just being nosy, I was trying to be certain Mrs. Cameron wasn't home. I didn't have my phone, so I couldn't exactly call her, now, could I?"

"Where was Jeff Cameron's body?" I asked.

"I was just getting to that," Rose said. "When I looked through the porch window it gave me a bit of a view into the kitchen. Those cottages aren't very big."

"You saw Mr. Cameron in the kitchen," Mr. P. spoke up from the foot of the bed.

Rose nodded slowly, her expression suddenly serious. "He was on the floor."

"Were his eyes open or closed?" I asked.

"I didn't see his face," she said. She paused for a moment, replaying the scene in her mind, I was guessing. "I saw his watch and a bit of one cheek. His head was slumped forward like this." She dropped her chin to her chest. "And of course those fire-engine red shoes."

The Newton Gravity IVs Jeff Cameron had been wearing when he'd been at the shop.

"What did you do?"

"I tried to get a better look. I banged on the glass. I tried the door, but it was locked." Rose was absently smoothing the bandage on her left arm. "Then something hit the back of my head—I'm certain it was that boat fender—and the next thing I knew I woke up to a very nice dog nudging me with his rather cold nose and I was two houses away." She turned to Mr. P. "Remind me to make some dog biscuits."

He nodded. I saw the lines pulling around his eyes and mouth again and knew Rose's story worried him.

Rose focused her attention back on me. "Sarah, someone else was in that kitchen, someone in a pink hooded sweatshirt. I just caught a glimpse of her."

"Her?"

"Yes. I think the person in the pink hooded sweat-shirt was a woman. And not just because it was pink."

"What makes you say that?" I asked.

Rose tugged at the neck of the hospital nightgown. "Will you think I'm being an old fool if I say I just have a feeling?"

"You're not an old fool, but I think it would help if you could put your reasons into words."

"All right." Her gray eyes narrowed. "That sweat-shirt." She lifted her hands to her shoulders. "It was baggy. Avery has one that she wears—the black one—and the shoulders were the same. The seam at the top of the shoulder comes down onto her arm. It was the same for the person wearing that pink one. It didn't fit right."

Rose was very observant. I didn't doubt for a moment that she'd caught that detail even though she'd gotten only a quick look at the person. "Anything else?"

"When the person—she—raised her head I keep feeling I saw something that made me think I was looking at a woman. Cheekbones maybe, or mouth. I can't be sure." She pushed back the blanket and swung her legs over the side of the bed.

I caught her by the arm. "Where are you going?"

"We can't waste any more time talking," Rose said, squaring her shoulders. "Leesa Cameron killed her husband. We have to do something."

Chapter 3

No one said anything. Rose pressed her lips together for a moment, and her chin came up. "You don't believe me."

Liz spoke first. "You were hit on the head pretty hard."

"Get out," Rose said.

"I'm not saying you didn't see something," Liz said, gesturing with one hand. "But it was starting to get dark, you said yourself you could only see a small bit of the kitchen and then somebody hit you over the head. You might not have seen what you thought you saw—that's all. The police didn't find any body."

Liz turned to me. "I talked to Mo's grandson. He was still here when I got here. He said he checked the yard at the Cameron's house, he knocked on both doors and he even looked through the window. He didn't see anyone—alive or dead."

Rose picked up the call button that had been lying next to her on the bed. She held it up, finger poised over the end as though she was about to eject us all out of our seats. "Get out of my room right now or I will have you thrown out."

Her voice was steady and even, which was an indication of how angry she was. Where most people got louder when they were angry, Rose became cool, quiet and focused. "I don't care if you are Elizabeth Emmerson Kiley French; you're not welcome here right now," she said.

Liz looked stricken, the color draining from her face. She got to her feet, her eyes never leaving Rose's face.

I stood up as well and put a hand on Liz's shoulder. "Just . . . just go. I'll take care of everything here and I'll call you later." She pressed her lips together and her eyes slowly slid to meet mine. "Go," I repeated. With one backward glance at Rose, she did.

Rose fixed her gaze on me, a clear challenge in her eyes. "Do you believe me?" she asked.

I folded my arms over my chest and tipped my head to one side to study her. The hospital gown and robe were several sizes too big, her hair was going in all directions and there was a large bandage on her wrist. But a mix of defiance and anger burned in her eyes. Rose may have been tiny, but I would have rather taken on a black bear over a picnic basket than get into a skirmish with her.

"Well, if I didn't, do you think I'd be stupid enough to tell you?" I asked. "And for the record, I do believe you, although you can't be certain Leesa Cameron killed her husband. You don't have any definite proof that Jeff Cameron is dead, let alone that she did anything. He could just be injured."

"Then we better get going." She looked at Alfred. "Could you get my clothes, please, Alf? I think they're in that closet." She pointed at a small locker on the wall opposite the end of the bed. Then she scanned the floor. "Does anyone know what they did with my shoes?"

"Rosie, what are you doing?" Mr. P. asked.

"I'm getting dressed so I can sign myself out of here and go back to the cottage so we can find out what happened to Mr. Cameron." She leaned sideways and shook a finger at a space just past my left shoulder. "Sarah dear, my shoes are by that chair. Could you hand them to me, please?"

I shook my head. "No."

That got all her attention. She straightened up. "You could go with Liz," she said, a warning edge to her voice.

"Not happening," I said. "As your *daughter*"—I put an extra emphasis on the last word—"I'm telling you that you're staying here until the doctor says you can leave. I'll call Michelle and the two of us will go over to Jeff Cameron's cottage and find out what's going on."

"You're not my daughter," Rose said. "Not really. That was just a ruse perpetrated by Liz."

"No, I'm not," I said cheerfully.

Both Rose and Mr. P. looked confused at my apparent unconcern.

I held up my cell phone. "But I would be happy to call Abby, who is your real daughter, so she can weigh in on all of this." I made a sweeping gesture with one hand as though I were a *Price Is Right* spokesmodel showing off the prizes for the Showcase Showdown. "Or have you already called her?"

For a long moment we stared at each other. Then Rose sighed and sat back down on the edge of the bed. "All right," she said. "But what are you going to do if Michelle is busy? You shouldn't go over there by yourself."

"People who live in glass houses, Rose," I said, raising an eyebrow.

"I get your point," she said. "But it doesn't really apply, because when I went over there I didn't know there was a killer in that house."

I exhaled slowly. "If Michelle isn't available, I'll call Nick. If I can't get him, I'll go get Mac. I won't go by myself." I nudged her legs with my knee. She swung them back on the bed and I pulled the sheet and blanket back over her again.

"I heard that tone," she said.

"Good," I told her, leaning down to kiss her forehead. "I'd hate to think I'd been too subtle." I moved to the bottom of the bed. "I'm going to call Charlotte so you'll have backup," I said to Mr. P. I jerked my thumb in Rose's direction. "If she tries anything before Charlotte gets here, sit on her."

Mr. P. gave me a smile. "Don't worry, my dear," he said, hiking up his pants, which were already up close to his armpits. "I'll watch her like a hawk."

I walked out to the nurses' station, pulled out my cell and called Charlotte, giving her the short version of what was going on.

"You're certain Rose is all right?" she asked.

"She kicked Liz out of her room and gave me a hard time about going over to the Cameron house by myself," I said. "She's fine."

"You aren't going over there by yourself, are you?" Charlotte immediately asked.

"No, I'm going to call Michelle," I said. "I think the police need to be involved. Rose was attacked by someone and it's possible something has happened to Jeff Cameron."

"I think that's a good idea. I'm on my way. Call me when you know anything, and be careful."

I promised I would and said good-bye. I knew I could count on Charlotte to handle things. She was a former school principal, sensible, dependable and unflappable.

It was busy by the nurses' station, so I decided to go out to my SUV to call Michelle, where it would be quieter. I wasn't sure how I was going to explain everything to her, and I was glad of the extra few minutes to think things through.

Detective Michelle Andrews and I had been best friends growing up, at least for July and August each year. We'd both been summer kids in North Harbor, and every July first we'd just pick up the friendship where we'd left off at the end of the previous summer. At fifteen Michelle had suddenly stopped talking to me. I'd only recently found out why. Now we were working on putting our friendship back together.

I slid behind the wheel and pulled my phone out again. My hands were shaking. I leaned back against the seat and closed my eyes for a moment. The rush of adrenaline that had powered me since Liz had called was wearing off. I pressed a hand to my chest and I could feel my heart hammering.

I took a couple of slow, deep breaths, in through my nose, out through my mouth, the way I'd learned at a stretching class Jess had dragged me to. Rose was all right. She was feisty and angry, but she was all right, and hopefully Michelle would be able to help me connect with Jeff Cameron and figure out what Rose had seen. And then I was going to make Rose phone her daughter. No excuses.

Michelle picked up on the fourth ring. "I heard about what happened to Rose," she said. "Is she all right?"

"She is. They're just waiting for the results from some blood tests and then they'll discharge her." I cleared my throat. "I'm in the parking lot at the hospital right now, and I need a favor."

"Sure, what is it?" she asked.

"I'm just going to give you the short version," I said. "Because if I give you the long one we'll be here half the night. Rose was making a very unauthorized delivery of a pair of candlesticks to a customer, Jeff Cameron—to his wife, actually. Rose was at the side door of the cottage they're renting at Windspeare Point and someone hit her over the head. Whoever hit her moved her a couple of houses away."

"Was anything taken?" Michelle asked. "Her purse? Her phone? Any of her jewelry?"

Liz had had both the gift-wrapped candlesticks and Rose's purse in the L.L. Bean bag. Rose had been wearing her watch, I'd noticed. And Avery had her phone. "Not as far as I know."

"I'll follow up with the officer who responded, see if he has any leads."

I raked my hand back through my hair again. "Thank you," I said, "but that's not the favor."

"Okay," Michelle said slowly. I could hear the curiosity in her voice.

I was beating around the bush and I needed to just say it. "Before she was hit over the head, Rose saw something in the Camerons' kitchen." I cleared my throat again. "Someone . . . in a pink hoodie dragging what she believes was Jeff Cameron's body."

For what felt like a very long moment, Michelle didn't say anything. "Are you certain?" she finally asked.

"Rose is."

"She thinks . . . what?"

"That Leesa Cameron killed her husband. Look, I know the officer who responded went to the Camerons' cottage and didn't find any body, but Rose insists she saw one."

I heard Michelle blow out a breath on the other end of the phone. I pictured her at her desk, head propped up on her hand, even though I had no idea where she actually was. "That's a pretty serious accusation."

"I know."

"Could she have misunderstood what she saw? Maybe it was some kind of . . . adult . . . game."

"For the record, yuck!" I made a face even though she couldn't see it. "As for what she saw, I don't know.

That's the favor. I want to go over to the Camerons' house and see if either of them is there. Will you come with me?"

"Right now?"

"If you can." I leaned my head back against the headrest and closed my eyes for a moment.

"I can do that. I'm just about ready to leave for the night," Michelle said. "Do you want me to pick you up or meet you there?"

"I'll meet you there." I gave her the address.

"Give me about twenty minutes."

I felt a little of the tension ease out of my body. "Thanks," I said.

"Hey, Sarah, anytime," she said.

I ended the call, tossed my phone onto the passenger seat and pulled out my car keys. I started the SUV and then looked over at my phone. Should I call Liz? No, I decided. If she knew where I was going, she was apt to show up with some questions of her own. I didn't need her butting heads with Michelle. I'd call her once there was something to report. And I fervently hoped there would be very little to report.

Chapter 4

The cottage Jeff and Leesa Cameron were renting was the last one of six nestled among the trees overlooking West Penobscot Bay. Beyond the bay were Deer Isle, Swan's Island and the Atlantic Ocean.

The road curved inland just past the little green house. I pulled over, just beyond the cottage, and shut off the SUV's engine. I could hear the mournful sound of the Deer Isle foghorn in the distance. Although it was almost twenty miles away across the water, something about the geography of the coast made the foghorn audible on this stretch of shoreline. It was a lonely sound in the near darkness.

Trees and the growing darkness obscured part of my view of the house, but I could see a light on inside and there was a car parked in the driveway. I fervently hoped that Michelle and I would find both of the Camerons at home with a perfectly logical, reasonable explanation for what Rose had seen. Because I knew she had seen something. Her mind was as sharp as it had been throughout her teaching career. So something had happened in that kitchen.

I studied the small house. It was surprisingly isolated, with trees on both sides and the cliffs leading down to the bay beyond the backyard. It would have been easy to sneak up behind Rose while she was distracted by whatever had been going on inside the kitchen.

Michelle drove up then, turning in the Camerons' driveway and parking in front of the house.

I got out of the SUV and walked over to her. "Thank you for doing this," I said.

She smiled. "I don't mind. I like Rose." She must have seen the surprise I was feeling on my face. "Really, I do," she said, locking the car and tucking the keys in the pocket of her gray skirt. Everything looked good on her. Michelle was tall and slim, with red hair and green eyes and the kind of quiet confidence that to me went along with being a police officer. "Okay, I'm not crazy about her detective work, but I kind of admire her persistence—and if you tell Rose I said that I'm going to deny it."

When their friend Maddie Hamilton had been arrested for the murder of the man she'd been seeing, Rose, Liz, Charlotte and Mr. P. had "investigated" and dragged me into their sleuthing. After they'd "solved" the crime, they had decided to open their own detective agency, Charlotte's Angels, Discreet Investigations, the Angels for short. Mr. P. had completed all the requirements the state had in place to become a licensed investigator. Now Rose was apprenticing with him. They'd set up their office in the sunporch at the store, which pretty much guaranteed that I'd get pulled into their cases.

I squeezed my thumb and index finger together and slid them across my lips like I was closing a zipper. Then I made a motion as though I was locking a tiny lock with an equally tiny key. I finished by pantomiming dropping the key into my bra. It was the same elaborate secret-keeping ritual we'd used when we were teenagers. Now that Michelle was back in my life, I realized how much I'd missed her.

She grinned at me now. "Let's go," she said, tipping her head in the direction of the Cameron house.

"How are you going to do this?" I asked as we started up the driveway. We couldn't exactly knock on the door and if Leesa Cameron answered ask her if she'd killed her husband earlier this evening.

"I thought we'd do good cop, bad cop," Michelle said. "I'll be good; you'll be bad."

"I don't know how to be the bad cop," I blurted. I looked at Michelle. She was laughing.

"I'm kidding, Sarah," she said. "We're following up on what happened earlier this evening. That's all."

"What if Jeff Cameron isn't here?" I asked, smoothing a wrinkle out of the front of my blue-and-white-striped T-shirt.

"Then we'll find out where he is." Michelle stopped in the middle of the driveway. "I'm sure there's some logical explanation for what Rose saw," she said. "I talked to the officer who responded to the nine-one-one call. He confirmed that no one was home here."

"How?"

"There were no cars here in the driveway or parked

nearby on the street. He knocked on both the front and the side doors and got no response at either one, and"—she put extra emphasis on the word—"*and*, yes, he took a look through a couple of windows and checked the backyard. He didn't see anyone or anything."

I opened my mouth to point out that just because no one answered the door or was visible through the windows, that didn't actually mean no one was home. Then I closed it again. I had no business telling Michelle how to do her job. She was a good police officer. But I couldn't help thinking that if I'd just killed my husband, I was pretty sure I'd stay out of sight when the police knocked at my door.

Michelle bypassed the front entrance, continuing up the driveway to the side door. As we passed the sleek silver Audi that was parked there, I rested my hand on the hood for a moment. It was still warm. Whoever had been driving the car hadn't been at the house very long. I crossed my fingers that it was Jeff Cameron.

Michelle gestured in the direction of the porch and spoke over her shoulder. "Officer Theriault did find a couple of sailboat fenders by the side steps. It's possible Rose tripped on those stairs, fell and hit her head on one of them. If she was dazed, she could have wandered up the road to where she was found."

She didn't believe Rose's story about being hit over the head from behind, I realized. She'd come out of friendship for me—and I was grateful for that—but Michelle didn't think Rose had seen Jeff Cameron's dead body or been attacked by someone.

I felt a surge of protectiveness. Rose wasn't the feeble old woman some people seemed to think she was. She'd saved my life the previous winter and barely broken a sweat. She hadn't tripped on the steps and hit her head. Maybe she hadn't seen Jeff Cameron's dead body being dragged across his kitchen floor, but she'd seen something.

Four steps led up to a small landing by the side door. Rose was right. It was possible to see through the porch windows—which didn't have any curtains or blinds that I could see—into part of the kitchen. I could see a section of floor and part of a doorway into some other area of the house. Because I have several inches on Rose, I could also see through the porch to the backyard.

Michelle knocked and I realized I was holding my breath, hoping that it would be Jeff Cameron who came to the door. But it wasn't. It was a woman. She was tall, with blond hair in a gamin pixie cut and blue eyes behind dark-framed hipster glasses. Michelle pulled out her badge and identified herself. "Are you Leesa Cameron?" she asked.

The woman nodded. "I am. Is something wrong?"

Michelle held up her ID. "I'm Detective Andrews. She gestured down the street. "There was an incident earlier this evening. A woman may have been hit over the head with a boat fender like that." She pointed at the white plastic bumpers sitting in a galvanized bucket beside the porch steps.

Leesa Cameron shrugged. "I'm sorry, Detective. I've only been home for about fifteen minutes. I can't help you."

I didn't want her to close the door. I put a hand on the painted wood. "Mrs. Cameron," I said. "My name is Sarah Grayson. I own Second Chance, which is a repurpose shop here in town." I glanced at Michelle and saw nothing in her expression that told me I should stop talking. "The woman who was attacked, Rose Jackson, works for me. She was dropping off a gift that your husband bought for you. I'm sorry, but it's possible your husband was hurt as well."

Leesa Cameron's expression changed from polite inquiry to something darker. Her blue eyes narrowed and her mouth pulled into a tight, thin line. It wasn't the reaction I'd expected. She sighed. "You better come in," she said.

We followed her through the small porch into the kitchen. It was very clean. The walls were white. So were the cupboards. The floors were pale white oak. There were no signs of a struggle, no blood anywhere.

An old farm table had been repurposed as an island in the middle of the room, and there was a retro aquamarine chrome table-and-chair set against the end wall—the only spot of color in the space. There were several cardboard boxes piled on the speckled Formica top of the table. A gray overnight bag was sitting on one of the matching aqua-colored chairs. We'd had a similar set in the shop a couple of months previously. The vintage table and chairs were in excellent shape and, like the whitewashed, solid-wood cupboards and granite countertops, suggested the cottage was high-end and likely came with a high-end rent.

"You're going somewhere?" Michelle asked.

Leesa Cameron nodded. "I'm going back to Boston."

She cleared her throat and looked from Michelle to me. "I appreciate your concern about Jeff, but he's fine. He's a scumbag, but no one has hit him over the head with a boat fender, although it sounds like a good idea to me."

Michelle frowned. "Excuse me?"

Leesa twisted the diamond-studded wedding band she was wearing around her ring finger. She was maybe a couple of inches taller than me although we looked the same height since I was wearing wedge-heeled sandals and she was in flip-flops.

"Jeff met someone else. He's gone, and so is everything that was in our joint investment account. If he'd been here when I got home, yeah, I might have hurt him, but he was already gone." A cell phone was lying on the chrome table. She picked it up, scrolled through several screens and handed the phone to Michelle. "See for yourself."

Michelle read the text without comment.

Leesa reached for an envelope on top of one of the boxes and passed that to Michelle, who raised an eyebrow. "It's the statement from our investment account. Go ahead. Take a look."

Michelle returned the phone and took a single sheet of paper from the envelope. She looked it over, then put it back in the envelope and handed that to Leesa. "Have you and your husband been having problems, Mrs. Cameron?" she asked.

Leesa's mouth twisted to one side. "I didn't think so," she said. "I lost my job three months ago—I was a buyer for a chain of home decor boutiques that went out of business—but Jeff was making good money, so we didn't have any financial issues. Part of the reason he took the job here was so that I could take some time to decide what I want to do next. When Jeff first started working for Helmark, we spent six months in India. This was supposed to be my time, my turn. And it was supposed to be a chance for the two of us to spend more time together, but he was always working." She laughed, but there was no humor in the sound. "I guess it's true. The wife is the last person to know." She turned to me. "I'm sorry about your . . . friend, but I didn't see anything. I wasn't here and clearly Jeff wasn't, either."

Michelle nodded, the motion almost imperceptible. "Do you mind telling me where you were?"

"I was with Jeff's sister, Nicole. I thought maybe she'd know where he went or who the other woman is, but she was as shocked as I am." She folded her arms over her midsection and rubbed her left shoulder absently with the other hand. She had the strong legs, wide shoulders and sculpted arms of a rower, and I'd noticed the prow of a scull in the backyard when I'd looked through the porch. "Nicole being here is why we chose North Harbor," she continued. "She's all the family Jeff has aside from . . . well, me."

Leesa turned her attention to me again. "What did he buy?" she asked. "You said he got me a gift."

It seemed odd to me to buy a present for a woman you were about to leave, but there was no reason not to answer her question. "A pair of candlesticks."

She laughed again, her face twisting into a semblance of a smile. "Let me guess. They were silver. Kirk & Son."

"Yes." How had she known?

"There's your proof," she said. "I don't know where Jeff is, but I promise you he's fine. When we first got married, we were broke. Eating-ramen-and-peanut-butter-for-dinner broke. So broke that I sold the only thing of value I had, a pair of silver candlesticks that had belonged to my grandmother. Those ones he bought? His snarky way of making this square between us. They definitely weren't any kind of a romantic gesture."

"I'm sorry," I said. "They're still yours. I'll make sure you get them."

"Thank you," she said. "Could you leave them with my sister-in-law?" She gave me a wry smile. "I suppose I should say my soon-to-be ex-sister-in-law."

I nodded. She grabbed a pad of sticky notes from the counter and scribbled an address and a phone number. I took the square of paper and put it in my purse.

Michelle pulled her phone out of her pocket. "Mrs. Cameron, what's your husband's cell number?" she asked.

Leesa Cameron recited the phone number and Michelle punched it into her phone. "He won't answer, Detective," she said.

She was right.

"The phone is turned off," Michelle said after a moment.

"Jeff hired a student from Cahill College as an assistant for the summer," Leesa said. "Chloe Sanders. She might know how to get in touch with him. She's very keen. Hang on a second." She grabbed her cell from the counter and swiped through several screens. Then she held up the phone and Michelle typed the number on it into her own phone. I repeated the digits silently to myself, hoping I'd remember them.

"Thank you," Michelle said. She cleared her throat. "Is there any possibility that your husband was involved with Miss Sanders?"

Leesa laughed. "None. Oh, I'm not saying she wouldn't have been interested. She hung on his every word and he's a very good-looking man, but Chloe wasn't his type. He called her a Roomba."

"You mean like the robot vacuum cleaner?" I said.

She nodded. "He said having an assistant was like having a Roomba. He could just leave all the grunt work for her."

I was starting to think Jeff Cameron was a first-class jerk.

Michelle glanced at me and gave a slight shrug; then she turned to Leesa and held out a business card I hadn't noticed her pull from her bag. "Thank you for your help, Mrs. Cameron. If you think of anything else, please call me." The other woman promised she would and we left.

"Do you think she's telling the truth?" I asked as we reached the street.

"You think she isn't?" Michelle raised an eyebrow.

"I don't know. Why would someone buy an expensive gift for a woman he was about to leave?"

She glanced back at the house. "You heard what she said. It was his crappy way of making things even so he could leave the marriage without owing her anything."

"So he clears out their investment account but buys her those candlesticks so they're even? That makes no sense." I pushed my hair off my face, wishing I'd pulled it back into a ponytail the way Michelle had with her hair.

She patted her pocket as if she was checking to be sure her phone was still there. "Sarah, one thing I've learned is that people do things that make no sense all the time."

"Maybe she killed him," I said, kicking a rock with the side of my sandal, sending it skittering down the driveway into the street. "Maybe the story she just told us is her way of covering it up. If people think Jeff Cameron has run off with another woman, no one will be looking for him."

Michelle exhaled softly but didn't say anything.

"What did the text say?" I asked.

"That it wasn't working anymore, he'd met someone else and he was going to start a new life."

I shook my head in frustration, pulling at the bottom of my striped T-shirt. "C'mon, Michelle," I said. "Who does that kind of thing? In the movies, maybe, but in real life? Who ends their marriage with a text?"

"You'd be surprised." She held up both hands. "That's how people do things now, with a cell phone. Not face-to-face."

I wasn't convinced, and it obviously showed in my expression.

"You don't honestly think Leesa Cameron concocted this elaborate story as a cover, do you?" she asked. "How do you explain the statement from their financial adviser? Their account is empty."

"That would be easy to fake."

"And just as easy to check on."

I made a face.

"Why don't we go talk to the people who found Rose?" Michelle said. "I'd like to know if they saw anything."

I nodded. "Okay." This conversation wasn't taking us anywhere.

We walked along the curve of the street past a small, pale blue cottage, identical to the one the Camerons had been renting. The next little house had been painted a deep shade of inky navy blue. An open porch stretched across the front like a welcoming smile.

"It's this one," Michelle said. She pointed to the brass numbers by the front door. "Number twenty-four."

Just then a woman came around the side of the house followed by a large black Lab. The dog's tail began to wag the moment he spotted us. The woman put a hand on its back. She said something to the dog I couldn't hear and then the two of them started toward us. She was tiny and curvy, no more than five feet tall, I guessed, with dark almond-shaped eyes behind round tortoiseshell glasses. Her hair was pulled up on her head in a messy bun and she was wearing khaki shorts, a red tank top and Birkenstocks. "Can I help you?" she asked with an inquiring smile.

Michelle pulled out her ID again. "I'm Detective Andrews," she said. "This is Sarah Grayson."

"You're here about Mrs. Jackson," the woman said.

"We're just following up."

"Is she all right?" The woman looked from Michelle

to me, concern pulling at the skin around her mouth. She gave her head a little shake. "I'm sorry. I'm Ashley Clark. Casey"—she put a hand on the head of the dog—"found her right over there." She pointed at the clump of trees that shielded the property from the house next door.

I nodded. "She has a lump on her head and a couple of scrapes on her arm, but otherwise she's okay. If she had her way she'd already be out of the hospital." My chest tightened unexpectedly and I had to stop and swallow before I could continue. "Rose is"—I made a gesture in the air—"like family. Thank you for everything you did for her."

Ashley smiled and the hand on the dog's head stroked his black fur. "I'm just glad we were here."

I gestured at the big Lab. "May I?" I said.

She nodded. "Say hello, Casey," she said to the dog.

I leaned forward and held out my hand, fingers curled into a loose fist. He sniffed it for a moment and then took a couple of steps closer to me, his tail wagging like a flag waving in a stiff breeze. "Hey, Casey," I said softly. "Thanks for taking care of my friend Rose."

His big brown eyes seemed to smile at me, and he nuzzled my wrist with his cold, wet nose. I scratched the top of his head.

Michelle was already running Ashley through finding Rose.

"I was in the backyard watering my tomato plants," she said. She gave a self-conscious laugh. "It probably sounds silly, but I knew by Casey's bark that something was wrong. He doesn't bark that much anyway, and it wasn't his 'Hey, play with me' bark or even 'The mailman is here with a dog biscuit' bark."

I thought about Elvis's ability to seemingly know when someone was lying. "I don't think it's silly," I said.

Casey cocked his head to one side and looked at me, almost as if he were trying to show his appreciation for my vote of confidence—or suggesting that I scratch behind his right ear.

"I came around the side of the house and saw Casey over there by that tree standing next to Mrs. Jackson," Ashley continued. "I yelled to Keenan—that's my husband; I'm sorry, he isn't here right now—to call nine one one and then ran over to her. I thought maybe she'd been walking and got hit by a car."

"Did you hear or see anything before the dog started barking?" Michelle asked.

Ashley frowned and shook her head slowly. "That's the thing," she said. "I didn't. I don't remember hearing any cars go by. There were no squealing brakes from someone stopping too fast and I didn't hear anything that sounded like a car hitting . . . her."

That seemed to support Rose's story. I looked over at Michelle but couldn't catch her eye.

Ashley took a couple of steps forward and pointed down the road in the direction of the Camerons' cottage. "The only car I saw or heard, aside from the police and the EMTs, was the Camerons' Jeep—his car; she drives an Audi—and that went by about half an hour before, when we were barbecuing. It's really hard to miss. It's Big Bird yellow."

Michelle asked about the neighbors in the pale blue

cottage next door. Ashley explained that they were out of town for the week.

I straightened up, giving Casey one last scratch on the head. He looked up at me and then went to sit next to his owner again. "Thank you," I said, reaching out to give her arm a squeeze. "I don't like to think about what could have happened to Rose if you and your husband and Casey hadn't been here." The dog lifted his chin and looked up at Ashley as if he wanted to make sure she'd heard the words of praise for him, too.

She smiled at me. "I think she would have been okay. She seems to be pretty feisty."

I laughed. "That she is."

Michelle had a few more routine questions; then she gave Ashley her card in case her husband thought of anything he wanted to add and we started back to our cars. I knew from those questions that she didn't believe Rose's story.

"Are you going back to the hospital?" she asked as we came level with her dark blue Honda.

I nodded. "I'm hoping Rose will be ready to come home." I folded my arms across my midsection. "What happens now?" I asked.

She fished her keys out of the pocket of her gray skirt. "I'll keep trying to contact Jeff Cameron and I'll verify that investment statement is the real thing in the morning. I'll talk to the assistant as well. Beyond that, Mr. Cameron is an adult. If he wants to walk away from his marriage, there's no law that says he can't."

"You think he's alive."

She sighed softly. "I haven't seen or heard anything that makes me believe he's dead."

I didn't say anything.

Michelle looked over at the house. "C'mon, Sarah," she said, shifting her gaze back to me. "You were in that kitchen. Did you see anything that would indicate a man had been killed there? There was no blood, no evidence of a fight or a struggle. I didn't smell bleach or vanilla-scented candles or anything that suggested someone had cleaned up a crime scene."

"That was one room," I pointed out. "And if he'd been hit over the head there wouldn't necessarily be anything to clean up."

Michelle narrowed her green eyes and studied my face. "You actually think Rose saw Leesa Cameron dragging her husband's body across the floor of that kitchen? Really, Sarah?"

I folded one arm over the top of my head like I was pulling up a hood. "I think she saw something. I won't go so far as to say that Leesa Cameron killed her husband, but I think it's a pretty big coincidence that he ran off with all their money and another woman the same night that Rose saw his body being dragged across the floor."

"Sometimes coincidences happen. You heard what Ashley Clark said about seeing his Jeep go by before the dog found Rose."

"It doesn't mean he was driving it," I said.

Michelle took a moment, as though she was sifting through her words before she spoke. "I think Rose believes she saw what she told you she saw," she said. "But I think she may have had a small stroke, wandered up the road and then fell and hit her head, knocking herself out. Maybe what she thinks she saw was just her brain trying to make sense of the gap in time, putting pieces together maybe from a movie she watched or a book she was reading." She touched my arm briefly. "I know how stubborn Rose can be. But I really think you should have her examined by a specialist."

I bit the inside of my cheek so I wouldn't say the wrong thing. Thankfully Michelle's phone buzzed then. She pulled it out, checked the screen and then looked at me again.

I made myself smile at her. "Thank you for coming out here with me," I said. "I should get back to the hospital and check on Rose."

"Anytime," Michelle said. She gave me a hug and I walked back to my SUV. Michelle got in her own car and I waved as she drove away.

I didn't agree with her. I didn't believe that Rose had had a small stroke and imagined seeing Jeff Cameron's body being dragged across the kitchen floor of that cottage by some mystery person dressed in a pink hoodie. It was less than a month ago that there had been a seniors' health clinic at Legacy Place, the former chocolate factory where Rose had lived before she was "invited" to move and took the third apartment in my house.

Charlotte had been one of the volunteers at the clinic, which had been held in the main entrance of the building Rose still snarkily referred to as Shady Pines. Rose had gone with me to help Charlotte get set up and, she admitted, to catch up on all the gossip. I'd dragged her around for the various tests—Rose did not like doctors. Her blood pressure, pulse and blood sugar had all been lower than mine.

I stuck the key in the ignition and took one last look at the cottage. "I really am turning into Rose," I said aloud. I couldn't explain it, but I couldn't shake the feeling that something had happened in that little house. The question was, what?

Chapter 5

My cell phone rang then. It was Charlotte. The hospital was ready to discharge Rose.

"I want her to come home with me, but she won't have any of that," Charlotte said. "She wants to go home to her own apartment." Charlotte had a spare room in her little yellow house that Nick had painted and installed new carpet in just a couple of months ago.

Rose's unwillingness to stay with Charlotte didn't surprise me.

"We'll take her home," I said. "If we have to, you and I and Mr. P. can take turns on guard duty all night."

Charlotte laughed and I told her I'd be there in about fifteen minutes and ended the call.

Rose wanted to know what had happened to Jeff Cameron and she wasn't going to rest until she got some answers. She wasn't going to like the answers I had so far. That persistent streak was what had gotten her involved when Maddie Hamilton had been accused of murder. And it turned out she had a bit of a knack for ferreting out clues, probably because she looked—and baked—like someone's sweet little grandmother and people just seemed to confide in her. Or maybe it was the cookies. It also helped that Mr. P. had all the computer expertise of a teenage hacking genius. Add to that the fact that Liz knew every bit of gossip going around town and Charlotte, after years of being a school principal, knew pretty much everyone in North Harbor, so it didn't seem completely crazy that they'd decided to start their own detective agency.

Of course, Nick wasn't happy about his mother and her friends investigating anything. I could still see the look on his face when he learned that Alfred had met all the requirements to get his PI's license and Rose had begun an apprenticeship with him.

I knew Rose wasn't going to let this go. I hadn't totally been joking when I'd told Charlotte we might have to guard the door to keep Rose from going out to investigate.

Mr. P. was watching for me when I pulled up to the emergency room doors. He raised a hand and I waved back to let him know I'd seen him. I came around the front of the SUV and opened the door for Rose. Charlotte was on one side of her and Mr. P. was on the other. She looked well. She'd combed her hair, her color was good and she seemed to be moving without pain. And she didn't like Charlotte and Mr. P. hovering. Her lips were pressed together in a tight smile.

"Where are we going, Sarah?" she asked as she reached the SUV.

"Home," I said.

"Whose?" Her gray eyes were fixed on my face.

"Yours and mine," I said.

She nodded. "Fine."

Alfred had already gotten in the back. Charlotte hesitated. "I wish she'd just come with me," she said quietly.

"I know," I said, putting an arm around her. In flats she was taller than I was. Since I was wearing a bit of a heel, we were the same size. "And if you suggest that, I'm almost certain Rose will jump out at the first stoplight we hit. And you'll be the one chasing her, because Alfred's knees aren't good and I'm not running in these things." I stuck out one leg so she could see my pretty wedge sandals.

Charlotte laughed and shook her head. Then she slid in next to Mr. P. I hurried around the back of the SUV and got behind the wheel again. Mr. P. touched my shoulder. "Sarah, you're in a no-parking zone," he said.

I leaned forward to look out the windshield. The no-parking sign was right in front of me. "I didn't even see that," I said. I'd been so focused on getting as close to the door as possible that there could have been a bear standing there holding the sign and I still wouldn't have noticed it.

"So put the pedal to the metal before someone sees you," Rose said from the seat beside me. Her hands were folded in her lap, shoulders squared. My own grandmother would have said she was loaded for bear.

I started the car, drove to the bottom of the lot, paid the parking fee and pulled out onto the street. No one spoke.

I glanced over at Rose again. She hadn't moved. "I'll tell you when we get home," I said.

"I didn't say anything," she said.

"You were going to." I touched the brake as a couple of laughing teenagers cut across the street in front of us.

"You don't know that," she retorted.

I took one hand off the steering wheel long enough to tap my temple with two fingers. "I'm very smart."

"You're very saucy."

I smiled but kept my eyes on the road. It was quiet the rest of the way home. I pulled into the driveway and we all piled out of the SUV, Mr. P. hurrying around to help Rose out of her seat.

The moment we stepped into Rose's apartment, Charlotte held up a hand. "No detective work until the tea's made." She looked pointedly at Rose.

"Fine with me," Rose said. "There are chocolate chip cookies in the blue tin." She started for the cupboard but Charlotte stopped her with a look.

"Sit," she said, making a shooing gesture with one hand. She had several inches on her friend, along with the bearing and tone of voice that went along with being a former school principal. Rose stood her ground for a moment and then took a seat at the table.

Once everyone had a cup of hot tea and a cookie, Rose turned to me. "You didn't talk to Jeff Cameron, did you?"

I shook my head. "No, we didn't."

"I knew it," she said, nodding for emphasis. "If you had, you would have said so the moment you picked us up."

She was right. That's exactly what I would have done.

"Did you talk to his wife?" Mr. P. asked, breaking a cookie in half and dipping the end of it in his tea.

"I did," I said. "She claims he left her for another woman and cleaned out their accounts."

Rose set her cup down. "You don't believe that, do you, Sarah?" The skepticism in her voice made it clear what she thought.

I took a bite of my cookie to buy a little time before I answered. "I don't know," I said, finally. "It seems like an awfully convenient coincidence."

"Coincidences do happen," Charlotte said.

I nodded. "I know. And Leesa Cameron did show us—well, Michelle—the text she got from her husband and a bank statement that showed their investment account had been emptied."

"Those things can easily be faked." Rose glanced over at Mr. P., who nodded in confirmation.

"Michelle is going to check with the bank in the morning. Leesa also told us that her husband had an assistant, Chloe Sanders. She's also going to talk to her."

"I had a Chloe Sanders as a student," Charlotte said. "She was on the debate team. Do you think it could be the same person?"

"Maybe," I said. "I know she went to Cahill."

"That sounds right," she said.

I rattled off the phone number I'd memorized when Leesa Cameron had showed it to Michelle. "Will you see if you can contact her in the morning? Maybe we'll get lucky."

Charlotte nodded. "Of course."

"You're a pretty good judge of people, Sarah," Alfred said. "What's your impression of Mrs. Cameron?"

I sighed and played with my cup, turning it around and around in the saucer. "She seemed genuinely hurt and angry," I said. "If she was lying, she's a darn good actress. And it looks like she has an alibi. She said she was with her husband's sister."

Beside me Rose made a frustrated sound.

"I saw Casey, by the way," I said. "He's a beautiful dog."

She smiled at that. "Yes, he is. Tomorrow I'm going to make him some dog biscuits."

"For what it's worth, Ashley Clark said she didn't hear or see any cars go by right before the dog found you."

"That's because I wasn't hit by a car," Rose said. "If I had been, I'd have broken ribs or at least bruises on this part of my body." She patted her midsection with one hand. I didn't know anything about injuries from being hit by a car, but it made sense to me.

"There is one problem, though," I continued. "Ashley says she saw Jeff Cameron's vehicle go by about half an hour before Casey found you."

Rose drank the last of her tea. She made a move to get up, but Charlotte immediately got to her feet and headed for the cozy-covered teapot on the stove. She poured a fresh cup for Rose and topped up her own. Mr. P. and I both shook our heads to more.

"Thank you, Charlotte," Rose said, reaching for the milk jug. "Did Ashley say Jeff Cameron was driving?" she asked.

I reached for another cookie. "No."

"It doesn't prove anything, then," Charlotte said. "It could have been Mr. Cameron who was driving or it could have been someone else entirely."

"So Detective Andrews will start investigating tomorrow?" Rose said. She added sugar to her tea and stirred. It seemed like an innocuous question, but I had a feeling Rose already knew the answer.

"Like I said, she's going to check with the bank."

"And?"

I pushed my cup back and shifted in the chair to face her. "And you already know the answer to that, Rose. The police aren't starting any investigation. They don't think there's anything to investigate. As far as they're concerned, Jeff Cameron left his wife and left town."

Rose's lips pulled into a thin, tight line. "So how does Detective Andrews explain what happened to me? What does she think happened? I hit myself over the head?"

I'd let myself get backed into this corner. There was no way out except to tell Rose what Michelle had said. I put both hands flat on the table and closed my eyes for a moment. It didn't change anything.

"Michelle thinks that you might have had a small stroke and fallen and hit your head. You were dazed and you got as far as the Clarks' house before you passed out. She . . . uh . . . thinks you should see a specialist."

"What a load of balderdash!" Rose exclaimed, gray eyes flashing. "She thinks I'm some feeble old fuddy-duddy, doesn't she?"

"She didn't say that. I think she's genuinely concerned about you."

"Bull crap!"

It struck me that if Rose did have some kind of heart

problem, she'd be having a stroke right now. Her hands were clenched and her face was flushed.

"Rosie, it wouldn't hurt to go see a doctor," Mr. P. offered.

I swung around to stare at him. He was leaning forward and he was frowning slightly.

"Alfred Peterson, you must have had a stroke yourself if you think there's anything wrong with my brain," Rose said.

"Rose Jackson, when was the last time you actually saw a doctor?" Charlotte asked. I could always count on her to be the voice of reason.

Rose looked up at the round red clock on the wall above the table. "About forty-five minutes ago," she said tartly.

"And before that?" Charlotte countered, her voice quiet in comparison to her friend's.

"I had my blood pressure and my blood sugar checked at that clinic at Shady Pines."

"Those were nurses, not doctors," Charlotte said. "When—other than about an hour ago—did you last see a doctor?"

"None of your business," Rose snapped. She really didn't like doctors. She went once a year for a physical checkup because Liz would nag her until she made the appointment and then show up on the day to drive her there.

"That's what I thought," Charlotte said. She brushed cookie crumbs into a little pile and swept them into her hand, dropping them onto her plate. "So make an appointment. Let the doctor check you out. It will prove to Detective Andrews that there's nothing wrong with you and maybe"—she stressed the word—"*maybe* the police will take a second look at what happened."

It was a sensible, logical suggestion because that was the kind of person Charlotte was, but I knew Rose was not in the mood for sensible and logical.

Mr. P. nodded. "I'll go with you." He reached across the table for Rose's hand, but she was already on her feet.

She looked from Alfred to Charlotte. "If Sarah had told you that she saw a body, neither one of you would be suggesting she see a doctor to have her head examined. I am deeply offended." She stalked out of the apartment, back rigid, before either of them could say anything.

After a moment of silence Mr. P. got to his feet. I caught his arm. "Let her go," I said.

"Rosie just got out of the hospital, Sarah. She shouldn't be walking around in the dark," he said.

"She isn't. She didn't even go outside. She's in my apartment talking to Elvis."

Mr. P. looked over his shoulder at the door. "I mean no disrespect, my dear," he said. "But how can you be sure? She's very angry."

"Rose is wearing the fuzzy slippers Avery knit for her. It doesn't matter how angry she is. She knows how proud Avery was when she made them. She's not going to wear them outside. Right now she's sitting on my sofa telling Elvis how mad she is at the two of you. And Michelle. And Liz."

Charlotte took a drink from her cup and set it down again. She got to her feet. "Stay here, Alfred," she said.

"I'll go talk to her. I'm the one who pushed her over the edge." She looked over at me. "It's not that I don't believe her. I just don't think it would hurt for her to go see her own doctor."

I gave her a half smile. "I know that and so does Rose underneath her dramatic exit." I looked from her to Mr. P. "Go home, both of you. Let me handle things. It will all look better in the morning. I promise."

"You sound like Isabel," Charlotte said, referring to my grandmother.

I smiled. "I wish she was here."

Charlotte smiled as well. "Me, too."

I stood up, brushing crumbs off my T-shirt. "Please. Go home," I said. I turned my attention to Mr. P. "I promise I won't leave Rose alone. I'll sit by her bed and watch her sleep if I have to."

Alfred managed a small smile. "That might be a little excessive, my dear," he said.

"All right. We'll go," Charlotte said. She picked up her cup and saucer and Mr. P.'s and carried them over to the sink. Then she came back to the table. She patted Alfred's arm. "Sarah is right. Rose needs some time to cool down, and I trust Sarah to take care of her."

He sighed softly. "All right," he said. He looked at me. "Please tell her I'm sorry."

"I will," I promised.

I put the rest of the dishes in the sink and wiped off the table. Charlotte and Mr. P. agreed to share a cab, and I went out on the steps to wait with them. As soon as the taxi pulled away from the curb I headed back inside.

Rose was on the sofa in my apartment. Elvis was sitting next to her. They both looked up when I came in the door. The cat licked his whiskers, which told me Rose had gotten him a treat. Probably more than one.

"Charlotte and Mr. P. have gone home," I said. I went into the kitchen, poured myself a glass of lemonade from the pitcher in the refrigerator and sat down on the other side of Elvis. "They're both sorry they upset you. All they want is to be sure you're all right."

"Sorry is as sorry does," she said, a little petulantly, it seemed to me.

"Don't give me that," I said, sucking on a chunk of ice. "Mr. P. wanted to go out in the dark to look for you, and Charlotte always has your back. She's been one of your best friends longer than I've been alive."

Rose stroked Elvis's fur but didn't say anything.

"And speaking of best friends who care about you," I began.

That got her hackles up again. "Sarah Grayson, are you taking Liz's side over mine?" she challenged.

I slid down until I was basically sitting on my tailbone. "I'm not taking anyone's side," I said. "I'm just stating a fact." I took another sip of my lemonade. "And for the record, if the tables were turned, we both know you'd be telling me to go see a doctor, just to prove there wasn't anything wrong with my head."

Rose leaned toward Elvis. "That's why I like cats," she said. "They don't have nearly as much to say as some people do."

The cat murped his agreement.

I tipped my head back and rolled my neck from side

to side. "They can't drive, either," I said. "So they can't take anyone over to see Jeff Cameron's sister in the morning."

I stared down into my glass and set the ice cubes swirling. Out of the corner of my eye I could see Rose struggling not to smile. She finally lost the battle and leaned against me, grinning. "Do you always get what you want?" she asked.

I rested my head against hers. "No," I said. "So I'm going to enjoy this little victory."

Elvis wiggled out from between us, shook himself and jumped down from the sofa.

Rose sighed. "Detective Andrews is a lovely young woman," she said. "And I do appreciate that she went over to the Camerons' house with you. She's a good friend."

I nodded.

"But she tends to think that the simplest explanation is the right one, and while that might be true most of the time, it's not true all of the time. Life just isn't that neat and simple. It's messy sometimes, and this is one of those times."

"Yes," I said. What I didn't say was that I had a feeling it was about to get a lot messier.

Chapter 6

Rose yawned and lifted a hand to cover her mouth. "I'm sorry, dear," she said. "I promise it's not the company."

"It's been a long night," I said. "We could both use some sleep."

"I'll see you in the morning, then."

"Stay here," I said, leaning forward to set my glass on the floor beside the sofa.

"I'll be fine," she said. "I'm just going to go home and go to bed. I won't do anything rash, I promise." She put her hand over her heart.

I stretched my arms up over my head. "I know that," I said. "But you did take an awful whack on the head."

"I'm fine," she repeated. "I don't even have a concussion."

"That's because you have an exceedingly hard head." I made a face at her and she laughed. "Humor me, please," I said. "I don't want to have to sneak into your place at two a.m. and hold a mirror up to your mouth to see if you're breathing."

Rose laughed again. "All right. I'll stay." She held up one finger. "As long as you sleep in your bed and I sleep here on the pullout."

"Deal," I said. The sofa bed had a good mattress and I knew Rose would be comfortable.

Elvis launched himself back onto the sofa between us. He poked the cushion a couple of times and then looked expectantly at Rose.

"You may have to share with Elvis," I said.

"That's not a problem," she said, reaching over to stroke his fur. "He won't be the first hairy male to share my bed." Her gray eyes twinkled.

I clapped my hands over my ears and shut my eyes. "Too much information," I exclaimed. I could hear her laughing anyway.

I made up the bed while Rose went to get her pajamas and toothbrush. "We have to make Rose call her daughter in the morning," I said to Elvis. He cocked his head to one side and gazed at me with narrowed eyes as if he were thinking, *How do you plan on doing that?*

I was pretty sure I could nudge Rose into calling Abby. I knew she cared about me as much as I cared about her, and in the end she'd do it for that reason alone.

I'd spent summers in North Harbor with my grandmother as far back as I could remember. The rest of the year I'd lived first in upstate New York and then in New Hampshire. Both my father and mother had been only children, so I hadn't had a pile of cousins to hang out with during the summer. My grandmother's friends, Charlotte, Rose and Liz, had become my surrogate extended family, a trio of indulgent and loving albeit opinionated aunts.

When the radio station where my late-night syndicated radio show originated changed hands, I was replaced by a music feed from the West Coast and a nineteen-year-old guy with a tan and ombré hair who gave the temperature every hour. I'd come back to North Harbor at the urging of my mother, who knew how much I loved the town. When I decided to open Second Chance, Rose, Charlotte and Liz had been almost as thrilled as my grandmother. They were family. I'd do anything for them.

Rose came back carrying her pajamas, her toothbrush and one of her ubiquitous totes.

"What's in that?" I asked.

She handed the bag to me. "Just a few things for breakfast. Would you stick it in the refrigerator, dear, please?"

I stuck the bag in my less-than-full fridge. Rose had been giving me cooking lessons for months now, and to everyone's surprise—especially mine—they seemed to be starting to take. Now I needed to work on making a grocery list and making time to hit the store.

I peeked in the bag as I set it on the shelf, catching sight of eggs and what looked like Canadian bacon.

"I could cook breakfast," I offered. Just because the doctor had said Rose didn't have a concussion didn't mean that she shouldn't take it a little easier.

"I know you could, dear," she said. She looked at the opened sofa bed. "Oh, that looks lovely and cozy."

"You can take the bathroom first," I said. "There's

lots of hot water for a bath. I want to check the store's Web site before bed."

Rose gave her head a little shake—which didn't seem to cause her any pain, I noted. "You work too much," she said. "At this rate the only hairy man you'll be sharing your bed with is Elvis."

I poked a finger in each ear. "La, la, la, la, la," I sang loudly.

All that got me was a smile. Rose picked up her pajamas. "I think I will have a bath," she said. "I do like that nice deep tub of yours."

"I put out some towels."

She nodded. "Thank you, dear. It's a bit late now, but remind me to call Abby in the morning."

"How did you know I was going to ask you that?" I said.

She tapped her right temple with a finger. "I'm very smart."

She started down the hall to the bathroom. "You listen at doors," I called after her.

"That, too," she replied.

I woke in the morning to the smell of coffee and bacon instead of a cat sitting on my chest breathing cat breath in my face. So much for me cooking breakfast instead of Rose. I padded out to the kitchen in my pajamas and bare feet. Rose was at the stove, one of my dish towels used as an apron and pinned around her waist with a couple of chip-bag clips. Elvis was watching her every move from a stool at the counter.

"Good morning," I said.

"Good morning," Rose said, giving me a sunny smile. Elvis gave me his usual murp in hello.

"Before you ask, I already called Abby."

"What did she say?" I asked.

"She told me what I'd done was dangerous and a little stupid."

"And?" I prompted because I knew there had to be more.

"And I told her she was right."

My eyebrows went up. "That must have surprised her."

Rose eyed the pan, giving it a little shake. "She's going to come for a few days at the end of the month."

"Good," I said. I edged past her to get a cup for my coffee. After I'd poured and added cream and sugar I joined Elvis at the counter. "What can I do to help?" I asked.

"I have everything under control," she said.

I propped my elbows on the counter and wrapped my hands around the mug. "How do you feel?"

"I feel fine." Rose gestured in the direction of the sofa with a spatula. "That bed is very comfortable." She absently rubbed the back of her neck with her free hand. I'd noticed her doing that a couple of times the night before.

I set my cup on the counter, slid off the stool and went over to her. "Does that hurt?" I asked.

She frowned. "What? Oh, you mean my neck. No. It's just a little irritated. I think I was probably dinner for some black fly last night."

"Let me take a look," I said. I put my hands on Rose's shoulders and turned her body a little so her neck was in the best light. A patch of skin on the left side of her neck, just at her hairline, was a little red because she'd been rubbing it. I leaned in closer.

"I'll just put a little calamine lotion on and it will be fine."

I straightened and she turned to look at me. "Did they give you any shots when you were in the hospital?" I asked.

"No." She shook her head. "They took blood from this arm." She raised her left elbow. "But that's all." She frowned. "What is it?"

"It looks as though there's a needle mark on your neck."

Rose's hand immediately went to the place. "A needle mark? I don't think so, Sarah. How on earth could I get a needle mark on my neck?"

"That's what I'd like to know. I think we should go back to the hospital."

"Well, I don't." She flipped the bacon with an expert toss. "What's that going to achieve other than waste a lot of time? I already told you they didn't give me any shot at the hospital."

I raked a hand back through my messy hair. "I wasn't thinking it happened at the hospital."

Rose moved the frying pan off the heat and turned off the burner. She wiped her hands on the tea towel and gave me all her attention. "Are you saying you think I was injected with something when I was at the Cameron house?"

I shrugged. "I don't know. Maybe that is just a bug bite." I looked at her neck again. "I'm far from an expert, but it doesn't look like one to me."

Rose moved to rub her neck again and then stopped herself. "That would explain how I could have been hit hard enough to be unconscious for several minutes but not have a concussion."

"We need to go back to the ER and have someone look at this who knows what they're doing," I said. "And maybe do some kind of blood tests."

"I'm not going back to the hospital," she said, a matter-of-fact tone to her voice. "If you tell me you see a needle prick, then that's what it is. Besides, we'll have to sit there all morning and we need to go see Jeff Cameron's sister."

"I'm not a doctor, Rose," I said. "I might be wrong."

She reached up and patted my cheek. "Nonsense. You're as smart as any doctor. You could have gone to medical school." She broke into a smile then and clapped her hands together. "Nicolas," she said.

"What about Nick?" I asked. I reached over and swiped a piece of the Canadian bacon from the pan.

"He'll know what that is—not that I doubt you for a moment."

She was right. Not only was Nick an investigator for the medical examiner's office, he also had a degree in biology and he'd been accepted into medical school. He'd worked as an EMT to put himself through college and had been offered a job teaching an EMT course before he took the investigator's job. I knew that short of tying Rose up with the cord of her bathrobe and stuffing her in the back of my SUV, there was no way I was going to get her back to the hospital. Nick was my best bet.

I nodded. "I'll call him after breakfast."

"Splendid," Rose exclaimed. She picked up the spatula and motioned me back to my stool with it. "Now, go sit down while I finish breakfast."

I hesitated, thinking I should have been the one doing the cooking. As if she had once more read my mind, Rose waved the spatula at me again. "I'm fine," she said, with just a tinge of annoyance in her voice. "Sit."

I leaned over and kissed the top of her head. "I'm sitting," I said.

After a bacon-and-egg sandwich on a toasted English muffin and a second cup of coffee, I called Nick.

"How's Rose?" he asked. "I'm guessing you spent the night in her apartment."

"Close," I said, pulling up the cotton blanket on the bed. I was multitasking, making the bed as I talked. "She spent the night here with Elvis and me."

"How did you manage that?"

"A bit of guilt, a bit of whining."

Nick laughed.

"I'm guessing Charlotte brought you up to speed," I said.

"Michelle, too," he said. "Is there anything I can do to help?"

I sat down on the edge of the half-made bed. "Yeah, there is. That's why I called." I explained about the mark on Rose's neck. "I might be wrong, but short of duct tape or chloroform, there's no way I'm going to get her to go back to the hospital. If I'm wrong, it doesn't matter. And if I'm right, maybe you'll have better luck convincing her."

"Well, of course, because my persuasive skills have worked so well on Rose in the past." He made no effort to keep the sarcasm out of his voice.

"Please," I said, stopping just short of begging—not that I wouldn't beg if I had to. But I didn't have to.

"I could stop by the shop sometime late morning," he offered.

"Thank you," I said, relief easing the knot in my shoulders.

"Hey, no problem." I could feel the warmth of his smile through the phone.

I told Nick I'd see him later and we said good-bye. I brushed my hair into a low ponytail, put on some lip gloss and grabbed my bag.

Elvis and I waited in Rose's kitchen while she got dressed. I'd called Mac the night before and brought him up to date on everything that had happened. He was opening the shop for me. Since he lived in the small apartment on the top floor, it wasn't a big inconvenience for him. I thought—for what had to be the hundredth time—how hiring Mac had been the smartest decision I'd made when I decided to open Second Chance.

My cell phone rang while I was sitting at the kitchen table. I checked the screen. It was my grandmother.

"Hi, Gram," I said. Hearing her voice wasn't as good as seeing her in person, but it was close.

"Hello, sweetie pie," she replied. "How's Rose?"

"Let me guess," I said. "Charlotte called you."

"Liz."

I leaned back in the chair. "Rose is fine, Gram. She spent the night with me. She snores, by the way."

Gram laughed. "I know. I shared a room with her when the four of us went to Florida."

"I'll call Liz when I get to the shop," I said. "I'm actually in Rose's apartment right now waiting for her to get dressed."

"They'll work it out," she said. "Do you know how many arguments they've had over the years?"

I shook my head even though she couldn't see the motion. "I don't have a clue."

She laughed again. "Neither do I, but I can promise you that it's a very big number."

"I miss you," I said.

"I miss you, too," she said. "But I'll see you in a bit more than a month."

Gram and her new husband, John, had gotten married almost a year ago. Jess and I agreed that John looked like actor Gary Oldman's slightly older brother. He had the same dark hair, streaked with gray, waving back from his face, and the same intense gaze behind dark-framed glasses. There were thirteen years between Gram and John—she being the elder—which had raised some eyebrows, but Gram didn't seem anywhere near her seventy-four years. And more important, she didn't care what other people thought.

They'd set out on their honeymoon in an RV that wasn't much bigger than a minivan, intending to travel along the East Coast and work on a project for the charity Home for Good. One house-building project had turned into several, and now after nearly a year away Gram and John were finally coming home.

"I can't wait to see you," I said.

"You, too," Gram said. "I have to go. John has breakfast ready. Give Rose a hug for me. And tell her I said to listen to you."

"I will," I promised. "Give John a hug for me."

"I will." She blew a kiss into the phone. "Love you, sweetie."

"Love you, too," I said.

Rose came bustling out of the bedroom then. "I'm sorry to be so much trouble," she said, fastening her watch as she came into the kitchen. Elvis had already wandered around the apartment, sticking his furry black nose into pretty much everything. Now he was sitting quietly at my feet washing his face.

"You aren't any trouble," I said. "I'd do the same for Jess or Nick."

Rose grinned and raised an eyebrow at Nick's name.

I felt my face get red. "You know what I mean."

"And you know what I mean," she countered.

"Yes, I do," I said, getting to my feet. "Which is why I'm not having this conversation with you."

"I know it seems like we're all a little pushy sometimes when it comes to Nicolas and you," Rose said, reaching for the green-and-white canvas tote she'd left on one of the chairs. I picked it up for her.

"A little?" I asked, narrowing my gaze at her.

She wrinkled her nose at me. "You know that I love that boy as though he were my own, but goodness, he is as slow as cold molasses when it comes to women. All we're trying to do is kindle a little spark so the two of you can get the fire lit." And then she wiggled her eyebrows at me.

All of them—Rose, Charlotte and Liz, not to mention

Gram, who wasn't even in town at the moment—had been trying to nudge Nick and me into a relationship since we'd both ended up unattached and back in North Harbor at the same time, telling me about Nick's great hair genes, and him about my good dental hygiene. We'd been spending a lot more time together lately now that Nick had started running with me when he wasn't working. I wasn't sure if I could call what was happening a romance, though. We had an easy familiarity that came from having known each other since we were kids. He was funny and handsome and I had no idea whether it would turn into something more—or if I wanted it to. I'd kissed him—more than once, and he seemed to like kissing me—but that was as far as it got. Rose was right; Nick could be as slow as cold molasses. But I wasn't exactly a speedster myself.

"Oh, I almost forgot," I said. I wrapped my arms around Rose and gave her a hug. "That's from Gram. She called while you were getting dressed."

"I'm sorry I missed her," Rose said. "I'll call Isabel tonight."

"She'd like that," I said as we moved out into the hall.

Rose pulled out her keys to lock the door. "Who finked me out to her?"

"Liz called her. I don't think she was trying to fink you out to Gram."

"Sarah, how long have Liz and I been friends?" Rose asked.

I shrugged. "I don't know. Since sometime just after the dinosaurs died out, I think."

She glowered at me.

I held the front door for her and we stepped outside. "What I do know is that in all the years you've been friends, Liz has always had your back, so whatever it takes to fix things, I think you should do. And by the way, Gram said to tell you that you should listen to me."

"I'm starting to see where your bossiness comes from," Rose grumped.

I laughed and unlocked the SUV.

I stuck the sticky note with the address and phone number for Jeff Cameron's sister on the dashboard. I decided we had a better chance of getting the information we were looking for if we talked to her in person, and if we didn't call first it was a lot harder for her to say no to talking to us.

Since we were going to Second Chance after we talked to Nicole Cameron, we took Elvis with us. He sat on the front bench seat of my SUV between Rose and me and watched the road the way he always did.

"I wonder who used to own Elvis," Rose said. "Do you think it could have been a long-distance truck driver?" The cat turned and eyed her as though he'd taken offense at the suggestion that anyone could claim ownership of him.

"Maybe," I said. "That would explain why he's a bit of a backseat driver."

Rose reached over and stroked the top of Elvis's head. "He's very intelligent," she said. "Look at how he can tell whether or not someone is telling the truth."

I was still making sense out of that skill. We'd all noticed that if someone was stroking the cat's fur and telling a lie, Elvis would get an expression on his face that, as Liz expressed it, looked like he'd just had one of Avery's kale smoothies.

Elvis's apparent lie-detecting ability had come in useful in more than one of the Angels' cases. Both Mac and Jess had theorized that somehow the cat was reading body reactions in much the same way that an actual polygraph machine did. Considering that he had an uncanny ability to figure out my mood, they were probably right.

"I know where you're going with this, Rose," I said. "We're not taking Elvis in with us when we get to Nicole Cameron's house. For all we know she might not even like cats."

"I wasn't suggesting that."

"Good," I said.

"Although I certainly don't see why anyone wouldn't like Elvis. He's handsome, he's an excellent mouser and as I just said, he's extremely intelligent."

Out of the corner of my eye I saw Elvis straighten up as though he'd understood every word Rose had said. And for all I knew, maybe he had. I talked to him all the time, and sometimes it really did seem as though he was listening. And other times he made it very clear that he wasn't listening to what I was saying at all.

Nicole Cameron lived on a tree-lined street about halfway up the hill from the main downtown. The houses were mostly Cape Cod style with a few two-story, older Federal-style homes.

"There it is," Rose said, pointing at a gray-shingled house with a tall maple tree in the front yard. A red Jeep Wrangler was parked in the driveway, its front wheels turned sharply to the right as though it were parked on a hill.

I pulled to the curb and parked. Up ahead, on the other side of the wide street, I saw a vehicle I recognized. I didn't point it out to Rose. "Guard the car," I said to Elvis as I got out of the SUV. The cat moved over to the driver's seat, reaching up to rest a paw on the steering wheel.

The front door of the house had a replica twist doorbell in an oiled bronze finish. I turned the knob and after a moment the door opened. Nicole Cameron was about my height. She had the same blond hair as her brother in a chin-length bob. Where Jeff Cameron had the lean build of a runner, Nicole was built more solidly, with the same strong, muscular arms and shoulders as her sister-in-law. She was probably a rower, too, I was guessing.

"Ms. Cameron, my name is Sarah Grayson," I began.

"You want to ask me about Leesa," she said. She was wearing a yellow T-shirt and gray cropped leggings and her feet were bare.

I nodded. "Yes."

Nicole Cameron turned her attention to Rose. "You're Rose Jackson, aren't you? You were delivering the candlesticks my brother bought for Leesa."

Rose nodded. "Yes, I am." She sent me a look that was as confused as I felt.

A frown creased the younger woman's forehead. "I'm sorry you were hurt. You're all right?"

"Yes, I am," Rose said, her voice gentle, as though she were talking to an animal that might spook at any moment.

Nicole sighed softly. "You should come in," she said. "I uh . . . I know you have questions."

She moved back and we stepped inside. The house opened into a small foyer. Ahead of us was a hallway that I guessed led to the kitchen and the stairs to the second floor. To our right was a coat closet, and the sun-filled living room opened to our left.

Rose took several steps into the room and then stopped so abruptly I almost bumped into her. Liz was sitting on the sofa.

"What are you doing here?" she asked, surprise evident in both her voice and the rigid way she held herself. So she hadn't spotted Liz's car on the street when I did.

"I know Nicole from Phantasy," Liz said. Phantasy was a spa that belonged to Liz's niece, Elspeth. "And I'm here because I wanted to find out if her sister-in-law was here last night."

Nicole Cameron wiped her hands on her leggings. "Leesa was here last night," she said. She shook her head and gestured in the direction of the sofa and a pair of boxy apple green Fillmore chairs. "I'm sorry. Please have a seat."

I sat down on the gunmetal gray couch and Rose took one of the chairs. Nicole sank onto a tufted brown leather ottoman. "Leesa got here sometime around six thirty. She was upset. You know that my brother left her?"

I nodded.

"I put the TV on and the news was just starting. We watched *Murder Ink*," she said, referring to the program known as water-cooler television because it was the show everyone was talking about the morning after it aired. "It was a rerun. It was after eight when Leesa left."

Rose had gotten to the Cameron house just before eight o'clock. There was no way the hooded figure she'd seen was Leesa Cameron.

"I was just asking Nicole if she'd heard from her brother," Liz said.

The younger woman shook her head. "The last time I talked to Jeff was Tuesday. I've been texting and calling since I got up, but he hasn't texted me back and the calls just go to voice mail."

"Did you have any idea your brother was going to leave his wife?" I asked.

She stared down at her feet for a moment. "No," she said. "I didn't see any sign that anything was wrong, and Jeff didn't say a word to me."

I glanced at Liz and one expertly groomed eyebrow raised about a millimeter.

"But . . . uh." Nicole hesitated. "That's the kind of person Jeff is. He wouldn't have let on what he was planning to anyone. He isn't good with emotions. We were raised by our grandmother. She died three years ago, and after it happened he just disappeared. He couldn't handle the grief. We just reconnected less than a year ago. At some point he'll call. It's just the way he does things." She was wearing a stack of bracelets on her right wrist and she slid them up and down her arm.

"When you talk to him, would you ask him to call Detective Andrews at the police department?" I said. I got to my feet. Liz and Rose stood up as well.

Nicole did the same, walking us to the door, still absently playing with her bracelets.

"Thank you for talking to us," Liz said.

"I'm sorry Jeff got you all mixed up in this," Nicole said. She turned to Rose. "And I'm very sorry you were hurt."

Rose smiled and patted her arm. "Thank you, my dear," she said.

No one spoke until we reached the street, and no surprise, it was Liz who had the first words.

"At some point he'll call." She snorted, turning to glance back at the house. "What a load of—"

I arched an eyebrow at her.

"—horse pucks," she finished.

"Liz is right," Rose said. "She doesn't seem very concerned about her brother being missing. Maybe that's because she believes he's alive."

"Well, if he's done this kind of thing before, that's understandable." I held up both hands before Liz and Rose could object. "I'm not saying I think Jeff is still alive. I'm saying I can see why Nicole might."

Liz rolled her eyes.

I pulled my keys out of my pocket. "So you think what? That Leesa Cameron killed her husband and his sister helped her cover it up?"

Liz shrugged. "Maybe."

Rose studied her friend, her head tipped to one side. "You believe me."

"Well, of course I believe you," Liz retorted, as if there had never been any question of it. "I wouldn't have gotten up at the crack of dawn to get here before the police and had one of those hideous smoothies Avery makes for breakfast if I didn't." She pulled a face. "I can't believe the good Lord intends for me to drink what is essentially a weed for breakfast, not when he created sausage."

I put my arms around her shoulders and pressed my cheek to hers. "We appreciate your sacrifice."

"Yes, we do," Rose said. She and Liz locked eyes for a moment, and I knew everything was all right with them again.

"So what are you doing now?" Liz asked.

"We're headed to the shop," I said.

Rose gave a melodramatic sigh. We eyed each other. The stubborn jut of her chin warned me I was in for an argument.

I crossed my arms over my chest. "We had a deal," I said, warningly. "You let Nick look at your neck and I don't drag you back to the hospital."

"What happened to your neck?" Liz immediately asked.

Rose turned and tipped her head forward. "Sarah thinks someone might have injected me with something."

Liz bent over her friend's neck. "There?" she asked, pointing with one finger.

I nodded. "Maybe that's why Rose was unconscious. Not because of the bump on her head."

She squinted and leaned in for a better look. "I think you might be right," she said. I could see the concern in her blue eyes, which she masked when Rose turned around.

"If you don't want to go back to the store to wait for Nick, we could just go over to the hospital right now," I said sweetly to Rose.

"Are you trying to blackmail me?"

I nodded. "Is it working?"

A smile pulled at the corners of her mouth. "It is, but only because at the moment Nicolas is the lesser of two evils."

I laughed. "I'm sure he'd be flattered to hear that."

"Fine," she said with a bit of a martyred sigh. "You win."

"Thank you," I said. Then I reached out to touch her arm. "You did have a head injury. I just want to be sure you're all right."

From across the street we heard a burst of laughter. There were children dancing on the front lawn of the two-story house across the street in what seemed like a loosely choreographed routine. A girl who looked to be about twelve was shooting a video with a small camera, gesturing madly when one of the dancers missed a step.

Rose followed my gaze. "If Nicolas was examining the back of your neck once in a while, you could have some little ones of your own," she said.

"It's a long walk back to the shop," I replied darkly.

She gave me a look that was all innocence. "Sarah, how could you, in all good conscience, leave a little old lady who, as you yourself just pointed out, had a head injury, at the side of the road?"

Liz jabbed me with her elbow. "How do you like it when the shoe is on the other foot, missy?"

I held up a finger in warning. "Watch it or you'll be

driving Rose to work and I'll be going to McNamara's for a lemon tart." Lemon tarts were Liz's favorite. "By. My. Self," I stressed.

She laughed. "The only place I'm driving is Phantasy for a fresh manicure and some gossip." She blew me a kiss. "Later."

Rose caught her hand as Liz moved past her. "Thank you," she said.

"Anytime," Liz said, and I noticed a suspicious sparkle in her eyes that I knew it was better I didn't comment on.

Rose and I climbed into the SUV. Elvis stretched and moved over. At the bottom of the street I turned left.

"This isn't the way back to the shop," Rose said, frowning as she looked through the windshield. I glanced sideways. Both she and Elvis were looking inquiringly at me.

"I know," I said. "We're going back to the scene of the crime to see if anything there jogs your memory."

"I had exactly the same idea." Rose smiled. "You know, it's uncanny how often we're in sync." She swept a hand through the space between us.

"Yes, it is," I agreed, keeping my eyes on traffic. It occurred to me that "scary" might be a better word.

Chapter 7

No one was home at the Cameron cottage. I parked in front and Rose and I got out. Elvis jumped up onto the back of the seat and peered through the passenger-side window. Rose stood at the bottom of the driveway and looked around.

"Tell me what you did, step by step," I said.

"I went to the front door," she said, gesturing with one hand.

"Did you knock or ring the bell?" We started walking slowly up the driveway.

"I rang the bell. When no one answered, I knocked."

"And then you went to the side door?"

Rose nodded. "There is no side doorbell, so I knocked. When I didn't get any answer there, either, I peeked through the window. That's when I saw Jeff Cameron's body. Then something hit me and the next thing I remember is the dog."

I nodded slowly. "Okay, I want you to back up a little. When you got out of the taxi, did you notice any lights on in the house?"

"No."

It would have been getting close to dusk when Rose arrived, about the time of day people turned their inside lights on, unless they were busy killing someone. "Wait a minute," I said. "What about the candlesticks?"

"They were in a box wrapped in that pretty blue paper with a silver bow. The box was in my L.L. Bean bag, the little one with the blue bottom and handles. My purse was in there, too." I remembered seeing Liz with the bag the night before.

I studied the front of the little house for a moment. Through the front window I could see a painting of the harbor on the living room wall. "Did you see anything through that window?" I asked.

Rose shook her head. "No, the curtains were closed." She turned to look at me. "I'd forgotten that. Do you think it's important?"

I shrugged. "I don't know. Maybe." I stood at the end of the walkway to the front door where it joined the paved driveway. "So you went to the other door and knocked."

"Yes."

"Where was your bag? Which arm?"

Rose frowned a little but she patted her left forearm. "Right here."

"Show me what you did, as close as you can," I said. I stood on the pavement, hands jammed in my pockets as Rose made her way to the side door of the house. She climbed the steps, knocked, waited and then went up on her tiptoes for a better view through the windows.

She turned to look at me over her shoulder. "Then whatever it was hit me. That's it."

"Back it up again," I said. "You're looking through the window." I made a turnaround motion with two fingers.

"Yes." She nodded slowly.

"What do you see?"

"The back of a chair, chrome like that table-and-chair set we sold last month to that couple from Portland."

"What else?"

"Shoes," Rose said. "Bright red sneakers—well, running shoes, I guess I should say." She turned around again. "I know what you're trying to do. You're hoping I might remember something else if I just tell you the first thing that comes into my mind, but it isn't working. I don't remember anything else." Her voice was edged with frustration.

I nodded. "Okay. It was worth a shot. But could we keep going so I can at least go over the details from beginning to end? I've only had them in bits and pieces up to now."

"Of course we can," Rose said, giving me a smile. She faced the porch again, put a hand on the railing and peered through the window.

"So you saw the running shoes," I said. "What happened then?"

Rose exhaled slowly. "I saw whoever it was in the pink hoodie. I think that person was dragging Jeff Cameron's body."

I moved a few steps closer up the driveway. "So that person crossed directly in front of your line of sight?"

"No. I just saw her—or him—from the side, and only for a moment."

"What did you do?"

"For a minute I didn't do anything. Then I stood on my tiptoes to try to get a better look and I called out and banged on the window. I tried the porch door, but it was locked. So I looked around for something I could use to break the glass, but I couldn't find anything. I was going to go to the front door when something hit me over the head." Rose raised a hand but didn't say anything. I realized she wasn't looking at what was right in front of her. She was seeing a memory replay in her head.

"Someone caught me," she said slowly. Her hand went to her neck. She looked at me, comprehension spreading across her face. "When I started to fall. Whoever it was stuck me with something, just as I passed out."

I nodded. "Yeah, I think so."

Rose came down the steps. "That's what you were trying to get me to remember."

I shrugged and gave her a smile. "I was hoping."

She put her hands on her hips in mock annoyance. "Very sneaky saying it was worth a shot so I'd think what you were doing hadn't worked and I'd relax."

I put my arm around her shoulders and laid my cheek against her head. "You taught me well," I said.

She reached up to pat my cheek. "You've always been a quick study, sweet girl," she said.

We walked back down the driveway. Elvis was still perched on the back of the seat, studying the house as if he could somehow come up with the answers we were looking for.

Rose got in the passenger side and Elvis jumped down to settle himself beside her.

"Ready to head for the shop?" I asked. Rose didn't answer. Her mind was somewhere else. She was stroking Elvis's fur, a faraway look on her face.

I watched her until she realized the SUV wasn't moving and turned her attention on me.

"Sarah, who was the other person?" she said.

Elvis scrunched up his nose as though he were considering the question.

"What do you mean?" I said.

"Let's say it was Leesa Cameron dragging her husband's body." Rose held up a hand. "And yes, I know she has an alibi, but for now let's say she doesn't."

I stuck the key in the ignition but didn't start the car. "Okay, let's say that."

"Who hit me over the head, injected me with—with whatever it was that knocked me out? She had help."

Elvis murped his agreement.

Why hadn't I thought of that before? In all the uproar, that little detail had slipped past me. I pounded lightly on the steering wheel. "Good question. Who was it?"

"Did you ever read Sir Arthur Conan Doyle?" Rose asked.

Conversations with Rose could easily veer off on a tangent, so I didn't bother asking how the creator of Sherlock Holmes was connected to Rose being hit over the head and most likely injected with something that knocked her out. "In an English class in college," I said.

"Then you probably know what he said about eliminating the impossible so that whatever is left, even if it seems preposterous, has to be the truth." She patted her white hair. "I'm paraphrasing, of course."

"I know the quote," I said.

Elvis nudged her hand and she resumed stroking his fur. "Well, I've always thought Sir Arthur was making things unnecessarily complicated. Instead of wasting a lot of time eliminating the impossible, in my experience it's better to look at the most obvious answer first."

If Nick had been with us, he would have rolled his eyes because I knew what she meant without any more of an explanation. "You think Leesa was involved with someone."

Rose nodded. "Exactly, and it's impossible to keep that kind of thing a secret in a small place like this. Not for very long."

"So if"—I put extra emphasis on the word—"*if* Leesa Cameron did something to her husband because she was involved with another man, and *if* we can find out who that man is, we can figure this whole thing out." Because of course that wasn't impossible or improbable at all.

Rose beamed at me. "Well, now we have a plan," she said.

On the drive back to the store, Rose and Elvis discussed cat treats. It seemed that she felt she should make some for him since she was going to make dog biscuits for Casey.

Second Chance is in a red brick building that was built in the late eighteen hundreds. We're located on Mill Street where it curves and begins to climb uphill, about a twenty-minute walk from the harbor and easily reached from the highway—the best of both worlds for tourists. Gram holds the mortgage on the building and I'm working to pay her back as quickly as I can.

As we turned into the parking lot at the shop, Nick pulled in behind us. He got out of his truck and walked over to the SUV as we got out. He shot me a quick smile and focused his attention on Rose, putting both his hands on her shoulders. "Are you all right?" he asked.

He was tall, over six feet, with Charlotte's eyes and smile. He was wearing a blue golf shirt and what I thought of as his work pants, ones that seemed to me to have at least a dozen pockets.

"I'm fine," she said, smiling up at him. She turned her head and pushed her hair to one side so he could check out where she'd been hit on the head, and then she held out her arm and let him check the bandage the nurse had put on in the hospital. "I can take that off tomorrow," she told him.

"Make sure you keep it dry for a couple more days."

Rose nodded. "I will. Sarah wrapped my arm in a couple of plastic bags before I got in the tub last night."

Nick glanced at me. "Very resourceful," he said. He turned back to Rose. "Any headaches, blurred or double vision? Are you nauseous? Have you eaten?"

Rose held up a hand and ticked off her fingers. "No, no, no, no and yes." She kept a completely straight face, so while I knew she was humoring him just a little, I didn't think he did.

Nick looked at me again. "Show me the place on her neck," he said.

Rose turned around and bent her head forward,

and I showed him the tiny red mark. It seemed to me it had already faded a bit more. Nick pulled out his cell phone and peered at Rose's neck through the phone's camera lens.

"Is that some kind of magnifying glass?" I asked, leaning over for a closer look.

He nodded. "Fifteen times magnification."

"You get all the cool toys in your job," I teased.

Nick straightened up. "Actually, this came from Liam."

"Liam my brother?" I said.

"Only Liam I know. Yeah."

Rose straightened up and turned back around. "So what do you think?" she asked.

"It's possible that spot is an injection site," he hedged, pretty much as I'd expected.

She nodded but didn't say anything.

"What do you remember?" Nick asked.

"Not a lot," she said. "Pain on the side of my head and my neck. The next thing I knew I woke up to a very nice dog nudging me with his nose." She looked at me. "Would you be able to drive me over after supper to take some biscuits to Casey?"

I nodded. "Sure." I looked at Nick. "So?"

He frowned. "It's possible Rose was drugged, but the only way to know for sure is a blood test." He looked at Rose. "You can go to the hospital and have it done. I can call them."

"Could you do it?" she asked. "I mean, if it wouldn't be too much trouble? I got poked a lot last night. I feel a bit like a pincushion." She gave him a guileless look that I probably would have fallen for myself if it wasn't for the fact that she'd used the same look on me about a dozen times before I got wise to it.

Nick hesitated.

Rose leaned over and patted his hand. "It's all right. I shouldn't have put you on the spot," she said. "I'm sorry."

"You didn't." He smiled down at her. "I can do it. I'll get my bag and be right there."

"You are a darling man," she said. She gestured at his cell phone. "Is that the magnifying thingie?" She took the phone from Nick's hand before he realized what was happening. "Oh, Alfred would love one of these. May I show it to him?"

Nick looked a bit uncertain, eyes darting from the phone to Rose to me. "Umm, all right."

"Thank you, dear," she said with a smile. "I'll see you inside." She got her tote bag from the front seat. Elvis jumped down and the two of them headed for the back door of the shop.

Nick opened the passenger door of the truck and from the backseat grabbed a black nylon backpack that I knew held all his medical supplies. He was trying to stifle a grin and not really succeeding.

"I know what you did," I said, crossing my arms over my chest.

"I don't know what you mean," he said, but the grin got loose and I knew for sure I was right. He was playing Rose just as much as she had been playing him. Sometimes seeing Nick and Rose interact was like watching Tweety Bird and Sylvester the Cat.

"I may have been born at night, but it wasn't last night," I retorted.

"Okay," he said, the grin turning a little sheepish. "I know how Rose is when it comes to doctors and hospitals. I figured if I suggested me taking her blood right off the bat she'd say no, but if the hospital was the first choice I'd look a lot better."

"Very sneaky," I said as we started for the door. And that might have worked if Rose hadn't been manipulating the situation to achieve the same end, although I had no idea what her reasons were.

He raised an eyebrow. "I prefer to think of it as resourceful." I didn't have the heart to tell him he wasn't quite as resourceful as he thought.

"So what will this blood test do?" I asked.

"Based on what Rose just told me, I suspect that she could have been dosed with methohexital."

"Which is?"

"A rapid-acting barbiturate. Dentists use it quite a bit. Rose could have been unconscious in seconds and awake again in as fast as five minutes. It can't be detected in the bloodstream after twenty-four hours, which is why I want to get a blood sample now."

"But they did blood tests last night," I said.

Nick nodded. "Those would have just been routine tests, most likely just a CBC—that's a complete blood count—and a creatine kinase test which they do to help rule out a heart attack. They wouldn't have had any reason to test for methohexital."

We stepped inside. Rose was talking to Mac. Elvis was on the workbench washing his face and ignoring both of them. There was no sign of Mr. P. Rose handed Nick his phone without comment.

"Why don't we use my office?" I said.

Nick smiled. "Good idea."

"Nick's going to take a blood sample from Rose," I said to Mac by way of explanation.

"I heard," he said. "I can hold down the fort."

"Thanks," I said.

There were no customers in the shop proper, which was a good thing because the moment Avery caught sight of Rose she bolted across the room and threw herself into Rose's arms. Her face was pale and unshed tears glistened in her eyes.

Rose gave me a baffled look and folded the teen into a hug. "My dear, what on earth is wrong?" she asked.

Avery pulled back, her eyes scanning Rose's face. She swallowed hard. "I'm sorry. I'm so, so sorry," she said. "It's my fault you got hurt."

"Nonsense," Rose said, brushing a strand of hair behind Avery's ear. "First of all, I'm fine, as you can see. And second, what happened to me is the fault of the person who whacked me over the head. Why would you think that has anything to do with you?"

"I took your phone." She pulled the cell from her pocket and held it out.

Rose smiled at her. "Child, that phone couldn't have saved me, but a lovely dog did. His name is Casey. Would you like to meet him?"

Avery sniffed, swiped at her nose with the sleeve of her plaid cotton shirt and nodded.

"Splendid." She reached into her bag and handed Avery a tissue.

I looked at Nick and dipped my head in the direction of the stairs to the second floor. He nodded and headed quietly for them.

Mac had come in behind us and was standing at the cash desk. I walked over to him while Rose explained to Avery how they were going to make dog biscuits for the Clarks' big black Lab.

"I knew something was wrong when she got here," he said, indicating Avery, who was smiling now as Rose held her hands and talked. "She wouldn't tell me what it was, but she made me swear on your life that Rose was okay."

"I guess that's why my ears were burning," I said with a smile.

Mac smiled back. He was Nick's height, all lean, strong muscle with light brown skin and cropped black hair. He smelled like Ivory soap and peppermints. "Do I want to know about this blood sample Nick is going to take?"

"Probably not," I said, "but I'm going to tell you later anyway."

He laughed.

"Thanks for opening this morning," I said.

"Anytime." Mac's eyes stayed locked on mine just a little longer than they needed to before he looked over at Rose. "I'll put Avery to work sorting that box of postcards you bought from Cleveland. You should probably get Rose upstairs before she changes her mind or Nick does."

I gave my head a little shake. "Umm, yeah, I should do that," I said. I looked around. "I thought Charlotte was coming in."

Mac nodded. "She was here. She and Mr. P. are working on something."

"Do I want to know about it?" I asked.

He came around the cash desk.

"Probably not," he said, raising an eyebrow, "but I'm going to tell you later anyway."

Like he had just a moment before, I laughed.

I walked back over to Rose and Avery and dropped a hand on Avery's shoulder. She turned and I could see that all the anxiety and fear were gone from her face. I smiled at her. "Kiddo, could you sort through that box of postcards that Mac has out on the workbench?"

"I was going to do that, Sarah," Rose said.

"You should take it easy today," Avery said, "shouldn't she, Sarah?"

"Yes, she should," I said, fixing Rose with a steely stare to make my point—which I knew she'd ignore.

"I'll do it, Sarah," Avery said. "Is it okay if I make the tea first?"

I nodded. "Absolutely."

She gave Rose a quick hug and dashed up the stairs, taking them two at a time.

I put my arm around Rose's shoulders and we followed at a slower pace.

"I can't believe Avery thought what happened was her fault," she said. She was still holding her phone, and she tucked it into the pocket of her pink cotton sweater.

"She loves you," I said. I hesitated, took a breath and let it out slowly before I spoke again. "You're not going to do anything again like last night, right?"

She didn't speak and she didn't look at me. She just gave her head a little shake.

We found Nick in my office holding a cup of coffee

and leaning against my desk. He gestured to the large mug beside him. "That's for you, and, Rose, your tea is coming."

I reached for the coffee and took a long drink, making a mental note to thank Avery for bringing the cup and Mac, who I knew had made the pot of coffee just the way I liked it.

Nick settled Rose on the small love seat in my office and very quickly and efficiently drew her blood. "I'm going to drop this at the lab," he said.

"Thank you," Rose said, reaching for the cup of tea that Avery had just delivered. "Nicolas is very good with his hands," she said to me, bending her head to take a sip.

Nick's mouth twitched as he tried not to grin. I glared at him and he wisely turned his attention to his bag.

"Good to know," I said.

Nick slipped the shoulder strap of the black nylon first aid kit over his shoulder. Then he leaned down to give Rose a hug. "If you need any help with that dressing, let me know," he said.

Rose kissed his cheek. "I will," she said.

"I'll see you and Jess tonight?" Nick said to me, raising an eyebrow.

I knew he was referring to Thursday Night Jam at the Black Bear Pub.

I nodded. "We'll save you a seat."

After Nick was gone, Rose stretched out her arm and studied the tiny bandage Nick had put in the crook of her elbow. "He really is good with his hands," she said.

I grabbed my mug from my desk. "You could at least try to be a little less obvious," I said.

"At my age I don't have a lot of time to waste on less obvious."

I made a face and Rose laughed. She studied her arm again. "How long do you think it will take before we get any results?"

"A couple of days, I'm guessing," I said. "I think it may all be a little faster because Nick is using the medical examiner's lab."

Rose gave me a knowing smile over the rim of her china teacup. "I know," she said. "That's why I let Nicolas think he was winning a victory by getting me to ask him to do the blood sample."

I shook my head.

She got to her feet and headed for the door, leaning over to kiss my cheek as she passed me. "Don't worry, dear," she said. "I would never use my powers for the forces of evil."

"I'm pretty sure Darth Vader said the same thing," I called after her. I could hear her laughing as she went down the hall.

I dropped onto the love seat and drank the last bit of now cold coffee in my cup. There was a knock on the office door. "C'mon in," I called.

Mac poked his head into the room. "I saw Nick leave," he said. "How did it go?"

"Nick's taking the blood to the lab. Now we wait," I said. "Not that I think that Rose is going to pass the time by knitting or baking a cake."

Mac smiled. "Based on the conversation she's having with Avery, she's planning on making dog biscuits."

"For Casey."

"Please tell me Casey is a dog," he said.

I nodded. "A very nice black Lab that found Rose by the side of the road." I pulled a hand back through my hair. I wasn't exactly sure what to do next. There was no way Rose was going to sit by quietly until Nick had the results of her blood work.

"What can I do?" Mac asked.

"Aside from sitting on Rose until we know more, I don't know."

He took the heavy pottery mug from my hands. "How about I head over to McNamara's in a little while and get lunch for all of us. Charlotte and Alfred will be here, you know Liz is going to stop in and Rose is going to want to start working on this case, because it is a case, isn't it?"

I nodded. "It is. Michelle doesn't seem to think so and I'm not certain Nick does, either, but I believe Rose, and I want to know what happened to her."

Chapter 8

I was about to go back downstairs to see if I had any messages when my cell phone rang. It was Michelle.

"How's Rose this morning?" she asked.

"She's fine," I said. "I'm guessing Nick told you about the needle mark on her neck."

"He said he convinced her to let him take a blood sample."

It was more like she conned him into taking the sample, but I didn't say that. "I'm hoping we'll get some results in a couple of days."

"Good. Maybe that will clear things up."

I could picture Michelle nodding as though those blood tests would settle everything.

"Sarah, the reason I called is I checked with the Camerons' financial adviser. Jeff Cameron did empty the account yesterday with some made-up story about needing the money because they had the chance to buy a piece of property they'd been looking at."

I propped an elbow on my desk. "It doesn't prove

he left town," I said. "Do you have any idea who this other woman is?"

"If you're asking did he show up at the bank with her on his arm, no. And I also spoke to his assistant, Chloe Sanders. She has no idea where he is, either."

It was pretty much what I'd expected. I thanked Michelle for everything she'd done and said good-bye.

I spent the rest of the morning out in our newly converted work space in the old garage cleaning a couple of wicker rocking chairs so I could paint them. I headed inside at about twelve fifteen. Avery had a small drop cloth spread on top of a section of Mac's workbench. She'd sorted the postcards into three piles.

"Hi, Sarah," she said when she spotted me. "I went through those postcards like you asked. I have a pile that are nice enough to frame, another pile that you can just sell one by one in the shop—tourists like that kind of stuff—and a few that are torn or have big water blotches on them."

"Good job," I said. "You can recycle the ones that are damaged."

She nodded, twisting the stack of bracelets on her left arm around her wrist. "Sarah, do you think I could maybe try framing some of those nicer postcards?"

Avery was very creative and I'd learned recently a pretty talented artist. I had no idea what she'd come up with, but I was sure she'd create something that would catch customers' attention. "Sure," I said. "There are a couple of boxes of frames on the top left shelf." I pointed to the storage unit along the back wall.

"Awesome," she said with a grin. "What do you need me to do now?"

"You could help me set up one of the folding tables and gather enough chairs for everyone to have lunch."

"Sure," she said, sliding off the stool she'd been sitting on. "Are you going to be talking about what happened to Rose last night?"

"Yes," I said. There wasn't any point in trying to keep what was going on from her. Avery had the kind of selective bionic hearing all teenagers had, in my experience. You could tell her something three times, and if she wasn't interested, she wouldn't hear a word. On the other hand, when she did want to know what was going on, she could make out a whisper from across the shop.

"I'll take my lunch and stay in the store, then," she said. "You're getting lunch for everyone, right?"

"Mac's gone to McNamara's," I said. "And thank you for offering to cover in the shop."

Avery's expression turned serious. "Rose is my family. We have to catch whoever tried to hurt her."

"We will," I said with a confidence I didn't quite feel. "Nick is helping and so is Detective Andrews."

We had the table ready when Mac came in the back door trailed by Mr. P. and Charlotte. It struck me that this was becoming a habit whenever the Angels had a case. Mr. P. raised a hand in hello and made a beeline for me. "Sarah, how's Rosie?" he asked.

"She's all right. I promise," I said. Charlotte joined us. I brought them up to date on the visit with Nicole Cameron and the possible needle mark on Rose's neck.

"Nicolas took a blood sample?" Mr. P. asked, frowning a little behind his wire-framed glasses. The few wisps of hair the man had were sticking out all over his head.

"I know what you're thinking," I said. "But there was no squabbling with Rose."

"And Rose agreed without squabbling with Nicolas?" Charlotte asked.

"Let's just say they each had an agenda, but if we're lucky we'll be able to prove that Rose was drugged, which will—I hope—show the police that Rose isn't some ditsy old lady."

Mac had given Avery her lunch and she'd gone into the shop. Now Charlotte took the take-out bag from him and began to set out the rest of the food. Rose came into the workroom then, and Liz was with her.

"Hello, pretty girl," Liz said to me as she reached the table.

I caught her hand. She'd gotten a pink French manicure. "Very pretty yourself," I said approvingly. I raised an eyebrow. "Was it worth the investment?"

"I think so," she said.

I walked over to stand next to Mac. "Thanks for getting lunch," I said. "What do I owe you?"

"Don't worry about it," he said.

"I can ask Glenn, you know."

Mac crossed his arms over his chest. "Won't work. It's a guy thing. We stick together."

"Really?" I said.

He nodded. "Really."

I'd found Jeff Cameron's business card on my desk.

I pulled it out of my pocket now. "I need a favor," I said.

"Sure," he said. "What is it?"

Mac had worked as a financial adviser before coming to North Harbor. I handed him the card. "This is Jeff Cameron's business card. He works for Helmark Associates. I Googled them. They provide temporary employees for businesses."

"I've heard of them."

"Do you have any contacts from your old life that might have heard of him?"

He swiped a hand across his mouth. "Maybe."

"Thanks," I said. "It struck me that if he was—is—having an affair, it's probably not with someone here in town. I don't think it would be possible to keep that secret for very long."

"I'll see what I can find out." He tucked the card in his pocket. "What's going on between Rose and Alfred? It looks like she's avoiding him."

I explained about Michelle suggesting Rose had had a small stroke and how both Charlotte and Mr. P. had wanted her to go to the doctor to prove her wrong. "She was . . . offended. She stalked out of her apartment into mine. I sent the two of them home. The good thing was once I had Rose at my place it wasn't that hard to convince her to spend the night. I'd been afraid I was going to have to sneak around the back of the house and climb through the window so I could watch her sleep."

Mac shook his head. "That would explain why I found Mr. P. waiting by the back door at quarter to eight this morning."

"He's crazy about her," I said. "And I know she feels the same way about him."

A slow smile spread across Mac's face. "And would you have predicted *that* would happen the day the two of you"—he cleared his throat—"encountered each other at Legacy Place? You're kind of responsible for the two of them getting together."

I laughed, putting a hand to my mouth. "Given that—as Gram would say—Mr. P. was naked as a jaybird, no."

I'd been doing a workshop at Legacy Place as a favor to my grandmother. I'd walked into the room we were using and, thanks to a miscommunication, discovered a naked Alfred Peterson, posing in the middle of the room.

"It wasn't his best look," I said to Mac.

I remembered walking across the floor to Alfred, keeping my eyes locked on the old man's blue ones, silently repeating, *Please don't let me see anything that isn't G-rated.*

When I'd asked what he was doing, Mr. P. had replied, "I'm posing, my dear."

Based on the position he'd assumed, I'd been fairly certain he was trying to approximate the *Farnese Atlas*, a marble sculpture of Atlas, partly down on one knee, with the world on his shoulders. In Mr. P.'s case it had been a red-and-white-striped beach ball with the logo of a beer company on his shoulders.

It turned out that he was posing for an art class, filing in for Sam, of all people. There had been some kind of mix-up. The class, it turned out, was drawing hands, not bodies.

I looked at Mac. I was shaking with laughter at the memory, my lips pressed tightly together. Luckily, Charlotte had been with me and had walked in and sent Mr. P. off to the washroom with an admonition to put his clothes on before—as she put it—the mystery was gone.

Mac glanced over at Alfred, who was talking to Charlotte, although his attention kept shifting to Rose. "The beginning of a pretty good friendship," he said.

I nodded. "Hard to believe, but yes, it was."

We settled at the table. Rose took the chair to my right and Liz sat beside her. Mr. P. and Charlotte were on my left and Mac leaned against the workbench with his sandwich and coffee, the way he often did when we had these kinds of meals. I glanced at him and he gave me a small smile of encouragement.

Mr. P. had set his computer bag on the table. He hadn't unwrapped his sandwich or touched the cup of tea Charlotte had poured for him. I'd noticed that he and Charlotte had exchanged a couple of looks when he wasn't watching Rose and trying not to be obvious about it.

I cleared my throat and they all turned their attention to me. I held up a hand in the old man's direction. "Mr. P., you're up," I said.

"Thank you, Sarah," he said. "First of all, Charlotte was able to get in touch with Mr. Cameron's assistant, Chloe Sanders."

"She was my student," Charlotte said. "She agreed to stop by this afternoon."

"Charlotte and I spent the rest of the morning trying to track down Mr. Cameron," Mr. P. continued.

"So did you?" Liz asked.

He pushed his glasses up his nose. "No, Elizabeth. We didn't. There hasn't been any activity on his credit or debit cards since late yesterday afternoon when he put gas in his vehicle at a station in Rockport. Calls to his cell phone go straight to voice mail."

"Wait a minute," I said. "I thought Jeff Cameron was at a meeting in Portland. That's what he told me yesterday."

Charlotte shook her head. "There was no meeting. It had been rescheduled."

"He was in town," Rose said.

"All we can prove for the moment is that his vehicle was here," Mr. P. continued, his eyes never leaving Rose's face. "As well as the transaction at the gas station, we also have him on video heading for the highway early in the evening."

"Do you believe he's dead?" Rose asked.

I turned to look at her, but like Mr. P. all her attention was focused on one person. Him.

"We have another theory," Charlotte said slowly.

Alfred nodded. He cleared his throat. "It is . . . more than a little outlandish," he said.

Mac pushed away from the workbench and moved forward so he was standing between my chair and Mr. P.'s. "What is it, Alfred?" he said.

"Do you think he's dead?" Rose asked again.

"I think he wanted you to think he's dead," Mr. P. said. "But I think he set up his wife to make it look like she killed him and then he ran off with all their money."

No one said anything for what felt like a stretched

moment in time. Then Rose spoke. "You're saying Jeff Cameron used me. He manipulated me into offering to deliver those candlesticks to his wife so I could be a witness to his alleged death." She was sitting upright in her chair, her hands folded primly in her lap, but anger flashed in her gray eyes.

Mr. P. nodded. "I'm sorry, Rosie. Yes."

"He thought I was some feeble, dotty old woman he could use as part of his scheme. If he wasn't dead, I'd smack him with my purse."

Liz made a snort of derision. "Clearly the man is a pretty lousy judge of people."

"Our theory is like a colander at the moment," Charlotte said, setting her cup on the table. "It has a few holes, mainly the why and the who. Why on earth would the man want to set up his wife like this, and who helped him?"

"He had to have had help," I said. "Someone to masquerade as his wife and someone else to assault Rose."

"That may work to our advantage," Mr. P. said. He gave me a small, sly smile. "Sarah, by any chance are you familiar with what one of our Founding Fathers, Benjamin Franklin, said about secrets?"

I nodded. "Three can keep a secret if two of them are dead." The words didn't leave me with a good feeling.

Chapter 9

That was all it took to wash away Rose's anger at Charlotte and Mr. P., although I suspected she wouldn't have stayed angry even without all the work the two of them had done to try to trace Jeff Cameron. Rose and Charlotte had been friends for a long time, and although she didn't talk about it, I knew her feelings for Mr. P. ran deep, just the way his did for her.

I reached for my coffee and shifted in my chair so I could look at Liz. "And do you have anything you'd like to share with the group?" I asked.

"As a matter of fact, I do," she said. "Leesa Cameron may"—she held up one finger—"may have been seeing another man."

"Why do you say that?"

"Well, apparently she's some kind of rower."

I nodded. "I saw a scull in the backyard."

"Her husband is a runner." She looked at me and I nodded. "Leesa Cameron had been working out with someone." She paused. Knowing Liz, it was for effect.

"For at least the past two months. And they'd been running."

"Why wouldn't she just go running with her husband?" Rose asked.

"You're sure about the running part?" I said.

"One hundred percent," Liz said. "Shannon, who did my nails"—she held up her hand like she was royalty—"said Leesa admitted she'd been running, but she said 'we': *We were running*." Liz reached for the insulated carafe that held the tea. Her eyes flicked in my direction. "Shannon said Leesa Cameron's feet reminded her of yours."

Liz had gifted me with a spa pedicure at Phantasy after a road race I'd done in May. It had been a wonderfully pampering experience and I'd been thinking of doing it again.

I made a face at her. "For the record there's nothing wrong with my feet, but we get your point. Do you know who Leesa was working out with?"

Liz shook her head. "Shannon didn't know, but I'm going for a massage. I'll see what I can find out."

Talk turned to what to do next. The consensus was to dig into Jeff Cameron's background to try to figure out where he was at the moment and who was helping him.

Rose decided to spend the afternoon in the Angels' sunporch office with Alfred, while Charlotte worked in the shop with Avery. Mr. P. looked as though a load had been lifted from his shoulders.

"I'm going to do some fact-finding," Liz said, slipping one arm around my waist and walking me to the stairs.

"The kind of fact-finding that involves scented oil and a massage table?" I teased.

"The kind that I hope will either verify Alfred's theory or put the kibosh on it."

"So you think the idea that Jeff Cameron set up his wife is a little too far-fetched," I said, lowering my voice so Charlotte and Avery didn't have a chance of overhearing.

Liz scrunched up her nose at me. "Child, I've been around long enough that there's very little that seems too far-fetched to me. But Detective Andrews and Nicolas, they don't have the same amount of life experience."

I smiled. "I love you," I said, knowing what she'd say before she answered.

She leaned over and kissed my cheek, waving one hand dismissively. "Everybody does," she said. And with that she headed out the door.

Chloe Sanders showed up around two o'clock. I was working out in the garage. Mr. P. came to get me. Charlotte and Rose were in the sunporch waiting with her.

"Sarah, this is Chloe," Charlotte said. She gave the young woman a warm smile. "Sarah owns Second Chance."

"Thanks for coming to talk to us, Chloe," I said.

"Mrs. Elliot told me what happened," she said. "I'm not sure I can help, but I'll try."

Chloe Sanders was tiny—barely five feet tall. Her shoulder-length brown hair had a deep blue streak of color in the front and she had three piercings in her left ear. In contrast, her clothes were conservative—

black trousers and a crisp white shirt with three-quarter-length sleeves.

"Do you have any idea where Mr. Cameron is?" Rose asked.

Chloe shook her head. "I got a text from him last night telling me that he was going out of town so I had the rest of the week off."

"Did he say anything to you yesterday?" I asked.

"I only saw him for a few minutes yesterday morning. He had me researching a list of companies. I was at the library and down at the town hall."

Elvis padded into the room, jumped up onto Mr. P.'s desk and bumped Chloe's arm with his head. She smiled down at him. "Hello," she said.

"That's Elvis," I said.

She held out her hand and after he'd sniffed it Elvis let her stroke his fur. "What happened to his nose?" Chloe asked, indicating the long scar on the cat's face.

"I don't know," I said. "It happened before I got him."

"Was it typical for you not to talk to Mr. Cameron all day?" Charlotte asked. Her hands were folded over the apron she always wore in the shop.

"It was if he had meetings most of the day. He'd just give me a list of what he wanted done." She continued to stroke Elvis's fur. He had a blissful expression on his face.

"He had a meeting yesterday?" I asked.

She nodded. "In Portland. You know that Helmark provides temporary employees for businesses?"

"I do," I said.

"Jeff was trying to convince more companies here to use Helmark. He had a lot of meetings."

Chloe Sanders was articulate, not surprising for a former debater, and she looked whomever she was talking to in the eye when she spoke. I couldn't see any reason not to believe she was telling the truth. I thought about Leesa saying Jeff called Chloe the Roomba. It was hard not to think of him as a jerk.

"How late did you work last night?" Rose asked.

"I think it was about quarter to six when I left the library. They close at six."

"Chloe, do you mind telling us what you did last night?"

She cleared her throat, pressing her free hand to her mouth for a moment. "No. I don't mind. Mom and Dad went to New Hampshire for a few days. They're big NASCAR fans. I went home, ordered a pizza and watched TV. Like I said, Jeff sent me a text giving me the rest of the week off. That was it."

I glanced at Elvis and then caught Rose's eye. I gave my head a little shake. I turned my attention back to Chloe. "Thank you for talking to us," I said.

"You're welcome." She gave Elvis one last scratch behind his ears and then she turned to Charlotte. "It was so good to see you, Mrs. Elliot. If you need anything else, call me, please."

"I will," she said. "I'll walk you out."

I waited until they were out of earshot, and then I turned to Rose. Elvis was washing his face.

"You saw that?" I asked.

"Yes," she said.

That blissful expression Elvis had been wearing while Chloe stroked his fur hadn't wavered until she'd told us she'd been home alone all evening watching

TV. Then it had changed to a look that was the antithesis of contentment.

"Chloe Sanders lied about what she was doing last night," I said.

"Do you think it's possible that lovely child had something to do with what I saw?" Rose asked.

"I hope not," I said.

"Alfred and I will see what we can find out about her."

I nodded, hoping that the young woman Jeff Cameron had derisively referred to as a Roomba hadn't gotten herself into a mess that couldn't easily be cleaned up.

Rose came up to my office at about four thirty. "I'm taking Avery home with me to bake," she said, standing in the doorway.

"Do you want a ride?" I asked.

She shook her head. "Liz is coming to get us. She didn't manage to find out anything about who Lessa Cameron has been working out with. She said she's not throwing in the towel, though."

I smiled. "That doesn't surprise me."

Rose yawned. "Would it be all right with you if we took the dog biscuits over to Casey tomorrow?"

"Sure," I said.

She smiled then. "Thank you, Sarah."

"Hey, I like Casey, too."

"I mean thank you for everything you've done in the last twenty-four hours." She paused for a moment. "I don't know what we'd do without you."

"I'm not planning on going anywhere," I said, "so you won't be able to find out."

"I love you, sweetie," she said.

"I love you, too," I said.

I stayed late to finish cleaning the wicker chairs so I could get them painted. Elvis was happy to curl up on my desk chair with a few fish crackers while he waited. I was standing back, admiring my handiwork, when Mac came into the garage.

"Hi. I didn't realize you were still here."

"I want to paint these tomorrow," I said.

He walked around the two fat chairs. "They look a lot better than when you bought them from Cleveland." Cleveland was a picker I bought things from on a regular basis.

I wiped my hands on my jeans. "Yeah, scraping off a layer of chicken droppings is pretty much guaranteed to spruce up anything."

Mac grinned.

"What are you working on?" I asked, pulling off the old flannel shirt I'd been wearing over my T-shirt while I worked.

"Just gluing the joints of that old nursery rocker. I already sanded it, so one of us will be able to paint it."

I stretched one arm up over my head. "Thanks," I said. "I couldn't do all of this without you, you know."

He turned and smiled at me. "Hey, you're the one who keeps finding treasures under layers of chicken poop."

"And you're the one who keeps all of this running while I'm off being Dr. Watson to the Sherlock Holmeses who have their office in my sunporch."

"What do you think about Alfred's theory?" Mac asked.

I blew a stray clump of hair back off my face. "I admit it seems like a bit of a stretch, but on the other hand it also seems like a bit of a coincidence that Rose would show up at the cottage just when Leesa Cameron was moving her husband's dead body."

"I had the same thought," Mac said. "The fact that there hasn't been any activity on his cards or his phone is unsettling, though."

I nodded. "I know. I only spoke to Jeff Cameron for a couple of minutes when he was here, and I spent maybe five minutes with Leesa Cameron when Michelle and I went to talk to her last night, but I can't help feeling there was something wrong in that marriage." I reached down and picked up the scrub brush I'd used on the chairs. "Which I guess makes sense whether you're setting your wife up for murder or killing your husband."

"It's more than that, though, isn't it?" he said.

I turned the brush over in my hands. "Let's say for a moment that Mr. P. is wrong. That means Jeff Cameron ended his marriage with a text message. And was cruel enough to send a gift to his wife to mark the occasion, because, let's face it, those candlesticks had nothing to do with remembering Leesa Cameron's grandmother on what would have been her birthday. Who ends what was supposed to be a lifetime commitment like that?"

He shrugged. "Sometimes people make a commitment and they mean it when they make it, but after a while they find out they just don't have what it takes to keep it."

I set the brush back down on the stool I'd been using

as a makeshift table. "As Avery would say, that doesn't mean that then they get to act like a glass bowl."

Mac grinned at my use of Avery's euphemism for the word "asshole."

"Maybe it would be better if we all waited to get married until we could keep our commitments," I said.

That made him laugh. "There probably wouldn't be nearly as many marriages." He lifted one of the chairs off the drop cloth I'd been using. I moved the other and bent down to pick up one end of the canvas. Mac reached for the other two corners. We had a length of clothesline cord stretched across one end of the old garage and we draped the drop cloth over it to dry.

"Do you believe in marriage, Mac?" I asked. "I mean, in the idea of it?"

"Yes," he said. He pushed back the sleeves of his chambray shirt. "I see it as a public affirmation of a private commitment."

"You think we need that."

He shrugged. "I can only speak for myself, and I know I want it. I want the person I'm with to know that I'm not going anywhere when things go bad, because at some point they will. That's just life." He narrowed his dark eyes and studied my face for a moment. "May I ask you something?"

"Sure," I said. "You've been around when things have gone bad around here. I think that means you're entitled to ask me pretty much anything you want to."

"Why didn't you and Nick ever become a couple?"

It wasn't the question I'd expected. I pulled the elastic free that had been holding my hair in a loose knot to buy a moment of time. "Timing," I finally said. "The summer we were fifteen I had a crush on Nick and he went to music camp and fell for a flute player, a cellist and a girl who played the bassoon from Nova Scotia. In that order. I came home from college my freshman year at Christmastime madly in love with a poet who wrote long poems with no punctuation or capital letters."

"You made that last part up," Mac said with a smile.

I ran a hand through my hair. "You have no idea how much I wish I had. But I didn't." I shrugged. "It's just never been the right time for Nick and me."

"You've both been back here for more than a year now. You're not seeing anybody, and as far as I can tell, neither is he."

A piece of a wooden dowel was lying on the floor. I bent down to pick it up. "Everyone wants us to be a couple," I said. "You've probably noticed that. Rose made a point of telling me what great hair Nick has. Charlotte actually worked the fact that he doesn't snore into a conversation, and they told him that I have good teeth. They'd all be so happy if Nick and I got together."

Through the open door I heard a vehicle pull into the parking lot.

"Would you?" Mac asked. He glanced outside. "That's the people Rose sold the bed to on Tuesday. I better go."

I nodded without speaking and watched him walk across the lot to the middle-aged couple getting out of a red half-ton truck. I thought about Mac's question and wondered how I would have answered if he'd waited to hear me.

I looked at my watch. I had just enough time to grab

Elvis, head home, change and meet Jess for Thursday Night Jam. And Nick, I remembered belatedly.

I was the first to arrive at The Black Bear. I stood just inside the entrance and peeled off my slicker. It had started to rain as Elvis and I were driving home, and I hoped the people who had bought the bed hadn't had far to go.

Sam waved from across the room and hurried over to wrap me in a hug. "Hi, kiddo," he said. "I saved you a table." He was tall and lean, his hair a shaggy salt-and-pepper mix and his beard was clipped close, a concession to the warmer weather. A pair of Dollar Store reading glasses was perched on his head.

Sam Newman not only owned and ran the pub, he'd been my late dad's best friend. Sam had been making music his whole life, and he'd known my father just about as long. Right after college, before what Sam referred to as the three "M's"—Mariah (Mom), marriage and the munchkin (me)—my dad and Sam had put together a band called Back Roads. They'd even had a minor hit, "End of Days." Even though I considered my stepfather, Peter, to be my dad, Sam still took on a kind of fatherly role in my life. I could count on him to be straight with me, and when it came to music and guitars I trusted him more than I did anyone else.

"Thanks," I said, looking around. There were photos on every wall of the space; Sam with the various bands he'd played in over the years and musicians who had played in the pub, including some celebrities. My favorite was a photo of Sam and my dad that hung behind the bar. They were squinting into the sunshine, grinning, with their arms around each other's shoulders, and it made me feel good every time I saw it.

The place was already three-quarters full and I knew by the time the band was ready to play there wouldn't be an empty seat in the house.

"You're early," Sam said as he walked me over to a small table with a RESERVED sign on it. "You want supper?"

I nodded. "Please." My stomach growled loudly for emphasis.

"How about spicy chicken and noodles?"

"That sounds wonderful."

"Do you want to wait for Jess?" Sam asked.

I patted my stomach. "No."

He grinned. "I'll put your order in." He turned toward the kitchen and then turned back to me. "I almost forgot. I heard what happened. How's Rose?"

"She's fine," I said. "I've been trying to get her to take it easy."

Sam laughed. "That's a fool's errand."

I laughed as well. "Tell me about it. She either pretends she can't hear me when I tell her to sit down or she plays the *I changed your diapers* card."

"I'll have to remember that one," he said.

I rolled my eyes. "You've never changed a diaper in your life."

He nodded in agreement. "But I have fed you smushed-up peas and I have the photos to prove it. Who knew smushed-up peas could also be used as hair gel?"

"One of these days I'm going to find those pictures," I warned, shaking a finger at him.

Sam just laughed again. "Are you driving?" he asked.

I nodded. "I am. It's raining. Why?"

"We have an amber ale from that new microbrewery, Grimcross. I just wanted to get your opinion."

"Ask Jess," I said. "She'd be happy to tell you what she thinks."

"Good idea," Sam said. "Tina will bring your order when it's ready." He headed for the kitchen.

I'd just picked up my fork when Jess slid onto the chair beside me. "I was not meant to live near the water," she said, shrugging out of a red raincoat, which she draped on the back of the chair.

"Hello to you, too," I said. "And why were you not meant to live near the water?" I knew Jess didn't really mean that. She loved being close to the ocean. She wasn't as fanatical about sailing as Mac was, but she liked to go out a few times each season on one of the big schooners that called the harbor home. I teased her that she'd been a pirate in a past life.

Jess put a hand to her hair. "This," she said.

"Your hair looks good," I said. She was wearing it back from her face in a loose braid.

"Well, it was like wrestling with a bear to get it to do anything." She held up her hands about three feet apart. "When it's humid, it gets this big." She peered at the bowl in front of me. "That smells fantastic. What is it?"

"Spicy chicken and noodles," I said, taking a bite.

"Ooo, I want some," she said.

I darted my eyes sideways to look at her.

"Don't worry," Jess said. "I'm not crazy enough to

try and take food away from you." She looked around the pub, and then I saw Tina making her way across the room toward our table.

I had no idea how Jess did it, but she was always able to get the attention of servers, bartenders and sales associates wherever we were.

"What could I get you?" Tina asked when she reached the table.

"I'll have what she's having," Jess said, pointing to my bowl, "with a fried egg on top."

"What is it with you and fried eggs?" I asked after Tina was on her way to the kitchen.

Jess shrugged. "I like them as long as I don't have to eat them by themselves." She reached over and swiped a breadstick from my plate.

"I saw that."

"I know," she said before taking a huge bite.

"How was your day?" I dipped the end of the remaining breadstick in the spicy sauce in my bowl.

"Good. Lots of tourists in the shop. No bus tours, but there was a group of people in camper vans traveling together. Did you get any of them at your place?"

I nodded.

"Hey, I saw Josh. He told me about Rose. Is she all right?"

I set down my fork. "She's fine. I think her head is harder than a cement block. How did Josh know?"

I had known Josh Evans since we were kids. He was a lawyer and had come to the Angels' rescue more than once.

Jess shrugged. "His mother's working for Liz now, remember?"

Jane Evans had worked for Daniel Swift, who was descended from the original family that had founded North Harbor, at Swift Holdings. Liz had persuaded her to come work for the Emmerson Foundation, Liz's family's charitable foundation.

"Liz probably told Jane," Jess continued. "She told Josh. You know how those things work."

Tina came back then with Jess's order, including a bottle of the amber ale Sam had mentioned to me.

"Sam wanted your opinion on that," I said, indicating the tall green bottle.

Tina smiled. "On the house."

"I can do that," Jess said with a smile.

We ate in companionable silence for a few minutes, Jess wordlessly handing over one of her breadsticks. "So is Nick coming?" she asked.

"As far as I know."

"Do you want me to remember a previous engagement and make myself scarce?"

I frowned at her. "Why would you do that?"

She raised an eyebrow. "So the two of you can have a little alone time."

I looked around at the rapidly filling room. "Because this is such an intimate romantic place," I said.

"Hey, I was just trying to nudge you two along a little," Jess said.

I rolled my eyes at her.

"Are you at least going to kiss him again? And I don't mean that little peck-on-the-cheek thing you do, which is more like kissing your brother."

"We're not talking about kissing Nick or my brother."

Jess opened her mouth to say something and I held up a hand. "Not. Doing. It."

She laughed. "Well, at least tell me if the earth moved when you kissed Nick."

"You've been watching *Outlander* again, haven't you?" I said.

"Love me some Jamie Fraser," Jess said. "I wouldn't mind kissing him."

I shook my head and bent over my bowl again.

"So have you figured out exactly what happened to Rose yet?" she asked after she'd devoured about three-quarters of her noodles and chicken. She'd tucked one leg underneath her and was leaning against the back of her chair, drinking the beer straight from the bottle.

I sighed and shook my head. "Not really." I explained what Rose had seen, what Michelle thought had happened and how I'd noticed the needle mark on Rose's neck, which had resulted in Nick taking the blood sample.

"So what do you think?" she said. "Do you believe Rose actually did see someone dragging that guy's body?"

"I think she saw something. I just don't know what. You know Rose. She's not above taking a little dramatic license to get what she wants, but she wouldn't make this up and she didn't have a stroke. First of all, they checked her out at the hospital, and second, she's as healthy as a horse. Her blood pressure is lower than mine."

"Well, for what it's worth, I don't think Leesa Cameron killed her husband, assuming that he's really dead."

I pushed my empty dish away. "And that would be because?"

"She's been in the shop about half a dozen times," Jess said. "And she just bought a vintage lace robe on Tuesday. It's not the kind of sexy purchase a woman makes if she's going to kill her husband the next day."

"True," I said. "But it is the kind of sexy purchase a woman makes if someone other than her husband is going to see her in it."

Jess made a face. "Good point. You think someone else was going to get a look at the goods, so to speak?"

"I don't know," I said with a sigh. "I wish there was a way to find out."

"What are you drinking?" a voice said behind us. Nick was standing there.

He really was cute, I thought, looking up at him as he shrugged out of his rain jacket. His hair was wind-blown, which made him look younger and less serious. He'd always had the kind of boy-next-door looks that made women swoon.

Jess turned the bottle so he could read the label. "So what's wrong with it?" he asked, snagging the third chair and pulling it closer to us before he sat down next to me. He smelled like Hugo, the aftershave he'd been wearing since high school, the aftershave he'd been wearing when I French-kissed him at fifteen.

I shook my head. It wasn't a good time to think about that.

"Nothing," Jess said. "It's great—rich, warm with a hint of caramel."

"So why the face?"

"We were talking about what happened to Rose," I

said. "Do you know if Michelle has managed to get a lead on Jeff Cameron?"

"Not as far as I know," Nick said. "What about Rose and her cohorts? Have they come up with anything?"

Jess tried not to smile and took another drink of her beer.

"They have a couple of theories," I said, choosing my words carefully.

"Are you going to tell me what they are?" Nick scanned the room but couldn't seem to catch the eye of any waitstaff. Jess looked up, and just like before, Tina was suddenly on her way to the table. "How do you do that?" he said.

"I'm cute," she said with an offhand shrug. "And I tip better than you do."

Nick ordered a cheeseburger and our usual chips and salsa, which we had winter or summer.

"And one of those?" Tina asked, pointing at the beer bottle in Jess's hand.

Nick made a face. "Sadly, I'm on call. Just coffee."

"Good choice," she said. She looked at me. "Another decaf?"

"Please," I said.

"And one for me, too, please," Jess added.

"It shouldn't take long," Tina said.

Nick leaned an elbow on the table. "So tell me, what are the Angels' theories about where Jeff Cameron is?"

"I'm not answering that question," I said. "It's just going to make you crazy if I tell you."

He gave me that little boy smile that after all the years of using it on me shouldn't have worked so well but often did. "Oh, c'mon, Sarah. Give me a break. I'm trying. I didn't say one word to Rose about getting involved in this case."

"Seriously? You didn't?" Jess said, skepticism clearly in her expression and her voice.

He turned to look at her, narrowing his brown eyes. "You're not helping."

She pointed a finger at his face. "It's so adorable how you think I was trying to." A smile tugged at the corners of her mouth, but she managed to keep it in check.

A different server appeared at the table with Nick's coffee, along with a pot of decaf and a heavy stoneware mug for Jess. I waited until he'd filled both of our cups before I answered Nick. "Okay," I said. "Rose and the others actually have two theories and they're working on both of them. One is that Leesa Cameron killed her husband."

"I thought she has an alibi."

"Alibis can be faked," Jess said, adding cream to her mug.

"Yes, Leesa Cameron has an alibi, but it's just the word of one person at the moment," I added.

"What's the other theory?" Nick asked.

I hesitated, reaching for a packet of sugar to buy a bit of time.

"Oh, c'mon, Sarah," he said. "Tell me."

"Jeff Cameron faked his own death," I said flatly.

I waited for him to laugh. To my surprise he just nodded.

"Wait a minute, you're not going to tell me how preposterous the idea is?" I asked.

"No," he said. "Because it's not. People have faked their deaths before. The problem is they tend to slip up in some way—they contact someone in their old life or their story makes the news and they get recognized. So if that's what happened, there's a good chance he'll get caught."

Jess leaned sideways out of Nick's line of sight and winked at me. I ignored her even though I was happy to see that Nick was trying to be less judgmental when it came to the Angels' detective agency. He'd been blindsided when Mr. P. had met all the state's requirements, become a licensed private investigator and taken Rose on as his apprentice. He seemed to think his mother and her friends should spend their time baking cookies and holding fund-raisers for the library.

Tina came back with Nick's food and the chips and salsa just as Sam and the rest of The Hairy Bananas came from the back and headed for the small stage. We didn't talk after that, although more than once Nick and I did sing—along with a lot of other people—much to Jess's amusement. Nick was actually a very talented guitar player and a couple of times had sat in for a few songs with the band. Anyone who could play was welcome to join the guys, although it didn't happen very often. Sam had asked me to join them, but I hadn't practiced in a long time and I'd never been as good as Nick anyway. I liked to play mainly because it made me feel closer to my dad. My guitar had been his, lost for years after his car accident.

The band ended their first set with a rocking version of Bachman-Turner Overdrive's "Takin' Care of Business." Classic rock songs were the most popular with the pub's clientele.

Jess got to her feet. "I see someone I need to talk to. Do you want anything?"

I shook my head.

"How about you, Dr. Feelgood?" She nudged Nick with her elbow.

"I'm good, thanks," he said.

I turned so I was facing him. "When are you going to bring your guitar and sit in with Sam?" I asked.

He swiped a hand over his chin. "When I have some time to practice first."

"You know every single one of the songs they just played."

He grinned. "I'll bring my guitar if you bring yours."

I shook my head. "No way. I don't play nearly as well as you do."

"'Peaceful Easy Feeling,'" he said. The Eagles song was the first one he'd taught me to play after I'd gotten my dad's guitar.

When I didn't say anything he bumped my leg with his knee. "You could play that with your eyes closed."

"And I'll sound like I'm playing it with my eyes closed," I retorted.

"I'll bring my guitar over and we'll practice it together." He leaned closer. "It'll be fun." His breath was warm against my cheek and I could smell his aftershave. Catching the scent always seemed to take me back in time.

It would be fun, I knew, playing with him again. Nick had finally agreed to come running with me, and the times we'd been out I'd laughed myself silly, mostly because he ran like a black bear chasing a picnic basket. "I'll think about it," I said.

He straightened up and gave me a triumphant look.

I waggled a finger in his face. "No, no, no! Don't think you've won any kind of victory. I said I'd think about it. Think. That's all."

He just kept grinning at me.

"I'm changing the subject," I said. "Any idea when you might get the results of Rose's blood tests?"

"Maybe tomorrow," he said. "More likely it will be Monday." He shrugged. "Once we get those results we'll have a better idea of what happened to Rose."

"What would make someone set up another person for murder?" I asked, reaching for my mug.

"Anger and revenge are the top two reasons."

"As far as I know there was no reason for Jeff Cameron to feel that way about his wife," I said. Jess was making her way back to the table.

Nick nodded. "Yeah, that theory does have more holes than a colander, but like I said, once we get Rose's blood work maybe we'll have a better idea of what's going on."

For a moment I couldn't move. Then I carefully set my mug back on the table. It was that or break it over Nick's head, and I knew Sam wouldn't be happy about the latter. "What did you say?" I asked. To my surprise my voice sounded perfectly normal.

"I said there are a lot of holes in the Angels' theory," he said.

"No, you didn't," I said. "You said their theory had more holes than a colander."

Nick looked at me blankly. "Uh-huh. It's the thing you drain spaghetti in. It has holes in the bottom."

"I know what a colander is," I said.

"So what's wrong?" he asked. "Because I can see that something is."

What had Michelle said to me on the phone about that blood work? *"Maybe that will clear things up."* Now I understood exactly what Nick's agenda had been.

Jess had reached the table, but instead of sitting down she stood by my chair. She was five-nine in her sock-covered feet, at least two inches taller in the heels she was wearing, and I felt as though I had a Valkyrie beside me.

"At lunch today your mother said the same thing; their theory had more holes than a colander."

Nick flushed and his mouth twisted to one side.

"She told you what to say to me."

He shook his head. "No."

I raised my eyebrows but didn't say anything.

"Okay, she did suggest I *not* say that I think Michelle is probably right about Rose."

Jess groaned. "I swear, Nick, sometimes you're about as smart as a bag of hammers." She sat down, gave me a look of sympathy and rolled her eyes.

Nick shook his head and gestured with one hand. "Both of you seem to be ignoring the fact that Rose could have had a stroke. A stroke. If she did, she needs to be under a doctor's care." He made a motion in the air between Jess and me. "You think you're the only ones who care about her? Yes, when you called I'd already talked to Michelle. I saw a chance to have a couple of blood tests run to make sure Rose is all right. And yes, the toxicology tests are being done as well."

"Rose was examined by a doctor at the hospital. And they ran some tests. She didn't have a stroke, Nick." I struggled to keep my voice down.

"Oh, c'mon," he said. "Do you really think Rose saw Leesa Cameron dragging her husband's body across their kitchen floor? Or are you going with Cameron and some mysterious girlfriend staging some kind of elaborate setup?"

I swallowed down the sour taste at the back of my throat. "I'm going with taking Rose at her word until I see some real evidence that tells me something else happened."

"Well, I'm not willing to let something bad happen that I could have prevented."

Jess touched my arm. "Please let me take this one," she said. She didn't wait for my answer. She fixed Nick with her blue eyes. "First of all, you've taken one too many hockey pucks to the head if you think misleading or pretending or whatever you want to call it with Sarah is a good idea. And second, who exactly appointed you the guardian of all the rest of us, the all-knowing, all-seeing oracle who knows what's best?"

Nick kept his eyes on me. "Stay out of this, Jess," he said. "This has nothing to do with you."

She gave a snort of laughter and moved her chair back a couple of inches. "I'm moving out of the way because I figure there's a good chance you're going to get hit with lightning for being such a hypocrite." She glanced at me. "You should move out of the way, too, Sarah."

Anger flashed across Nick's face. Jess didn't give him a chance to speak. "You're right about one thing. This"—she made a motion in the air with one hand—"doesn't really have anything to do with me. Just the way Rose's health has nothing to do with you. She's a grown adult perfectly capable of making her own decisions, even if no one else likes them."

Nick opened his mouth and closed it again. Jess was on a roll and wasn't about to stop until she was done.

"You keep doing this," she said. She made a fist with her left hand and moved it up and down in a chopping motion. "Beating your head against the wall when all you have to do is walk around. You think you know better, better than Rose, better than your own mother, because they're old. And maybe you do. I don't know. The thing is, even if you do, you don't get to choose because it's not your life. We don't want to hear it. We want to screw up our own lives our own way." She took a breath and let it out; then she looked at me. "Can I get a ride home?" she asked.

"Sure," I said.

She smiled. "Thanks." Then she scouted the room, found Tina and pointed at the empty beer bottle on the table, holding up a finger.

Nick leaned toward me, resting one hand on the back of my chair. "Sarah, I'm sorry I wasn't straight with you, but I can't apologize for caring about Rose." The marimba ring tone of his phone interrupted before I could answer him. He stood up, took a step away from the table and pulled the phone from his pocket.

Tina came then and delivered Jess's beer. "Could I get you anything else?" she asked.

"Another order of chips and salsa," Jess said. She glanced at me. "This one's on me."

Nick ended his call and came back to the table. From the corner of my eye I saw Sam and the rest of the band making their way back to the stage. Around us people began to clap and cheer.

Nick leaned over my chair. "I have to go," he said. "But this isn't over."

I watched him walk away. I knew it wasn't over. I just wasn't so sure we had even gotten started.

Chapter 10

I woke up the next morning feeling like I hadn't slept at all, the sheet and a cotton blanket both wrapped in a tangle around one leg. After I'd gotten home from the pub I'd been too wired to watch TV. I'd spent some time searching around online, trying to learn more about Jeff Cameron. I'd remembered his sister saying he'd disappeared once before, after their grandmother died. I called Chloe Sanders, who told me Jeff had mentioned his grandmother only once. She was fairly certain the woman's name had been Catherine, but that was all she knew. I didn't have any luck finding an obituary for the woman.

I made coffee, scrambled an egg in the small cast-iron skillet Rose had insisted I needed, and ate it with a dish of stewed rhubarb that had grown in my back-yard. Charlotte had been horrified that I'd been pulling out the plants and composting them because I thought they were a weed. Elvis hopped onto my lap to mooch a bite of egg.

My cell phone rang. I slid it across the counter and

checked the screen, smiling when I saw who was calling. "Hi, Mom," I said. I leaned back, shifting Elvis sideways on my legs. He made a grumble of annoyance.

"Hi, sweetheart," she said. "How are things?"

"Things are fine," I said. I'd just talked to her and Dad less than a week ago. I had a feeling I knew what had prompted this call. "Have you been talking to Gram?"

I heard her laugh on the other end of the phone. "Guilty as charged. I just wanted to hear it straight from you that Rose was all right."

Elvis had jumped down to the floor to investigate what I'd put out for his breakfast.

"Rose is all right, Mom, I swear," I said.

"Isabel said someone hit her over the head with a boat fender?"

"Liz claims the fact that it was Rose's head is what saved her."

Mom laughed. "Not that anyone would ever suggest that Liz herself can be a little hardheaded."

I laughed, too. "Oh no, never."

"Is there anything I can do?"

"Not you, but maybe Dad. Is he around?"

I heard her take a sip of her tea, iced, I guessed, because of the time of year. "He went out for a run, but I can pass on a message. What do you need?"

My stepfather had been an award-winning newspaper reporter for many years. Now he taught journalism and writing at Keating State College in New Hampshire.

"Would you ask him if he could find out anything about the death of a Catherine Cameron? He'd be looking about three years ago. I don't know if that's Catherine with a 'C' or a 'K.' She would have been about eighty and she had two grandchildren, Jeff—probably Jeffrey—and Nicole. I don't know where in New Hampshire they lived."

"Does this have anything to do with what happened to Rose?" she asked.

"Maybe," I said. "Rose was doing a favor for a customer. I'm not sure whether or not he was being straight with her. I'd just like to know a little bit more about his background. Mr. P. has been searching online, but sometimes face-to-face works better."

"I'll give your father all the information as soon as he gets home." I heard a squeak, which told me she was at her desk in her office, which overlooked the backyard.

"Are you working?" I asked. Mom wrote an elementary school series of books that featured a talking gerbil named Einstein.

"Copy edits," she said. "Where do you stand on serial commas?"

"Umm, for them?" I said uncertainly.

"Well, of course. If only I could convince my copy editor that they're important. Or your father, for that matter."

"I have faith in your persuasive skills," I said.

She laughed again. "I may be able to make the copy editor see the light, but I think your father is a lost cause." I heard her shift once more in her squeaky desk chair, probably reaching for her tea. "I better get back to work, sweetie," she said.

"I'm glad you called, Mom," I said. "Talk to you

soon." I ended the call and set the phone back on the counter as Elvis came across the kitchen floor.

Since he'd finished his own breakfast, he jumped onto the stool next to me and eyed my plate expectantly.

"I already gave you a taste," I said.

He hung his head, giving me a mournful look while making sure I could see the scar that cut diagonally across his nose. That maneuver always worked on visitors to the store.

I gave him another bite of the egg. Clearly it worked on me, too.

Elvis murped a thank-you, ate the egg and then proceeded to wash his face. I cleaned up the kitchen and was about to go brush my teeth when the cat suddenly swung his head in the direction of the door. He jumped down, crossed the room and looked pointedly at the door before looking back at me.

I waited, half expecting to hear a knock, half expecting it would be Nick. There was no knock. Elvis sat down and continued to stare at the door. Feeling a little foolish, I walked over and checked the peephole. No one was there.

"Your radar is off," I said, bending down to give his head a scratch as I went past. He made a disgruntled sound in the back of his throat.

I finished getting ready, grabbed my bag and my keys and discovered Elvis was still sitting in front of the door. "You're persistent. I'll give you that," I said.

I stepped into the hallway and there was Mr. P. in a blue golf shirt and a Red Sox ball cap, his messenger bag over one shoulder. Elvis looked up at me, and the look on his face plainly said *I told you so.*

"Hello, Sarah," Mr. P. said. He smiled down at the cat. "Hello, Elvis."

I smiled back. "Good morning."

Rose came out of her apartment then, carrying not one but two tote bags. Mr. P. hurried over to take one of them from her. "You're here," she said, beaming at him. She turned to me. "Sarah dear, I told Alfred he could drive over to the Clarks' with us." She held up a paper bag. "I have Casey's dog biscuits."

Mr. P. pushed his glasses up his nose. "Are you sure it's all right, my dear?" he asked. "I don't want to take advantage."

"You're welcome to drive with us anytime," I said, setting down my own bag long enough to lock the door. "And you aren't taking advantage. I enjoy your company."

"So do I," Rose said.

Elvis meowed loudly.

"It's unanimous," I said with a grin.

We started out to the SUV with Elvis leading the way.

"You know the cat tower you built is still his favorite place," I said to Mr. P. "I think the only thing that could make it better was if it were in front of the TV so he could sit at the top and watch *Jeopardy!*"

One of the cat's little quirks was watching the game show every weeknight. He had some kind of internal clock that told him just when the show was beginning. My best guess was that he'd watched the show with his previous owner. I had no idea what the cat's life had been like before he'd turned up along the harbor front more than a year ago now.

Elvis looked back over his shoulder, meowed and bobbed his head as though in agreement about his affection for his tower.

"I'm glad you like it, Elvis," Mr. P. said.

I opened the back driver's-side door and the cat jumped onto the backseat. Rose climbed in beside him. Mr. P. took the front passenger seat.

"We don't have to pick up Avery," Rose said as she fastened her seatbelt. "She's gone to a very early movie, part of that film festival the library is putting on." She smiled. "I'm glad she's making some friends her own age."

"Me, too," I said.

"What's the plan for the day?" I asked once we were headed for Windspeare Point.

"I'm going to do a little more digging into Mr. Cameron's background. His work history so far seems to be very spotty," Mr. P. said.

"Charlotte is going to an aquacize class at the gym and Liz is having a massage," Rose added from the backseat.

We were at a stop sign so I glanced at her in the rearview mirror. "And what are you going to do?" I asked.

"I'm going to charm tourists into spending a lot of money," she said with a completely straight face.

"I have no doubt about that," I said.

"I didn't tell you—it turns out that Maddie Hamilton lives two houses away from Chloe Sanders' parents. Charlotte is going to talk to her, too."

I had a soft spot for Maddie. She was the reason I had my father's guitar. She'd found it at an estate sale, had it restrung and given it to me on my fifteenth birthday.

Rose had called Ashley Clark, and she and Casey were waiting on the front step of their little cottage. Rose fished one of the dog biscuits she and Avery had made out of the paper bag. The dog sniffed it and then took it from Rose's hand. The look he gave her was pure adoration.

When we got back in the SUV, Elvis had positioned himself on the far side of the backseat. He was looking out the passenger window at the street, ignoring the rest of us. It was pretty clear he was sulking.

Rose took another small bag from one of her totes and set it on the seat. I caught the distinctive smell of sardines. So did the cat. He turned to look at Rose, whiskers twitching. "Did you think I forgot about you?" she asked.

He walked across the seat and poked the bag with a paw.

"Is it all right if I give him one?" Rose asked.

"Yes, go ahead," I said.

She took out a star-shaped cracker and set it on the seat. The smell of sardines grew stronger. Elvis sniffed the treat and must have liked what he smelled because his green eyes all but closed in bliss. I made a note to use my own nose next time I was offered a plate of Rose's star-shaped cookies.

When we got to the shop, Avery was set up on an old table outside, painting picture frames. Mac was inside.

"I talked to a couple of people about Helmark Associates," he said.

I could tell from the expression on his face that he hadn't come up with anything useful. "No luck?" I said.

He shook his head. "Helmark was formed when People Plus and JobCore merged about a year and a half ago. That's when Jeff Cameron started working there, along with quite a few other people. JobCore offered a buyout, which a lot of their staff took advantage of. People Plus did the same kind of thing with an early retirement package. The new company hired a lot of people in a short time."

I made a face. "It was worth a shot. Thanks."

"I did learn one thing," Mac said, "although I'm not sure how it will help. Jeff Cameron had only been at his previous job about a year. Before that he had a gap in his résumé, which he explained by saying he was traveling around Europe working at different jobs for a few weeks or a few months. Apparently he didn't have any references or contact information from any of them. Helmark was short staffed and that really didn't make a difference to them."

I frowned. I wasn't sure how the information would help, either. "It's something for Mr. P. to look into," I said. I smiled. "Thanks for trying."

"Anytime," he said. He gestured at a large cardboard box on the cash counter. "How do you feel about accordions?"

"They worked for Lawrence Welk and Weird Al Yankovic," I said. "Why?"

"I helped Glenn move a sofa for his uncle last night. The old man offered me a couple of accordions that Glenn said have been in the house since Adam was a cowboy. Now I'm starting to think I should have taken the bottle of homemade beer instead."

I made a face. "Accordions are tricky. There's not a very big resale market and there's a lot of junk out there."

"I knew I should have gone with the beer," Mac said. He smiled, which told me he really didn't mean it.

I set my things down on the cash desk. "Hang on a minute," I said. "Let me take a look. The big thing with old accordions is whether they can still be played."

I pulled the smaller of the two instruments out of the box. It was made of red plastic and I knew at once it was a child's toy. "You might get a dollar for this at a yard sale," I said.

Avery was just coming through the shop, probably headed for the second-floor staff room to see what Rose had brought to eat in her overstuffed tote bags. "Can I have it?" she asked. She fished three quarters out of the pocket of her jeans and held them out to Mac. "I don't have a dollar."

"You can have it," he said. "But you don't have to pay me."

Avery took the accordion from me and held the quarters out to Mac. "Nonna will have a cow if she thinks I'm taking advantage."

"All right, then," Mac said taking the money from her hand.

Avery beamed with happiness, clutched the plastic accordion to her chest and took the stairs two at a time.

Mac walked over to me.

"What is she going to do with that?" I asked.

"I have no idea," he said.

"I like that she isn't worrying so much about what other people think."

"You can thank Rose for that," Mac said. "And you deserve some credit, too." He gave me a nudge with his elbow.

"You know, I'm glad it's worked out, Avery moving here with Liz." I looked up at the ceiling, half expecting to hear the sound of the toy instrument coming through from upstairs.

"Liz is going to have a cow when Avery takes that thing home, you know."

I held up both hands. "Don't look at me. You're the one who sold it to her."

Mac shook his head and laughed. Then he gestured at the box. "What are we going to do with that one?"

"Hang on a second," I said. "At least let me take a look." I lifted the second accordion out of the box. It was black, a bit larger than the one Avery had just disappeared upstairs with. I slipped my hands through the straps and squeezed. It was still playable, and to my uneducated ear the sound was fine.

I turned the instrument around to check the name, although I had a feeling what I was going to see. HOHNER STUDENT IVM it said on the front of the accordion. "We should be able to get a few dollars for this one," I said.

"Well, that's good," Mac said. "How much are you thinking?"

I shrugged. "Four, maybe five . . . hundred dollars."

His mouth actually fell open a little. "You're not serious?"

"Yes, I am," I said, grinning at him. "I know about

this much about accordions." I held up my thumb and index finger about half an inch apart. "But I know that Hohner is a quality instrument and this particular accordion is in very good shape. I'll see what Sam thinks, but this is better than a growler of Clayton McNamara's beer."

Rose came downstairs then, carrying two mugs of coffee. She handed one to me and the other to Mac. "There's rhubarb cinnamon coffee cake in the staff room," she said. Then she smiled up at Mac. "I'm going to miss you."

"I'm not going anywhere," he said slowly, frowning in confusion.

She patted his arm. "Liz is going to kill you when she finds out you sold that accordion to Avery," she said. She turned to me. "I'm just going to put out those quilts you washed," she said. "We should get two bus tours today."

I nodded and managed not to laugh until she'd gone into the workroom. Then I bumped Mac with my hip. "I'm going to miss you, too," I said, grabbing my things and heading for the stairs.

I knew it was wrong to compare two people with very different personalities, but I couldn't help noticing how easy everything was with Mac. I couldn't help wishing it was that way with Nick.

Half an hour later I'd just finished printing out the orders that had come in via our Web site when Mr. P. knocked on my door. "Sarah, do you have a minute?" he asked.

"Sure," I said, gesturing at the love seat across from my desk. "Have a seat."

Mr. P. sat down and I leaned forward, propping my elbow on the arm of my chair. "What's up?"

"I discovered some interesting information about Jeff Cameron's young assistant, Chloe Sanders."

"Interesting how?"

"This job was just for the summer."

I nodded. "Chloe's a student at Cahill College."

One eyebrow went up. "That's the interesting part, my dear. She isn't."

I frowned at him. "What do you mean she isn't?"

"I mean she didn't take any classes last semester."

I leaned back in my chair. "Did she fail the previous term or did she drop out?"

"As far as I can determine, she took a one-term deferment at the very last minute. She said it was for personal reasons."

"Do I want to know how you know that?" I asked.

Mr. P. smiled. "I don't think that you do," he said. "What I find interesting is that she left that information off her résumé and off the job application she filled out for Helmark online."

"She wouldn't be the first person who fudged a résumé," I offered.

He nodded. "True. But it's more than that. Jeff Cameron was a guest lecturer in the Global Studies Department back in March. The lecture was only for students and faculty."

"Chloe was at the lecture."

"She was. It piqued my curiosity, so I did a little digging."

I could tell from the beginnings of a smile on his face that his digging had unearthed something.

"So what did you dig up?" I asked.

"Two weeks after he was at Cahill, Jeff Cameron was at a business roundtable at the University of New Hampshire. There were photographs on the university's Web site."

It was obvious where he was going. "Chloe was in the audience."

Mr. P. nodded. "The tickets were sixty-five dollars. I don't like to generalize, but how many young women would spend that amount of money to attend a talk on outsourcing?"

"Not a lot." I pulled my hands back through my hair. "Do you think she was having an affair with Jeff?" I remembered what Leesa Cameron had said about Jeff calling his assistant a Roomba. Would he have been having an affair with someone he saw as the equivalent of a vacuum cleaner? I was starting to dislike the man even more.

My office door moved then and Elvis padded into the room. He jumped onto the love seat next to Mr. P., who smiled at the cat and reached over to stroke his fur. "I don't know," he said. "According to Rosie, the young woman didn't seem that upset at the idea that her boss had run off with another woman."

He was right. Chloe Sanders had seemed a bit concerned, but she had showed none of the emotion that Leesa Cameron had displayed.

"I'd like to know more about why Chloe took a semester off and why she left that information off her résumé. She used her faculty adviser as a reference on that résumé."

I linked my hands behind my head. "You're thinking a road trip to Cahill College?" I asked.

Mr. P. smiled. "I'm thinking a road trip to the library, my dear." He glanced at his watch. "In about half an hour."

"For?" I prompted.

"A half hour talk on the changing face of the European Community by Dr. Isabella Durand, assistant professor of government and Chloe Sanders' faculty adviser."

We agreed to leave for the library in ten minutes. When I got downstairs I expected to find Rose waiting with Mr. P., but he was alone. "Where's Rose?" I asked.

Mr. P. gestured in the direction of the Angels' office. "She said she has other irons in the fire. It's just going to be the two of us."

I frowned, looking past him to the door to the back of the building. "What do you mean 'other irons in the fire'?"

He shook his head. "Those were her exact words. Other than that I don't know." He followed my gaze. "Sarah, you do realize that we have exactly"—he looked down at his watch—"twenty-one minutes to get to the library?"

And Rose wasn't going to tell anyone what she was up to until she was good and ready. Mr. P. didn't say the last part, but it was implied.

I made a face. "We should go," I said.

Far more people in North Harbor were interested in the changing face of the European Community than

I expected, although the strawberry shortcake they were serving after the talk may have had a little to do with the good turnout. Isabella Durand was much younger that I had expected. She couldn't have been more than a year or so out of graduate school. She was tall and curvy, with a mass of curly blond hair and dark eyes behind her gray-frame glasses. She was wearing a chambray sundress and black lace-up glad-iator sandals that showed off her runner's calves. She was also an excellent speaker, advancing her argument that a European economic and political union made the case for a similar construct in our part of the world.

Mr. P. and I waited until the crowd had thinned before we approached Isabella Durand. Mr. P. offered his hand. "Dr. Durand, I enjoyed your talk very much, although we disagree on the influence of a resurgent Russia."

Resurgent Russia? Mr. P. never ceased to amaze me.

The professor smiled. "You're not the first person to challenge my reasoning in that area."

"And I'm certain I'd enjoy hearing more about your logic, but I'd like to talk to you about one of your for-mer students, Chloe Sanders." He extended one of his business cards.

Isabella Durand's expression changed even before she read the card. Her body stiffened and the smile on her face tightened. "Is Chloe in some kind of trouble?" she asked.

"She's been working for a man named Jeff Cam-eron," Mr. P. said. "He's been out of touch with his family."

"You mean he's missing." Her dark eyes narrowed. "You can't believe Chloe had anything to do with that?"

Mr. P. cocked his head to one side. He reminded me of a curious bird, eyeing a worm. "Dr. Durand, why did Chloe attend a lecture by Mr. Cameron which was supposed to be for students and faculty when she was taking a semester off?"

For a moment the professor didn't say anything. Her mouth moved and then she seemed to swallow whatever response she'd been about to make. She exhaled softly. "Mr. Peterson, the reason Chloe took last term off is between her and the university. You obviously don't have Chloe's permission to have that information or she'd be here right now."

Mr. P. didn't say anything. He'd told me once that people didn't like silences and if you left one, the other person would often step in to fill it.

"But it's not a big secret," the professor continued. "Chloe was a little overwhelmed with the amount of work global studies requires. She needed a bit of a break; that's all. As for Mr. Cameron's lecture, Chloe had written an excellent paper on outsourcing—his lecture topic—for my class the previous term. I thought coming to the talk might encourage her to return to classes in the fall. That's it."

She looked around before giving us a polite smile. "Now, if you'll excuse me, there are other people I need to talk to." She started for the table under the window, where there was coffee and some of what looked to be Glenn McNamara's cinnamon-raisin muffins.

Mr. P. turned to me. "I'm ready to leave if you are," he said.

We started for the door. "Do you think she was telling you the truth?" I asked.

"Not for a moment." He pushed his glasses up his nose. "What about you, my dear?"

I thought about all the evasive behaviors I'd seen from Dr. Durand: how she'd stiffened, hesitated, swallowed down her words. The professor was definitely keeping something from us. "Me, neither," I said.

He reached over and patted my arm. "Now all we have to do is find out why."

Chapter 11

We returned to the shop to find Rose using her considerable charm on a couple—a man and woman who looked to be in their early thirties.

"Thank you for accompanying me to the library, Sarah," Mr. P. said. "I'm going to see what I can find out about our professor." He headed for the sunporch, and since everything seemed under control, I went up to my office.

I spent the next while working on an estimate for a family that wanted us to handle the clearout of their mother's house. Mom, it turned out, was on a South Pacific cruise and was moving into an apartment when she got back. After about forty minutes I shut off the computer and delivered a cup of tea and a butterscotch oatmeal cookie to Mr. P. in the sunporch office.

"Any luck?" I asked.

He broke the cookie in half and took a bite. "Not yet. Dr. Durand doesn't appear to take part in any form of social media." He reached for his tea. "However, there are still some more rocks to turn over."

"I forgot to tell you earlier; I talked to my mom this morning," I said. "I asked her to ask Dad if he could find out anything about Jeff and Nicole's grandmother. I thought it might help if we knew a bit more about his background."

"That's a very good idea," Mr. P. said.

"I'll let you know what I find out."

Avery came in the back door then. "Hey, Sarah, I'm done painting for now. What do you want me to do next?"

"Help Rose in the shop, and when you have time, change the tablecloth and the dishes on the round table, please."

"Okay," she said. "What do you want me to use on the table?"

"Whatever you decide," I said. "I trust your judgment."

She clapped her hands together like a little kid. "I know exactly what I'm going to do."

"Can't wait to see it," I said. I headed outside. There was no wind and it seemed like a good time to work on my chairs.

I opened the big front doors to the former garage work space and put down a large tarp on the pavement in front of the building. Then I got out my homemade spray box, which was nothing more than the cardboard carton a commercial washing machine had come in with the bottom and front cut out. I'd scrounged three of the heavy cardboard boxes when the Laundromat one street over from Jess's shop had been renovated.

I'd just set one of the wicker chairs in the box when Charlotte came walking up the sidewalk. I brushed off my hands on my old shirt and walked down to meet her. "Hi," I said. "How was the gym?"

"Educational," she said. "I learned I'm way too uncoordinated for aquacize."

I slipped my arm around her waist. "I do not believe that," I said.

Charlotte smiled. "I appreciate the vote of confidence, but it's true. That class was like the Rockettes' kick line in water. I did learn a few things, though."

"How to kick your foot up as high as your nose?" I teased.

"Heavens, no," she said. "If I tried that—even in the water—I'd be in traction."

I held open the back door for her and we went inside. Mac was on his way out.

"I think I found a pair of hinges that will work for that old hope chest," he said to me. He smiled at Charlotte. "Yell if you need me."

Charlotte waved hello to Mr. P., who was still bent over his laptop, and we headed for the shop. We walked in to find Avery high-fiving Rose.

"What's going on?" I asked.

"I sold that dresser and bed that came from Edison Hall's house," Rose said. She looked pleased with herself, and for good reason. We'd been trying to sell that bedroom set for months.

"Rose is a selling ninja," Avery said, nodding for emphasis.

"That's good news," I said.

"I got the full price," Rose said tipping her head to one side to look at the heavy mahogany head- and footboards, which were resting against the back wall along with the side rails and dresser.

"Full price? Avery is right. You are a selling ninja," I said, giving her a hug. "I'll get a check ready and let Stella know it's here." We didn't take many items on consignment, but the bedroom set was a special case. The money would go toward Stella's niece's medical bills.

"I saw Stella and Ellie at the grocery store last weekend," Charlotte said. "Ellie is getting around with a walker now." Stella Hall was the late Edison Hall's sister. Ellie had been his daughter-in-law.

"That is good news," I said. Ellie Hall had had surgery on her back about six weeks earlier. She had little ones at home. I was happy to hear she was doing well.

"Sarah, can I use some stuff in the boxes under the stairs?" Avery asked. Her eyes darted to Charlotte. "I mean, *may* I use some stuff in the boxes under the stairs?"

I nodded. "Go ahead."

She headed for the storage space. Rose brushed her hands on her apron. "Alfred told me about your conversation with Dr. Durand."

Charlotte looked from Rose to me. "Who's Dr. Durand?"

Rose waved a hand at her friend. "I'll explain later. What I want to know is, how was aquacize?"

"Remember when Maddie convinced us to try Zumba?" Charlotte asked.

"Oh, I'm sorry," Rose said. I was clearly missing

something, not the least of which was that I didn't know Rose and Charlotte had tried a Zumba class.

"Maddie takes Zumba?" I said. "Maddie Hamilton?"

"Yes, dear. It's very good exercise," Rose said. She turned back to Charlotte. "What did you find out?"

"Nothing as far as another woman goes."

Rose sighed.

"Jeff Cameron arrived at the gym to change and run, and that was it," Charlotte continued. "No one saw him with a woman. Or anyone else, for that matter. He was pleasant, but he kept to himself for the most part."

"They hadn't been here that long," I said. "It's not surprising."

Charlotte nodded. "The only thing anyone noticed about him was that he's very competitive. He did some of the weekly timed runs the gym ran, and he always wanted to be the top person in his age group."

"What about Leesa Cameron?" I asked.

Charlotte shook her head. "No one I spoke to remembers ever seeing her there. I think she pretty much kept to herself."

"Maybe it was because she was doing Reece's father," Avery said. She was sitting cross-legged on the floor in front of the storage space under the stairs.

"Excuse me?" Charlotte said.

Avery turned to look at us over her shoulder. "Sorry," she said. "Maybe because she was sleeping with Reece's father." She made air quotes around the words "sleeping with."

"Sweetie, who's Reece?" Rose asked.

"She goes to my school."

"Why do you think her father was involved with Mrs. Cameron?" Charlotte said, frown lines forming between her eyebrows.

Avery shrugged. "I saw them, two or three weeks ago, maybe. I didn't know who she was until I saw the photo of her that Mr. P. had."

"Saw her where?" Rose said.

"Running." Avery made a face. "She pretty much sucked at it, by the way." She looked over at Charlotte. "I know, I know, you hate the word, but she did suck. Her arms and legs were going all over the place and she had to keep stopping." Avery looked at me. "She didn't look like you when you run."

"Thank you," I said. She seemed to have meant the remark as a compliment. "When exactly did this happen?"

"Sometime between five thirty and six."

"In the morning?"

"I like mornings," Avery said with a shrug.

Charlotte and I exchanged a look. Avery had to be the only teenager in town who willingly got up at five thirty during the summer.

"I like to get up and make a smoothie and sit in the elm tree in the front yard. I like it there. I saw Mrs. Cameron and Reece's dad go by a bunch of times—at least five or six. When she had to stop, she'd be all bent over like she couldn't get her breath and he'd rub her back. Seemed kind of personal to me." She looked up at Rose, who had walked over to the stairs. "I'm sorry. If I'd known it was important I would have said something sooner."

Rose leaned down and put her arm around Avery's shoulders. "It's enough that you said something now."

"What's Reece's last name?" I asked.

Avery turned to look at me. "Vega."

I nodded. The name, Vega, soundly vaguely familiar, but I couldn't figure out why.

My cell phone rang in my pocket. I held up a finger. "Hang on a second." I pulled out the phone. It was Dad.

"I need to take this," I said. "Excuse me." I walked over to stand by the front door to the shop.

"Hi, Dad," I said.

"How's my favorite daughter?" he said. I could hear his smile.

"I'm your only daughter."

He laughed. "Well, didn't that work out well for everyone?" He and my mom had gotten married when Liam and I were both in second grade. Dad had always treated me as though I was his biological child. I'd heard someone ask him once if he had any children of his own. He'd given the woman a blank look and said, "But Sarah is *my* child."

I hadn't just gotten a father. I'd also gotten a big brother. There was a month between Liam and me, him being the elder. He could be a pain-in-the-butt, overprotective big brother when I wanted to date someone he thought was a scuzzbag, but he could also be my biggest ally.

"Your mom gave me your message," Dad said.

"What did you find out?" I asked, leaning both elbows on the counter.

"I prowled around the archives at the paper. They're online now. I couldn't find any obituary for a Catherine

Cameron. Not with a 'C' or a 'K' or several other spellings I tried. I went back a year and forward a year."

"Crap!" I said.

"I did find a death notice for a Catherine Hennessy. It was three years ago and she was survived by her two grandchildren, Jeff and Nicole Hennessy."

"That's a weird coincidence," I said.

"I don't think it's a coincidence, Sarah," Dad said. "Are you sure the woman's last name was Cameron?"

I shook my head even though he couldn't see me. "No. But Cameron is the last name the grandchildren are using."

"This has something to do with what happened to Rose, doesn't it?"

"Yeah," I said. "Jeff Cameron—or whatever his name really is—bought a pair of candlesticks for his wife. Now no one can find him."

"Maybe you should start looking for Jeff Hennessy instead."

"Maybe we should," I said.

I thanked him for his help and said good-bye. Rose and Charlotte were in deep discussion about something, probably the trip Mr. P. and I had made to the library. We'd discovered a lot of information, but I had no idea how it fit together.

I went out to the sunporch to find Alfred. I explained what Dad had discovered and what Avery had told us about Leesa Cameron and her running partner.

"Interesting," he said. "I'll see what I can discover about the Hennessys and about Mr. Vega."

"Let me know what you find," I said, heading back outside.

The paint sprayer was being temperamental, and it took me the better part of the next hour to get it working properly. I went inside for a cup of coffee before starting on the chairs. I had just come down the stairs with a mug in my hand when Mr. P. came in from the back.

Rose took one look at him and immediately said, "You found something." She glanced at me. "Alfred told me what your father discovered."

Mr. P. had a satisfied smile on his face. "I did," he said. "Jeff Cameron changed his name. I couldn't find much about him beyond about three years ago, so I did a little digging into his sister. Nicole Cameron got her RN as Nicole Hennessy. Northeastern Medical Center issues her paychecks in that name. Although she goes by Cameron, she didn't actually change her name."

Mr. P. looked at me. "Don't worry, Sarah," he said. "I didn't do anything illegal."

"I appreciate that," I said.

"Both of the Camerons were raised by their grandmother," Mr. P. continued. "Their parents were killed in a car accident."

"That's awful," Charlotte said, shaking her head.

"Jeff left New Hampshire when his grandmother died and moved to California. He changed his name from Jeffery Cameron Hennessy to Jeff Cameron—no middle name."

"Why would he do that?" Rose asked.

"Maybe he was running away from his old life," Avery offered from across the room. She was still sitting cross-legged on the floor and didn't even look up from the box she was investigating.

"That's as good an explanation as any," I said. "And if he walked away from a life before . . ."

"Maybe he was going to do it again," Rose finished.

Chapter 12

I went back out to the garage to work on my chairs. I was just getting the paint sprayer adjusted when my cell rang again. This was why I usually left it in my office. I pulled it out to see who was calling.

Glenn McNamara. Glenn owned McNamara's, a sandwich shop and bakery that was popular with both the locals and tourists. I wasn't sure why he'd be calling.

"Hi, Sarah, did I catch you at a bad time?" he asked.

"Hi, Glenn," I said. "No, you didn't."

"I need a favor."

"Sure."

"You're supposed to ask what it is first," he said.

"Oh darn," I said. "Does that mean I've been doing it wrong all this time?"

Glenn laughed. "You're funny."

"Seriously," I said, walking over to the main door to the garage so I could stand in the sunshine. "What do you need?"

"What's your cat like when it comes to catching mice and other furry things?"

"Good," I said. "I use him as an advance crew in most of the old places we clear out."

"Could I borrow him?"

"You have mice down there?"

"Here? Good Lord, no. I have a pest-control company that checks the place regularly. It's my uncle Clayton's place where there's a problem. At least I think there is. Did Mac show you the accordions?"

The sun was warm on my bare arms. "He did," I said. "One of them is a Hohner. It's worth a bit of money."

"Good for Mac, then," Glenn said. "If either one of you is thinking of returning it, please don't. We're trying to get things out of that house, not vice versa."

"So you saw a mouse, or mice, or evidence of them?"

"Not me. My cousin, Beth. She's petrified of mice. If it's small and furry, you can pretty much be sure she'll be up on the table."

"You think the cat is a better idea than your pest-control people?" I asked.

He laughed. "Definitely. Beth is also the back-to-nature type. She doesn't want to share the house with any little critters, but she doesn't like the idea of any kind of chemicals or poison being used, either. And I don't want to have to keep checking if we set traps."

I blew out a breath. "Okay," I said. "The problem is Elvis isn't going to take whatever he finds by the paw and escort it outside, if you get my meaning."

"I get it," Glenn said. "It seems that's okay. It's part of the circle of life."

"Good to know," I said. "Sure you can borrow Elvis. When do you want to do this?"

"Now, if you have the time. I'm sorry for the rush, but Beth's only here for another week and there's still a lot she wants to do. Plus we're trying to strike while Clayton is agreeable."

"Got it," I said. He wasn't the first person to say something like that about an older relative. The funny thing was, just as often it was the younger people in a family who didn't want to let things go. "Where does your uncle live?" I asked.

Glenn had loaned me his van when we moved Rose into my place. He'd let the Angels set up a sting in the sandwich shop. I was actually glad to be able to do something for him for a change.

Glenn named a street at the far end of town along the coast, hugging the shoreline where it curved down toward Rockport and Camden.

"Elvis and I could meet you there in about half an hour if you can make that work."

"I can," he said. "I owe you."

"Don't worry about it," I said.

I put everything back in the garage, then went back inside to find Mac. He was at the workbench. I explained where I was going.

"The house is piled," he warned. "I don't mean like a hoarder. It's just that the old man has a lot of stuff."

I leaned against the workbench. Elvis was sitting near Mac, watching both of us.

"Do you think Glenn and his cousin would be offended if I see anything that would work here in the

shop and offer to buy it or bring it here on consignment?"

Mac set down the screwdriver he'd been holding.
"Just the opposite. I think they'd both be happy to get
some things out of there. I can't vouch for Clayton,
though."

"C'mon," I said to Elvis. "Rodent patrol."

The cat licked his whiskers, jumped down from the
workbench and headed for the back door.

Glenn's truck was parked on the street in front of
his uncle's house when I got there. He was leaning
against the front fender, arms folded over his chest.
He was tall, with wide shoulders, and he still wore his
blond hair in the same brush cut he'd had as a college
football player.

I pulled in behind the truck, picked up Elvis and
got out.

Glenn smiled at me. "Thanks for doing this, Sarah,"
he said. He looked at the cat. "You, too, Elvis."

Elvis made a low meow of acknowledgment.

We walked up the driveway to the back door of the
story-and-a-half house. It was set back from the street
on what looked to be a large lot. "This is a really beautiful spot," I said, looking around.

"It is," Glenn agreed. "Clayton and his father—my
grandfather—built this house. Beth lives in Portland—
the other Portland, out west. She's not interested in it,
so I'm hoping that Clayton will eventually sell it to me."

"I can see why you'd want to live here," I said. I
could hear the ocean in the distance. The soothing
sound of the waves hitting the shore seemed to pull
the tension out of my body.

Glenn opened the aluminum screen door and knocked on the inside wooden door. Then he opened it and stuck his head inside. "Clayton, are you here?" he called.

"No, I'm here," a raspy voice behind us said. A large, barrel-chested man came around the side of the house. He was easily as tall as Glenn, with the same broad shoulders and strong arms. But Clayton McNamara must have had fifty pounds on his nephew. He smiled at me and held out his hand. "You're Isabel's grand-daughter," he said.

I smiled. His hands were massive and his hand-shake was strong but not crushing. "I am," I said. "It's nice to meet you, Mr. McNamara."

"Call me Clayton, child," he said. "'Mister' makes me feel old. Now, I am old, but I don't like to be reminded about it."

"You know my grandmother?" I said.

He pulled off his Patriots cap and smoothed a hand over his bald head. "Yes, I do. She broke my heart."

I raised an eyebrow. "I think there's a story here I've never heard."

"Me neither," Glenn said.

"It was a long time ago," Clayton said. "Isabel was my first love. But first love is a fickle thing. I caught her kissing another man."

It seemed as though Gram had a past I knew noth-ing about.

Clayton fitted his hat back on his head. "Though to be fair the other man did have two peanut butter cook-ies in his lunchbox." He grinned at us. "And we were six."

I laughed. "You went to school together."

He nodded. "First through twelfth grade. How is Isabel? I hear she's been on her honeymoon for most of the last year."

"She has," I said. "I just talked to her a couple of days ago. She'll be home in about a month."

"Next time you talk to her, please give her my best."

"I will," I said.

He looked at Elvis and held out a hand. It was bigger than my head. "Hello, puss," he said. Elvis sniffed his fingers and then looked up at the big man and murped hello.

"How did he get the scar on his nose?" Clayton asked.

"I don't know," I said, stroking the top of the cat's head. "He had it when I got him. There are a couple of more scars that are covered by his fur. The vet said the other guy probably looks worse."

"He's a good mouser." It wasn't really a question.

I nodded. "He is. He lived down along the harbor front for several weeks before he came to live with me. He wasn't exactly scrawny."

Elvis turned and looked at the little house. And then, to everyone's amusement, he licked his whiskers.

Clayton stroked his long, shaggy beard. He may have had no hair on the top of his head, but he more than made up for it with the beard. "I'm thinking it may be a squirrel that's in that back bedroom. I did have the window open one day without the screen, but it doesn't make a lick of difference to Beth. She's scared witless of anything like that." He pointed at the house diagonally across the street. "That was the Williams house when Beth was a kid. Dillon Williams had a pet rat."

Beside me Glenn was nodding wordlessly.

"Beth was five. It bit her." Clayton held up the little finger on his right hand. "Took the tip right off the end of her finger."

"Whatever's in there, Elvis can get it," I said.

"Let's get to it, then," the old man said. He led the way into the house. Mac was right. The place was piled, but it was clean. It was just that there wasn't a bare surface anywhere. I followed the two men up to the second floor.

There were two bedrooms up there, one tucked under the peak of the roof on each side of the house. Clayton opened the bedroom door on the right. Like the rest of the house, it was piled with furniture. A double bed, a tall chest of drawers, a mirrored dresser, an armoire with double doors, a full-size rocking chair and heaps of women's clothing filled the room.

I set Elvis down on the floor just inside the door. He immediately began to sniff the air. "Go for it," I said. He started picking his way across the floor. "We should keep this door closed," I told Glenn.

"Okay," he said. "But how are we going to know if he catches anything?"

"We'll know. Trust me," I said.

The cat was already heading for the small closet in the far corner like a feline with a purpose. I closed the door.

"Would you like a cup of coffee?" Clayton asked.

"I should stay close by," I said, gesturing at the door.

"Not a problem," he said. "I'm perfectly capable of carrying a mug of coffee up these stairs."

"Then, yes, thank you," I said.

"How do you take it?"

"Cream and sugar, please."

He turned to Glenn. "You, too?"

Glenn nodded. "Do you need any help?"

"I'll ask if I do," Clayton said. "Stay here and keep Sarah company." He made his way back down the stairs, turning left at the bottom.

"He makes a good cup of coffee," Glenn offered. "I've always been a bit afraid to ask him what he puts in it, though." He looked around and sighed. "I don't know how on earth Beth thinks we can get this place organized in a week."

"I don't know if it would help, but we take things on consignment at the shop."

He ran a hand over his close-cropped hair. "How would you feel about my backing a truck up to the front door, putting about half the stuff in this house inside it and driving it down to your store?"

I shrugged. "Fine with me."

Glenn laughed. "Be careful. I might just do it."

I heard a thump behind us. I turned and looked at the door. There were no other sounds. "Not yet," I said. I turned my attention back to Glenn. "I'm serious," I said. "If we can help, let me know." I smiled at him. "I'll give you the friends-and-family discount."

"That's no way to run a business," he said.

"Yeah, kind of the same as giving away bread." I

raised an eyebrow. Glenn just smiled and shook his head.

It wasn't common knowledge, but I knew that Glenn had been the first to step up when the elementary school had begun their hot-lunch program. My grandmother had been one of the organizers. Glenn had offered to supply rolls for the program one day a week, and when Lily's Bakery had closed he'd also stepped in to fill the gap.

Clayton came back with a big mug of coffee for each of us. Glenn was right. His uncle made a good cup of coffee. "I'll be out at the woodpile if you need me," the old man said.

Glenn took his coffee and sat down on the top stair, leaning his back against the wall. I sat down next to him. He took a sip of his coffee and glanced over at the closed bedroom door.

"Don't worry. Elvis will catch whatever critter is in there," I said.

"How did you end up with the cat?" Glenn asked. "You said he was wandering around the harbor front before you got him."

"Sam," I said, wrapping both hands around my mug. "The band was doing their Elvis Presley medley and he noticed there was a black cat just inside the front door. He swore the cat stayed there for the entire set."

"Good taste," Glenn said.

"The next morning Sam was out in the alley putting a bunch of cardboard boxes in the recycling bin, and there's the same cat. Sam named him Elvis and fed him breakfast." I took another sip of my coffee. "No one seemed to know who Elvis belonged to. He showed up at the pub every few days and Sam fed him, but no one ever came looking for him. I took a guitar down one morning to get Sam's opinion. Elvis was there having breakfast."

I smiled, remembering how I'd asked Sam, "Why Elvis?"

Sam had shrugged. "He doesn't seem to like the Stones, so naming him Mick was kinda out of the question."

"How did you go from having breakfast with a cat to owning a cat?" Glenn asked. He held up a hand. "Not that I'm judging."

"Personally, I think it was a conspiracy," I said. "The two of them walked me out and the next thing I knew Elvis was in my truck and Sam was giving me a sales pitch on why I needed a cat."

He laughed. "Well, from my perspective it's working out well."

"Mine, too," I said. "Now I'm not the person who walks around her house talking to herself. I'm the woman who talks to her cat."

Glenn took a sip of his coffee and then held up a hand. "I forgot to ask you. How's Rose? I heard she was in the hospital."

I nodded. "She's fine. She was out on Windspeare Point. Someone hit her over the head."

"She was mugged?"

I hesitated. "Not exactly. Someone attacked her, but she wasn't robbed."

He squeezed one of his massive hands into a fist. "What the hell happened?"

I let out a breath. "Truth? I don't know. We've been trying to figure it out. Before she was . . . attacked, Rose might have seen a body."

"Hang on a minute. What do you mean 'might have seen a body'?" He leaned forward, propping his elbows on his knees.

"Long story," I said, tracing the rim of my cup with a finger. "Short version: The person Rose saw might be dead or he might have taken off and left his wife holding the bag." I took another sip of the coffee. "Do you know a guy named Jeff Cameron? He and his wife are new in town. They've been renting a cottage out on the point while they look for a house."

Glenn nodded. "Yeah. Runner, right? Always wearing running shoes, never stands still."

That pretty much described the man I'd met. "That's him."

"He's been in for coffee." A frown formed between his eyebrows. "It was his body Rose saw?"

"Looks like it. Whether he's alive or dead is another question."

"What do the police say? You're friends with Michelle Andrews."

I brushed my bangs back off my face. "Between us?"

He nodded. "Sure."

"She thinks Rose imagined the whole thing, maybe had a stroke."

"I bet that went over well," Glenn said with a wry smile.

"Pretty much how you'd expect," I said. "She's healthier than most people half her age, and they checked her over thoroughly at the hospital. I just . . ." I shrugged. "I just don't think she had a stroke. And I don't think she imagined what she saw, either."

"She's not that kind of person."

It was good to hear those words from someone who wasn't so close to the situation.

"I take it no one's been able to get hold of Cameron."

I shook my head. "No, but if he did run off with another woman, you can see why he might not want to be reachable."

"For what it's worth, I saw him early yesterday morning and there was no woman with him."

I stared at him. "You saw Jeff Cameron *yesterday* morning?" Rose had seen what she thought was Jeff's body Wednesday night. If it was him Glenn had seen, it added credence to the theory that Jeff Cameron had faked his death.

"Uh-huh. I came out here early—I don't know, maybe five thirty—and I saw him drive by. He's kind of hard to miss in that bilious yellow Jeep."

Before I could ask him any more questions I heard another thump followed by a muffled meow from the room behind us. I got to my feet.

Glenn followed suit. "I take it that's the all-clear signal."

"It should be," I said.

Elvis was on the other side of the bedroom door holding something, large, furry and I hoped dead in his mouth. He had a look of satisfaction in his green eyes. He gave a muffled meow of thank-you when I opened the door and he started down the stairs carrying his prize.

"Can you get the back door?" I said to Glenn.

"Oh yeah, sure." He followed Elvis down the stairs and opened the door to the backyard for him; then he came back up the stairs. I was still standing in the bedroom doorway. "That was not a squirrel," he said.

"Didn't exactly look like a field mouse, either." I raised my eyebrows at him.

He made a face. "I should look around."

"Good idea," I said. The quilt on the bed was rumpled, hanging down much longer on one end. I pointed at it. "You might want to wash that."

"I think we might want to wash everything in here," he said.

The closet door was partly ajar. I didn't remember it being like that when we'd let Elvis inside.

"Glenn, try the closet," I said, pointing in that direction.

"If there's something else in there, you're going to rescue me, right?" he said over his shoulder.

There was a feather duster on the nightstand closest to me. I picked it up and held it in front of me like I was a knight holding up a sword about to go into battle. "I'll save you. Go for it," I said.

He looked back at me and laughed. Then he opened the closet door. There wasn't anything inside as far as I could see, except more clothes. Glenn mumbled a swearword. "These are my grandfather's suits." He held up the sleeve of a gray wool pin-striped jacket. "Clayton would have to lose about a hundred pounds to fit into these. My grandfather was a beanpole."

He rummaged around, trying to push the hangers to one side, but there just wasn't room. I kept my feather duster at the ready, just in case.

"Okay, all right, that's where it is," he said.

"Are we talking alive it or dead it?" I asked.

Glenn pulled his head out of the closet.

"Neither," he said. He pointed to the ceiling. "I found a hole from the attic. I'm going to have to go up there."

"That's probably how whatever that was that Elvis caught got in here."

Glenn ran his hands back over his hair. "There's no way Beth and I can get this place straightened out in a week." He blew out a long breath. "Were you serious about what you said before? That you could sell some of this stuff at Second Chance?"

I struck a Statue of Liberty–style pose with the feather duster. "Don't I look serious?" I asked.

That made him laugh. I set the duster back on the night table. "We can do pretty much whatever will work for you. You can bring things to the shop and we'll get them ready and sell them for you. We can come out here and pick things up. We can even take over the cleanup. Talk to your cousin. And talk to Clayton. Then let me know what you need."

"Thanks," he said. "I owe you."

"No, you don't," I said, shaking my head. "You let your business be used for a sting, for heaven's sake. I still owe you."

"Hey, that was the most excitement I'd had on a Tuesday afternoon in years."

"You need to get out more," I said.

He laughed. Then his expression grew serious. "I mean it, Sarah, I appreciate this."

Glenn went downstairs and came back with a box of steel wool. He jammed about half the package into the hole in the closet ceiling. "That's going to have to do for now. I'll come back tonight and do something a bit more permanent."

We found Elvis out on the back stoop with Clayton McNamara. The cat was licking his whiskers. He smelled like fish.

"I hope you don't mind, Sarah," Clayton said. "I gave him a couple of sardines."

Elvis looked at me, seemingly daring me to say that had been a bad idea.

"I don't mind," I said, picking up the cat. "I think he earned them.

Glenn looked around. "Where is the—?"

"Evidence?" his uncle said dryly. "Don't worry. I took care of that."

"There's a hole in the ceiling of the closet in that room," Glenn said. "I stuck some steel wool in there for now, but I'll be back after supper to fix it properly."

"I appreciate that," Clayton said. He turned to me. "And it was very good to meet you and Elvis."

I smiled at him. "It was nice to meet you, too."

Glenn and I walked back to our vehicles.

"Glenn, are you sure it was yesterday morning that you saw Jeff Cameron?" I asked as we stood next to my SUV.

"I'm positive," he said. "Beth got here on Wednesday, and since Clayton gets up at the crack of dawn, I said I'd come out for breakfast and see what we could work out for a plan of attack." He pulled the keys to his truck out of his pocket. "Like I said, I recognized the Jeep, and it was definitely a man driving. I'm pretty sure it was Cameron." He narrowed his blue eyes. "Is it important?"

"I don't know," I said. "Maybe. It wouldn't hurt to mention it to Michelle."

Glenn shrugged. "Sure."

I unlocked the door of the SUV and set Elvis on the seat.

"If you're not in a hurry, why don't you follow me back to the shop?" Glenn said. "After all this, you at least have to let me give you half a dozen of those chocolate cupcakes with the mocha frosting you like."

"There's no way I'm going to say no to your cupcakes," I said.

I slid behind the wheel. Elvis had settled himself in his usual spot on the passenger side. He looked at me and yawned. "Tiring work," I said.

"Mrr," he said in agreement.

"You did a good job," I told him as we started for the sandwich shop. "What do you say? If Glenn ends up hiring us to clear some of the things out of that house, are you willing to go back for another safari?"

He looked up at me and licked his whiskers. I took that as a yes.

Chapter 13

There was very little traffic on the way to the sandwich shop. I'd already decided I was going to get another big cup of coffee to go along with my cupcakes. As usual Elvis was watching the road intently. We both saw the moving van blocking the street at the same time, which was, unfortunately a little too late to take a different direction.

I looked in the rearview mirror. There were three cars behind me. "It's just backing up," I told the cat. "It shouldn't take long."

There was just enough space in the alley for the truck to back up. I watched how skillfully the driver used his mirrors as he inched his way back. Glenn had taken a different route, and up ahead I saw him pulling into his parking lot. And then I caught sight of Liz. She was standing on the sidewalk in front of McNamara's with . . . Michelle? As I watched, Liz gave her a hug. Michelle crossed the street and Liz got in her car, which was parked right in front of the shop.

"What were they doing?" I said to Elvis.

He gave me a blank look.

"Please tell me Liz isn't trying to get information out of Michelle."

The cat almost seemed to shrug. I tipped my head back and looked at the roof of the car. There were no answers up there, either.

Glenn sent me back to my own shop with a large cup of coffee and six of his chocolate mocha cupcakes—which became five very quickly.

I was in my office changing my shoes when Rose poked her head around the door. "Sarah, do you have a minute?" she asked.

"Sure," I said. "What is it?"

"Did you know Cleveland has a younger sister?"

"Our Cleveland?" I asked. I'd been buying from the trash picker since Second Chance opened.

She nodded. "Actually he has three younger sisters and four younger brothers, all half-siblings. Cleveland's father was not the poster child for monogamy."

"Duly noted," I said. "Why is Cleveland's sister important?"

"Because she goes to Cahill College." Rose gave me a knowing smile. "I won't bore you with all the details about Logan's friends—that's Cleveland's sister's name, Logan. Lovely young woman, by the way."

"Is this the reason you didn't come to the library?"

"I was waiting for one of them to call me back."

"And?" I nudged.

"And it seems that Chloe Sanders was what we would have called a teacher's pet in my day, although that's not the expression Logan used."

I had a pretty good idea what expression Cleveland's sister had used. "Dr. Durand," I said.

She nodded. "It appears that Chloe was an excellent student. She even did a couple of projects for extra credit." Rose twisted the thin gold wedding ring she still wore around her finger. "Unfortunately that kind of thing doesn't always make you very popular with your fellow students."

"What does this have to do with Jeff Cameron?"

"It seems that when he was giving that lecture at Cahill, he said he was planning on hiring an assistant for the summer. Two of Logan's friends said that Chloe really wanted that job. She called it her big chance."

I rubbed the side of my neck. "Big chance for what?"

"I'm still working on that," Rose said. "I just wanted to keep you in the loop."

"I appreciate that," I said. "Before you go, Glenn told me something that may or may not be important."

Rose raised an eyebrow. "What did he say?"

"That he saw Jeff Cameron early Thursday morning."

She couldn't stop the smile that spread across her face. "More evidence that he faked his death."

"You know what Nick and Michelle will say," I said.

"That people mistake identities of people in cars and mix up dates all the time and this kind of information is very unreliable. As my mother used to say, 'Horsefeathers!'" She reached over, plucked a dust ball out of my hair, patted my cheek and left.

It was a busy afternoon. It seemed as if every tourist passing by North Harbor decided to visit the store.

No one had specifically asked me if I'd call Michelle so we could update her on what Mr. P. had learned about Jeff Cameron. By the end of the day they just all seemed to decide that that's what would happen.

Rose and Mr. P. were having dinner with Charlotte. "Why don't you join us?" Charlotte said.

"Thank you," I said. "But I want to go for a run. Next time, though."

Mac was crewing for someone who'd lost one of his regulars when the man had eloped to Las Vegas. I'd sent him off an hour earlier.

"Is your grandmother picking you up?" I asked Avery.

She shook her head. "Nonna's having dinner with Mr. Caulfield."

I did a double take. "Channing Caulfield?"

"Yeah. The money guy. Nonna said he wore her down." She had her backpack and the accordion in a brown paper shopping bag.

"Do you need a ride?"

She hiked the backpack up onto one shoulder. "Nope. I'm going to the library. This is totally the best day of the anime festival—*Mr. Dough and the Egg Princess*, *Mei and the Kitten Bus* and two films from the Dragon Ball series."

"Have fun," I said.

Elvis was waiting for me at the back door. "Looks like it's just you and me," I said. He climbed into the front seat of the SUV and I set a bag of tea towels on the floor of the passenger-side seat. The cat eyed the brown paper bag, whiskers twitching. Then he looked at me.

"Yes, the cupcakes are in there," I said.

He licked his whiskers.

"Cupcakes are people food."

His green eyes went to slits, making his skepticism very clear.

"What should we have for supper?" I asked once I'd backed the SUV into the driveway at home and gotten out.

Elvis eyed the paper shopping bag still on the floor at his feet.

"Cupcakes are not supper," I said.

"Merow," he said, and I could have sworn I could detect sarcasm in his tone. Did cats even understand sarcasm? I wondered.

"Yes, I know we've had cupcakes for supper before, but I'm trying to turn over a new leaf."

He tilted his head to one side and regarded me unblinkingly. I was pretty sure this cat, at least, got sarcasm.

I leaned across the seat to grab the bag of tea towels. I was going to wash and iron them and Jess was going to make pillow covers out of them for me. Elvis walked along the seat and jumped down to the driveway. I backed out of the car. "Hey, where are you going?" I said.

"Murp," he said, and then he disappeared around the side of the house. Translation: backyard.

Friday night and even my cat seemed to have plans. I thought about my brother, Liam, teasing me about my lack of a love life or a social life. He'd been back and forth for the last several months, consulting on a development project for part of the harbor front that after too many delays and roadblocks would finally be getting under way at the end of August.

"I'd say you live like a little old lady, but Rose is a little old lady and she gets out way more than you do," he'd said the last time he'd been in town, as he sprawled on my sofa eating a bowl of chocolate pudding cake that Rose had dropped off on her way to meet Mr. P.

Since I didn't have a comeback, I'd stuck my tongue out at him. That had made him laugh, and then he suggested I could stick that tongue in Nick's mouth and maybe that would spice up my life. I'd thrown a pillow at him.

Nick. Even Liam thought we should get together, although his idea of getting together didn't seem to involve me in a lacy white dress and Nick in a suit the way Charlotte, Rose and Liz's did.

I changed into my running gear and went out onto the back verandah to see where Elvis was. He was sitting on a small wrought-iron bench next to the raised flower bed that Rose and Mr. P. had planted with sunflowers.

I held the door open. "Are you coming in?" I asked. He ignored me, looking in the direction of my neighbor, Tom Harris's yard. I may as well have been talking to the sunflowers. "I'm going running," I said. "We can eat when I get back." I felt a little foolish explaining myself to a cat.

I decided it was a good chance to take a longer, more challenging route than I'd picked the times Nick had gone running with me. He wasn't a runner, and it had been harder than I'd expected to rein myself in and not leave him behind.

I needed to talk to him. I couldn't avoid him much longer. Charlotte would notice. Or Rose. I thought about Mac asking me why Nick and I had never gotten together. I hadn't been lying when I'd told him our timing had been off. But Mac had been right when he'd pointed out that we'd both been back in North Harbor for more than a year and still nothing had happened. And it wasn't like all three of my fairy godmothers hadn't been pushing us together.

What was stopping me from pursuing a relationship with Nick? At fifteen that was all I'd wanted. What was different now? We'd made tiny moves toward each other, but they never seemed to go anywhere. Was Nick even interested? He'd come running with me. He'd eaten my cooking. The latter had to mean something.

I had a headache. Why did relationships have to be so much work?

I showered when I got home and pulled on a T-shirt and a pair of baggy cut-off sweatpants. Since my only company was going to be Elvis—at least I was assuming he'd be spending time with me—I decided I might as well be comfortable. This time when I walked out onto the verandah he immediately came across the grass. He followed me back inside and joined me in front of the refrigerator while I tried to decide what to have for supper.

"Spaghetti or salad?" I asked the cat.

He yawned.

"Pizza it is," I said.

Once we were settled on the sofa with a big slice for me and some of Rose's treats for him, I called Michelle. "Could you stop by the shop sometime on Monday?" I asked. "The Angels have some information about Jeff Cameron they'd like to share."

"Have you spoken to Nick?" she asked.

"No," I said. "I was out of the shop this morning. And by the way, did Glenn McNamara call you?"

"He did." She hesitated for a moment. "You know what the odds are on the reliability of this kind of witness sighting?"

"I know," I said. I didn't say "horsefeathers," but I was thinking it.

"Are you taking on some kind of job for Glenn?"

I popped two black olives in my mouth. It was clear Michelle wanted to change the subject. "Maybe. For his uncle, actually."

"So are you angling to get paid in blueberry muffins?" she teased.

"Chocolate cupcakes, actually," I said.

"The ones with the mocha frosting. They are good."

I waited for her to say that she'd been at McNamara's today, but she didn't. Odd.

"How was your day?" I asked, feeling a twinge of guilt for fishing.

"Full of meetings and paperwork. I didn't even go out for lunch."

I could have asked her straight out what she'd been doing with Liz, but I decided not to. Maybe Liz had been pushing over what had happened to Rose. Maybe

Michelle didn't want to tell me that she'd had to ask Liz to back off.

"Anyway, Nick should have the results from the blood work on Monday," she said. "The lab is a bit backed up. That's why he didn't get them today."

It seemed as though Nick hadn't told her about our argument. I decided I wasn't going to, either.

"Thanks for telling me," I said. I held out a piece of bacon to Elvis. At least when I spent the evening with him I could have exactly what I wanted on my pizza.

"I could stop by late morning on Monday," Michelle offered. "Would sometime around ten thirty be okay?" Once again I suspected she was motivated more by our friendship than by the desire to find out what Rose and her cohorts had come up with.

"That would be great," I said. "Thank you."

"See you Monday," she said.

I ended the call but held on to the phone. I hadn't been able to figure out why the name Vega had sounded familiar when Avery had told us it was the last name of the man she'd seen with Leesa Cameron. Jess knew a lot of people. Maybe the name would mean something to her. She was probably out on a date, but I decided to call her anyway. She answered on the fourth ring.

"Hey, what are you doing home on a Friday night?" I said.

"A last-minute fix on a wedding dress." She muttered something I didn't catch. "Bride and her mother brought it in. I'm not sure which one was crying harder."

"When's the wedding?"

"Next Friday night."

"Ouch!" I said.

"It's not that bad," Jess said. "I've pretty much got the skirt fixed, and the bride is coming in Monday so I can fit the bodice. What are you doing home on a Friday night?"

"Eating pizza with Elvis. He didn't feel like going out."

Jess laughed. "I think he said that last Friday night, too."

"I have a quick question for you," I said.

"Shoot."

"Why does the last name Vega seem familiar to me? Do you know anyone in town who's a Vega?"

"Michael Vega," Jess immediately said. "He's a sports massage therapist. And I'm pretty sure he takes a few clients as a personal trainer. Elin went to him last year after she broke her arm." Elin was one of her partners in the store.

"That's it," I said. I remembered Elin telling me how the massage therapist had helped restore the full range of motion in her arm.

"I thought Nick was going running with you," Jess teased. "Is the big guy not willing to rub you the right way?"

"I'm hanging up now," I said.

Jess was laughing. "I'll see you Sunday," she said before ending the call.

It was busy from the moment we opened the shop on Saturday. The tourists never seemed to stop coming. I only had time for half a sandwich at lunch. Thankfully, Mr. P. kept us supplied with coffee.

"How do you feel about Chinese food?" Liz asked as I locked the front door at the end of the day. She'd arrived a few minutes earlier to pick up Avery.

I blew a stray strand of hair back off my face. "Do you mean authentic Chinese cuisine or the American takeout version?"

Liz narrowed her gaze at me. "I mean Chinese food that you don't have to cook."

"Love it," I said.

"Good," she said. "It's the last night of that film thing at the library so it turns out Avery won't be home for supper and I probably ordered enough food for half a dozen people."

"Merow!" Elvis interjected from his perch about halfway up the stairs.

Liz waved a hand in the direction of the steps. "Yes, you're invited, too."

Elvis bobbed his head in acknowledgement.

"Hey, I missed you yesterday," I said to Liz. "Where were you?"

"I had Emmerson Foundation business. Did you want something?" No mention of meeting Michelle.

I explained about being out at Clayton McNamara's place. "I didn't know that Gram had a connection to the McNamaras."

"Those two were thick as thieves when they were kids," Liz said. "Clayton McNamara could have been your grandfather."

"I don't know what to say to that," I said.

She laughed and started for the workroom to collect Avery. "I'll see you later, toots."

Elvis and I ended up spending the whole evening with Liz. Charlotte had found a box full of old photos of herself, Liz, Rose and Gram, taken when they were teenagers. She'd organized them by year and left them with Liz to go through, to see which ones Liz wanted copies of.

"Hey, you were a babe," I teased, holding up a black and white snapshot of Liz in a one-piece swimsuit, standing on a rock by the shore, one hand on her hip, the other behind her head.

"Give me that!" She reached across the table for the photo.

I grinned and shook my head, holding the picture up out of her reach. "No way. I think I've found my Christmas card for this year."

"You are a wicked child," Liz said, glaring and pointing a finger at me. "I'm going to find one of those droopy diaper photos of you and that's going to be *my* Christmas card this year."

I laughed, thinking that spending the evening with Liz was way more fun than making awkward small talk on a date. Not that *that* had actually been an option.

Jess and I went prowling around several flea markets on Sunday and came home with the back of the SUV loaded. Elvis spent the day with Rose and Mr. P. and came home smelling like fish cakes.

I headed in early on Monday. Liz was bringing Rose and Alfred later. I wanted to spray the wicker chairs before it got busy, since I'd never actually gotten to it on Friday or Saturday.

I pulled into the lot to find a white extended-cab half-ton backed up to the rear door. Mac was helping two men in white shirts and loosened ties load a huge walnut armoire into the bed of the truck. He shook hands with both of them and they climbed into the cab and pulled out of the lot. I smiled and raised a hand in greeting as they came past me, and they did the same even though I had no idea who either of the men was.

Mac brushed off his hands and walked over to me. "Hi. You're up early," he said. He reached over to scratch the top of Elvis's head.

"You, too," I said. "You sold that armoire that's been in the front window for the last month. Or we were just robbed by two very well-dressed criminals."

"I sold the armoire." He gestured toward the street. "They were driving by, saw it in the window and then noticed me in the garage and came to ask me about it. I took them inside to have a look and they asked if they could buy it." He shrugged. "I didn't think you'd mind me saying yes."

Elvis squirmed in my arms and I set him down. He headed for the back door. "I don't mind," I said. "I was beginning to wonder if we were ever going to sell that thing. It's a nice piece of furniture but it's so big."

"I know. That's why they wanted it. They just bought a bed-and-breakfast in Camden—Herrier House. Does the name mean anything to you?"

I nodded.

"They're redoing the entire place and I thought since they're in the market for more furniture and other things it would be a good idea to accommodate them today. They were on their way to a funeral in Portland—that's why the ties and starched shirts. They stopped for coffee and ended up driving by because they were trying to get back out to the highway." He smiled. "Lucky for us."

"More like lucky for me that you were here," I said as we started for the back door, where Elvis had positioned himself, staring expectantly as though he could somehow will it to open. "I owe you for this."

"No, you don't," he said. "If I worked anywhere else I wouldn't be able to arrange my days to get to sail as much as I do. You make that work. I owe you for that."

"Mac, I rearrange things so Rose and her band of merry angels can chase bad guys. Adjusting the schedule so you can sail is a piece of cake."

Mac held the back door open for Elvis, who meowed a thank-you and headed inside. "Do you know what's on their schedule for today?" he asked as we stepped inside.

"Michelle is going to stop by sometime around ten thirty. Mr. P. says he doesn't want to sneak around behind her back. He wants to share what we know about Jeff Cameron changing his name."

"Do you think that might convince the police that Rose really did see his body?" Mac asked. I handed him the bag of clean dish towels and he set it up on the workbench.

I exhaled loudly. "Between you and me? No. And Rose isn't going to stop until she proves that she did." I rubbed the bridge of my nose between my thumb and index finger. "There's something I need your opinion on."

"What is it?"

"Glenn told me Saturday that he saw Jeff Cameron driving early Thursday morning."

One eyebrow went up. "Thursday morning? Is he certain?"

"That's the thing. He's certain about the day. He says it was Jeff's Jeep—that glow-in-the-dark yellow color is pretty distinctive. And he's positive it was a man driving. Heck, he's positive it was Jeff driving."

Mac studied my face. "But you're not so sure."

"It was early and he saw the Jeep from a distance."

Mac put a hand on my shoulder. "What's really bothering you?"

"If Jeff Cameron is alive, why hasn't he used a credit or a debit card?"

"Because he's trying to keep the charade that his wife murdered him going."

"But why?" I held out both hands. "That's what I can't figure out. Why?"

"Would a cup of coffee help?" Mac asked.

"Yes," I said. "Or maybe you should bring the pot and a straw."

Mac laughed. "It'll work out in the end."

"What makes you so sure of that?" I asked.

He smiled. "Because it always does."

I managed to get both chairs sprayed and was just cleaning up when I looked up to see Nick getting out of his truck. I waited, one paint-speckled hand on the top of my makeshift spray box, as he walked over to me.

"Hi," he said. "Michelle asked me to come by to hear what Rose and the others came up with."

I nodded. "Okay."

Nick shifted awkwardly from one foot to the other. "I'm sorry for what happened Thursday night. I should have been straight with you."

I believed him. I could see that he was sorry in the way he was standing, in his voice, in the way his fingers played with his watchband. But what he was sorry about was pretending he agreed with me. He wasn't sorry for not believing Rose.

"Thank you," I said.

He opened his mouth to say something else and I caught sight of Rose headed toward us.

She gave him an expectant smile. "Do you have any results yet?"

Nick shook his head and pulled his gaze away from me. "No. I'm sorry it's taking so long. The lab is busy, but I should have something this afternoon. I promise I'll call as soon as I know anything."

"Thank you, dear," she said. "We missed you Saturday night. Alfred planked a salmon."

"I know. Mom fed me the leftovers for lunch yesterday." He smiled at Rose. "I have to give my compliments to the chef. He's a good cook."

"Alfred has many talents," Rose replied.

I made a mental note to ask her later what planking a salmon meant and to stay away from any conversation about Mr. P's many other talents. I picked up the cut-down cardboard box and set it inside the garage. Then I stood in the doorway for a moment watching Rose and Nick talk. The conversation seemed to be about cooking, although I couldn't hear every word.

I reminded myself that Nick loved Rose. She was family to him just as much as she was to me. He was loyal and protective and funny and kind and a lot more. And there was something wrong if I always had to be reminding myself of that, I thought as I joined them again.

Michelle arrived then, pulling her car in next to Nick's truck. She walked over to us. "How are you feeling?" she said to Rose.

"I'm fine. Thank you," Rose said. She patted her white hair. "I guess I am as hardheaded as I've been told I am."

"Well, this is one of those times I'm glad about that," Michelle said. "I hope it's all right that I asked Nick to join us."

"Of course it is," Rose said. "We're always happy to have Nick around, aren't we, Sarah?"

Nick swiped a hand over his mouth to hide a smile.

"Always," I agreed, "especially when he brings muffins from McNamara's." I smiled sweetly up at Nick, hoping he'd get my reference to a past disagreement we'd had when he'd apologized with one of Glenn's muffins.

"So you're suggesting I should stop in at McNamara's the next time I'm headed here?" he teased.

"You're so thoughtful," Rose said. "We all like Glenn's blueberry muffins, but this time of year the rhubarb streusel muffins are hard to say no to." She smiled at him.

Michelle had a hard time not smiling as well. "Is Mr. Peterson inside?" she asked.

I nodded and we started across the lot to the back door. Mr. P. got to his feet as we stepped into the sunporch. "Hello, Detective Andrews," he said, offering his hand. "Thank you for coming."

"I'm interested in what you've learned," Michelle said, dipping her head in the direction of his laptop.

Mr. P. smiled up at Nick. "Hello, Nicolas," he said. "Are you joining us?"

Michelle immediately spoke up. "I asked him to. I hope it's all right."

"Of course," Mr. P. said. He quickly explained what the Angels had learned about Jeff Cameron, how he'd changed his name and walked away from his life after his grandmother died. How no one had seen him with any other woman in North Harbor.

"His name was Hennessy?" Michelle said. She seemed to be taking what he'd told her and Nick seriously.

Mr. P. nodded. "Two 's's,' two 'n's,'" he said.

"Do you have a theory as to where Jeff Cameron is right now?" she asked.

"We have two," he said. "One is that he's dead. The other is that he set up his wife to make it look like he's dead, although we don't have any idea why."

Nick's and Michelle's cell phones both rang then. "Excuse me," she said, pulling hers from the pocket of her cotton sweater and turning around so her back was to us. Nick had already stepped out of the room to answer his.

The conversation was brief. Michelle's face was expressionless when she faced us again. "Well, Mr. Peterson, I'm sorry to tell you that one of your theories is wrong. Jeff Cameron definitely didn't fake his death."

My heart sank. Nick was putting his own phone back in his pocket, his lips pulled into a thin line.

"What makes you so sure?" Mr. P. asked, although I suspected he knew the answer, too.

"A couple of rock climbers on Johnson's Reach found him. I'm sorry. He's dead."

Chapter 14

"Dead," Rose repeated, and not in the form of a question.

I saw Nick's gaze flick in her direction.

"The poor man," she said quietly. I was probably the only one who saw the knowing gleam flash for a moment in her gray eyes.

"I have to go," Michelle said.

"Thursday?" I asked, referring to Thursday night jam at Sam's.

"I'll try." She pushed past Nick. "See you there?" she asked.

He nodded. "I just need a second."

She nodded and left. Nick caught my arm and drew me out by the back door. "I have to go. Are we okay?"

"Yes," I said. "Go."

He hesitated.

"Go," I repeated. This time he went.

I rejoined Rose and Mr. P.

"Johnson's Reach is a couple of miles from the Camerons' cottage," Rose said. "How did his body get there?"

"I don't know," I said, scraping a couple of spots of sage green paint off the back of my hand. "Michelle will figure that out." I couldn't help thinking that it was a heck of a lot closer to Clayton McNamara's house, which added credence to Glenn's recollection of having seen Jeff on Thursday.

"Sarah's right," Mr. P. said, sitting back down and opening his laptop.

I had a feeling Michelle wouldn't be the only one working on how Jeff Cameron had ended up at John-son's Reach.

"Before I go, did you find out anything about Michael Vega?" I asked.

Mr. P. shifted in his seat to look at me. "As Jess told you, he's a massage therapist and he has several clients that he trains."

"Leesa Cameron was one of them."

"Yes," Rose said.

"All of Mr. Vega's clients are women," Mr. P. added, "not that there's anything wrong with that."

"Anything"—I struggled to think of the best word to use—"improper happen with any of his clients?"

"Oh no," Rose said. "Mr. Vega is by all accounts a gentleman."

"No one has an ill word to say about the man," Mr. P. said. "He's so clean he squeaks."

He and Rose exchanged a quick glance.

"But," I said. I pointed my finger at them. "You found out something."

"Maybe." There was caution in Mr. P's voice. "Michael Vega ordered a woman's BodiBudi last month."

I frowned. "A what?"

"A BodiBudi," Rose said. "A fitness tracker."

"You think he bought it for Leesa Cameron."

"We know he did," Mr. P. said. "The online account associated with that particular BodiBudi is registered to her."

"How do you know all this never mind," I said, running the words together. I pulled a hand over my neck. "Do you think they were involved?"

Mr. P. looked at Rose. "I think we need to talk to him."

She nodded.

"Me, too," I said. "Let me know when."

Mac and I were looking at paint after lunch, trying to settle on a color for the rocker, when Avery stuck her head around the door. "Hey, Sarah, Nonna just called me. She wants you to call her. She tried your cell but you didn't answer."

"What does she want?" I asked.

Avery gave me a blank look. "I don't know," she said.

"Go call Liz," Mac said. "We can figure this out later."

I went up to my office and called Liz back. "Hi," I said. "Avery said you called."

"Nicole Cameron called me," she said. "She wants to see us."

"Us?" I said.

"Rose. You. Me."

"Why?"

"Don't have a clue," Liz said. "I think it has to have something to do with her brother's body being found, though."

"It probably does." I looked at my watch. "I could bring Rose and meet you there later this afternoon.

"Nicole suggested four o'clock. Will that work?" Liz asked.

"I can make it work."

"Thank you, darling girl," she said. Elvis had come upstairs and jumped onto my desk. I hung up the phone and reached over to stroke his fur. "Something's up," I said.

He wrinkled his nose and looked up at me.

"I don't know, either," I said.

Rose and I pulled to the curb in front of Nicole Cameron's house about five minutes before four o'clock. The kids at the house across the street appeared to be making another movie. "Is the little boy wearing the two bath mats supposed to be Bigfoot?" I asked Rose.

"I think so," she said, "although I think one of his feet just fell off." She pointed at a large fuzzy slipper at the edge of the driveway. "Ask Alfred what they're doing."

"How does he know?"

Rose indicated a woman who looked to be in her late thirties sitting on the front steps of the house. "Because he talked to the mom to see if there was anything useful on their security camera. He wanted to confirm Leesa Cameron's alibi."

"You didn't tell me that," I said.

She shrugged. "There was nothing to tell, dear. The

camera wasn't aligned properly. All it recorded was some blurry footage of the peonies."

Liz pulled in in front of us then and we got out of the car. "Let's get this show on the road," she said.

Nicole must have been watching for us because she opened the front door before we reached it. She was pale and serious in a gray T-shirt and black walking shorts. "Please come in," she said, holding the door open.

"I'm so sorry about your brother," I said.

"Thank you," she said. She seemed a little nervous, rubbing her right wrist with the other hand.

"Is there anything we could do for you?" Liz asked.

Nicole shook her head. "No. Thank you for suggesting the funeral home to handle things on this end. I wouldn't have known who to call. I . . . uh haven't been able to get in touch with Leesa. I'm not even sure she's still in North Harbor."

"Why did you want to see us?" Rose asked.

Nicole stared down at the ground for a moment, then lifted her head. She glanced at Liz and me but focused her attention on Rose.

"I have to apologize to you," she said.

Liz gave me a knowing look.

"I lied," Nicole continued. She was still rubbing her wrist as though she was twisting a watch or a bracelet around her arm. "Leesa left earlier than I told you she did." She swallowed hard. "The truth is, Jeff and I didn't always get along, especially after our grandmother died, but the last six months things had been good. Then Leesa showed up here Wednesday night and said he was gone. She showed me the text he sent her and the statement she'd gone online and printed out from their investment account."

She made a helpless gesture with both hands. "I know I shouldn't have, but all I could think of was how he left me to deal with everything after Nana died and now here he was doing the same thing to Leesa. I was signed in to the hospital server, doing some in-service training. I just figured, who would know if I said she was here. Stupid, I know."

Rose reached over and laid a hand on Nicole's arm. "It's understandable that you would feel that way," she said. "Try not to be so hard on yourself."

"That's nice of you to say that when I protected the person who assaulted you," Nicole said.

"You didn't know that," Rose said.

Nicole shook her head. "It doesn't make what I did right." She looked at me. "Leesa called me after you and the detective went to see her. I . . . I offered her an alibi because my first thought was that Jeff had cut out on her." She swallowed hard. "My brother was dead and I was so quick to think the worst of him."

"Rose is right," I said. "You couldn't have known that something had happened to your brother."

She shook her head. "It doesn't matter. I should have given him the benefit of the doubt. He was my brother." She looked at Rose again. "And I should have done the same to you. I am so sorry."

"Thank you," Rose said. "I'm sorry for your loss."

Nicole Cameron got to her feet. "I wanted to apologize and explain to the three of you first. Now I'm going to call the police and explain what I did to them."

She walked us to the door and Liz reminded her to call if there was anything we could do to help. Rose was quiet as we walked down the driveway, seemingly lost in thought. Finally she looked at Liz. "You said she wasn't telling us everything. You were right."

Liz raised an eyebrow. "It happens." She looked at me. "At the risk of Rose swinging her purse at me, I think she should go home and maybe take it easy. This is a lot to digest."

"I wouldn't hit you with this bag," Rose said, patting the wicker roll bag with tan leather handles she was carrying. "Alfred bought it for my birthday. Your big melon head would probably leave a big dent in it."

"I agree with Liz," I said. "Can you just humor us for once and take it easy?"

Rose glanced at Liz and then looked at me. "Fine," she said. "I'll go home and take it easy, but this is a onetime thing and should not be construed as setting a precedent."

Liz rolled her eyes.

"Don't give me that look just because I like to watch CNN," Rose said.

"Go back to the store," Liz said to me. "I'll take Rose home."

"Are you sure?" I said.

"Go." She made a move-along gesture with one hand. "I'll be there later to get Avery."

"All right," I said. I leaned over and kissed Rose on the cheek. "I'll see you later."

They got into Liz's car and I waited until they had pulled away from the curb before I walked back to my

SUV. I looked at Nicole Cameron's house again as I unlocked the driver's door. By now Michelle would know that Leesa Cameron's alibi was fake. Rose had been vindicated.

I wasn't even halfway back to the shop when my cell phone rang. It was lying on the seat and I glanced sideways to see who was calling. Rose. I put my blinker on and pulled over to answer.

"Hello, dear," she said. "Could you please say hello to Liz? She's right next to me."

"Hi, Liz," I said, wondering what on earth was going on now.

There was some kind of noise in the background I couldn't identify. Then I heard Rose's voice, seemingly a distance away from the phone, say, "There. Are you satisfied?"

"Rose, what's going on?" I asked.

She came back on the line. "I was just showing Liz that I had in fact called you because she didn't believe me." She raised her voice at the end of the sentence.

"And why did you call?"

"I think I might remember something—something from the night I saw Jeff Cameron's body."

I leaned my arm against the door and propped my head on my hand. "What did you remember?"

"It doesn't exactly make sense," she said. "Do you remember when we cleared out the Cooper house?"

"I remember," I said. It wasn't likely I'd forget that.

As I'd told Glenn, we'd developed a bit of a side business at the shop, clearing out apartments and houses, most of the time for the families of seniors who needed or wanted to move but were just overwhelmed by dealing with everything they'd accumulated over a lifetime. The Cooper house was a rambling farmhouse with more rooms than was apparent from the outside. And every one of them filled with stuff. I wasn't sure how the house was connected to Jeff Cameron.

"When we were at Nicole Cameron's house I was going over what happened that night, and those tea chests we found in the attic at the Coopers' kept coming into my mind. I don't understand why."

"I don't see the connection, either," I said. "I'm sorry." We'd found several vintage wooden tea chests from Indonesia with the original wooden strapping, and in the case of one of them the original foil lining with bits of tea still clinging to it, in the attic of the old house. One of them contained several bolts of silk that Jess had bought and used to make beautiful robes for her clothing store.

"I need to go over there," Rose said. "I don't know why this matters, but I know it does."

I knew she meant the cottage, not the Cooper house. "Bad idea," I said.

"You sound like Liz."

"Great minds think alike, then."

"And fools seldom differ, dear," Rose countered.

"I heard that," Liz said in the background.

"Well, obviously I meant you to," Rose retorted.

I knew how this was going to play out. "Okay, hang on," I said. "Let's just skip the step where we argue back and forth and go right to the bottom line."

"I need to go over there, Sarah," Rose said. "I could have just let Liz take me home and then headed over once she was gone, but I didn't."

She had me. I closed my eyes for a second and tried to exhale quietly so she wouldn't hear me sigh.

"How about this? You and Liz drive over and park in front of the Clarks'. I'll be right behind you. Then we'll figure out what we're going to do."

"Hang on a minute, dear," Rose said. I heard voices again just far enough from the phone that I couldn't make out the conversation. Then Rose came back on. "Liz wants to talk to you," she said with what sounded like a touch of self-righteous indignation in her tone.

"Fine," I said.

After a moment Liz's voice came through the phone. "Are you crazy?" she asked.

"It's a possibility," I said lightly. "I've never been officially tested."

"Well, maybe you should be so we can get confirmation."

I laughed. "I'm right behind you. Less than five minutes, I promise. If Rose tries to do anything rash, get the dog to sit on her."

"Easy for you to say." Liz gave a snort of skepticism.

Rose came back on the phone. "Thank you, darling girl," she said. "I'll see you in a few minutes."

When I got to the Clarks' I turned in the driveway and parked behind Liz. She and Rose were standing in the driveway with Ashley Clark and Casey. The big Lab was sitting beside Rose and her hand was in his fur. It was pretty clear she had a friend for life.

I walked over to join them. Ashley smiled. "Hi, Sarah," she said. "It's good to see you again."

"You, too," I said. Casey turned to look at me and I reached over and scratched the top of his head.

"Ashley says she just saw Leesa leave about forty-five minutes ago," Rose said.

Liz pressed her lips together and narrowed her eyes at me but didn't say anything.

"Okay," I said, gesturing with my sunglasses. "We'll go down there for five minutes." I held up five fingers. "If it doesn't trigger any kind of a memory, that's it."

Rose nodded. "That's fine."

"Do you want to take him with you?" Ashley asked gesturing at the dog. "He's a softie, but people who don't know him don't know that."

"Will he go with us?" I asked.

The big Lab was leaning his head against Rose's leg.

His owner laughed. "I think he'd happily live with Rose." She walked over to the front steps and picked up the braided leather leash that was lying on the top one. She snapped it on the dog's collar and handed the end to Rose. "He knows how to heel and sit and stay," she said.

"Thank you," I said. "We'll only be a few minutes."

Ashley reached over and patted the dog's head. "Take care of Rose, boy," she said.

We walked along the road to the Camerons' cottage. Casey stayed by Rose's side and I got the feeling that if anyone gave her any trouble the dog would cheerfully chew their arm off.

There were no signs that anyone was home at the small green cottage. Nonetheless, being there made me antsy. Rose stood in the middle of the driveway. "Sit," she said to Casey, who did as he was told. She looked around the yard and then she closed her eyes for a moment.

Liz and I waited. "This is a waste of time," she muttered.

"Do you have a train to catch?" I whispered back.

Rose opened her eyes. She looked at us and shook her head. "I'm just going to stand on the steps," she said.

I glanced back down the road. There was no sign of any cars coming. I walked the rest of the way up the driveway looking for anything that might have made Rose think of those old tea chests. Nothing twigged.

Rose stood on the steps and, just as she had on Wednesday night, peered through the window. She sighed. "I don't know why I thought of those old tea chests," she said. "I guess it doesn't mean anything after all." She came down the steps, and she and Casey started down the driveway toward Liz, who was standing in the shade of a tall maple tree.

I climbed the stairs and took a quick look in the sunporch. There wasn't anything in it or the kitchen beyond that looked like a wooden tea chest. I turned, and as I did something on the small deck on the other side of the porch caught my eye. I stopped and took a second look.

Someone seemed to be sitting on a wooden Adirondack chair looking out toward the water. Something about the angle of the person's head made the hairs come up on the back of my neck.

"Just stay there a second," I called to Liz.

"Why?" Rose asked.

I was already on my way down the few stairs. "Just please stay there for now and I'll explain in a minute," I said.

I started around the side of the house. I only went far enough so I could see what I already suspected. Leesa Cameron was slumped in the chair. And it was clear she was dead.

Chapter 15

I called 911 and we waited for the police at Ashley Clark's small house. She took one look at Rose and Liz and invited them inside for iced tea.

"Go," I said. "I'll wait out here for the police."

I leaned against the SUV and wondered if I should call Michelle. Or Nick. Ashley came out with a tall, frosted glass of tea for me. "Thank you," I said, taking it from her and taking a long drink.

Ashley looked over her shoulder down the road. "You . . . um . . . you found Leesa, didn't you?" she asked. Her hair was loose around her face and she wasn't wearing any makeup. She didn't look any older than Avery.

There wasn't any reason not to tell her the truth. I nodded.

She blanched and swallowed a couple of times. "She's dead, isn't she? I mean, she has to be because otherwise you wouldn't be here."

"She's dead. Yes."

Ashley shivered even though the sun was warm

and wrapped one arm around her midsection. She shook her head. "I would have sworn that was her who drove by barely an hour ago."

"And maybe it was," I said. "The police will figure all of that out." I gave her a smile I didn't really feel. "Thank you for the tea and for taking Rose and Liz inside. Why don't you go in and wait with them? The police won't be very long. I'll come and get you."

"Okay," she said, and she headed back across the lawn to the house.

The police arrived less than five minutes later, a patrol car followed quickly by the forensic van, Michelle's small sedan and Nick's truck.

"Bring me up to speed," Michelle said. Nick stood silently beside her, his hands in his pockets.

I gave them a brief rundown of our visit with Nicole Cameron and how we'd ended up at the cottage. "I took a quick look through the porch window, thinking maybe I'd see something that might explain Rose's memory. I caught sight of . . . Leesa Cameron on the deck. There was uh . . ." I stopped and cleared my throat. "The angle of her head and neck seemed wrong. There was an empty bottle of vodka on the table beside her." I had to stop again for a moment. "And a pill bottle."

Michelle said nothing; she just nodded as I recited how I'd called 911 and we'd come back here to wait. After I finished I took her inside and she talked to Rose and Liz and Ashley Clark. We waited maybe another twenty minutes while she went down to the Cameron cottage before she came back to tell us we could leave. Nick had stopped long enough to put a hand on my shoulder and ask if we were all okay before he'd headed to the cottage as well.

We ended up back at Rose's apartment. I'd called Mac and he'd taken care of closing up the store. Jess had been there picking up the tea towels that she was going to make into pillow covers for me. She drove Charlotte, Mr. P. and Avery over, and when Rose urged her to join us, she'd come in and seamlessly started helping, washing lettuce in the sink and clipping chives from the pot in Rose's kitchen window.

Rose had coached me through the recipe for rhubarb crumble and it was cooking in her toaster oven. I sat down next to Liz at the table. Elvis was sitting on the chair next to her as though he expected one of the places to be his. Charlotte and Avery had gone to get extra chairs from my apartment.

"I can't believe that young woman killed herself." Liz shook her head.

"Maybe once her husband's body was found she felt the walls were closing in on her," Mr. P. said.

"I still don't understand why she killed him in the first place," Rose said. She kissed the top of Avery's head. "Will you put out the knives and forks for me, please?" she said.

Avery smiled at her. "Sure."

Rose went back over to the counter and I got up to peer in at my rhubarb crumble. "It's going to be fine," Rose said quietly in my ear.

I wasn't sure if she meant my dessert or everything associated with Jeff Cameron's death.

We all squeezed around the table for Rose's Chinese chicken salad. "I need the recipe for this dressing,"

Jess said, gesturing with her fork. "It's so much better than the one I'm using."

"The secret is a good balsamic vinegar and a bit of Dijon mustard," Rose said. "I'll write it down for you."

Rose came to help me when I dished out the rhubarb crumble. "Does it look all right to you?" I asked.

"It looks delicious," she said. "I'm so glad we discovered that patch of rhubarb in the backyard before you dug it all up."

"It wouldn't have happened if that birch tree hadn't come down in the middle of that windstorm," I said, carrying the first two bowls over to the table. "There was no way I could move it by myself. It was way too heavy. If Cleveland hadn't come over with his chain-saw to cut the tree up and haul it away, I never would have known I was digging out rhubarb and not some weed that looked like red celery."

I turned around, and Rose was staring into space, holding up the serving spoon like it was a magic wand. She shook her head and looked at me. "Say that again, please."

"I never would have known I was digging up rhubarb."

She shook her head. "No, the part about the tree."

I frowned at her. "There was no way I could move it by myself?"

She smiled. "Exactly." She walked over to the table. "How did Leesa Cameron move her husband's body? We still don't have an answer to that question. It was found at Johnson's Reach. It's the other end of town from the Camerons' cottage. There's no way she could have done that by herself. I couldn't." She looked at me. "Could you?"

I shook my head. "No."

"So she was having an affair with Michael Vega and he helped her," Jess said.

"Convenient, isn't it?" Rose said.

"What are you suggesting, Rosie?" Mr. P. asked.

"Leesa Cameron killed her husband, and when his body is found she kills herself." She looked at us all. "All the loose ends are tied up in a neat little bow. Whoever else was involved—whether or not it's Mr. Vega—just walks away."

"You think there's something we missed," Charlotte said. "Something that will help us find that person."

Liz sighed loudly.

"Yes," Rose said, ignoring her friend.

"What?" I asked.

"Why was Chloe Sanders so gung ho about working for Jeff Cameron?"

"She needed a summer job?"

"Why that particular job?" Rose said. "She had a professor who was very much her advocate. Why did she put so much effort into getting Jeff to hire Chloe?" She folded her arms over her chest. "And why did Michael Vega buy an expensive fitness tracker for Leesa Cameron?"

"So we keep digging," Mr. P. said.

Rose nodded. "We keep digging."

Chapter 16

The Angels spent most of Tuesday morning checking out Michael Vega. The more they found out, the harder it was for any of us to believe he'd been having an affair with Leesa Cameron. Everyone, it seemed, said the same thing about the man; he was a good guy and a straight arrow.

"I talked to Ann at the library," Charlotte said when she arrived for her shift, referring to the head librarian at the North Harbor Public Library. "Michael Vega built the new puppet theater in the children's department. Not only did he volunteer his time on a Saturday; he had the kids helping."

"He sounds like a nice guy," I said.

"If you're talking about Mr. Vega, it seems he's pretty much perfect," Liz said. She'd just come in the front door and she walked over to us, her high heels clicking on the wooden floor.

"What did you find out? What did Elspeth say?" Charlotte asked.

"I haven't talked to her yet," Liz said. "It occurred

to me that maybe Jane Evans might know the man."
She looked at me. "Jess said he was a sports massage
therapist. Remember? Jane injured her back last winter
when she fell on the sidewalk. I know she went to
someone for a massage."

"I remember," I said. What I also remembered was
how Liz had arranged for a weekly cleaning service
at Jane's house until she could get around.

"Well, small town, small world—it was Michael
Vega who worked on her back."

"What did she say?" Charlotte asked.

"Oh, Jane pretty much thinks he walks on water.
Not only did he do wonders for her back, but he's also
a devoted family man. She told me about this romantic dinner he planned and pulled off for his wife's
birthday." She gave us a wry smile. "He and their four
kids took her on a scavenger hunt to all the important
places in their life—where they went for their first
date, where he proposed, the little chapel where they
got married. It ended with a catered picnic up at the
park." Liz rolled her eyes. She wasn't exactly a
romantic.

"That doesn't sound like the kind of thing a man
having an affair would do," Charlotte said.

"It doesn't sound like the kind of thing most of the
men I know would do," Liz countered. "He had to have
been up to something. No man is that perfect." She
looked over at me. "And don't tell me I sound like a
cynical old woman."

"I would never do that," I said, putting a hand to
my chest in umbrage.

"Good," she said.

I leaned over and kissed her cheek. "I'm not stupid enough to ever tell you you're old." I could hear Charlotte laughing as I headed for the door.

I went outside to talk to Mac, who was sanding a small metal cabinet. I had a couple of questions about my plan for Clayton McNamara's house. He agreed with my estimate for the cost of the job and we talked for a few minutes about when we could fit the work into our schedule.

I was back in my office, working on a plan of attack for Clayton's house, when Nick called.

"Hi," I said.

"Hi," he said. He sounded a bit off.

"Are you all right?" I asked.

"I got the results from Rose's blood tests. I'm sorry it took so long to get back to you."

"That's all right."

He didn't say anything.

"What did you find out?"

"I owe you an apology," he said. "And Rose and, hell, probably Jess, too."

"Rose didn't have a stroke." I didn't make the words a question because I already knew the answer.

"No. You can say 'I told you so.'"

I pictured him shaking his head and probably raking a hand back through his hair. "I'm not going to do that."

"Jess will."

I laughed, leaning back in my desk chair. "Yep. She probably will."

"I still don't think Rose and my mother and the rest of them have any business getting involved in

Michelle's cases," he said with just a little *I know I'm right*-ness in his voice.

"I get that," I said. I didn't add that that was the problem. "More importantly, though, was Rose drugged?"

"She was. Methohexital. They found very small amounts of it in her blood."

I couldn't help it. "I knew it!" I said, pumping my fist in the air.

"She was attacked," Nick said. "I should have listened to her. I should have listened to *you*. I'm sorry."

I took a moment before I spoke. "I know you are. Maybe from now on just try to keep an open mind when it comes to Rose and the others."

"I am trying, Sarah," he said quietly.

I nodded even though he couldn't see me. "I know."

"I already gave everything to Michelle. You'll probably hear from her. And if anyone was helping Leesa Cameron, we'll find them. I promise you that."

"Do you know yet how she died?" I asked. I didn't really expect him to tell me.

"The autopsy hasn't been done," Nick said. "But you saw the vodka bottle."

"And the pill bottle."

"Sleeping pills. She had a prescription for them."

"What about Jeff Cameron?"

"C'mon, you know I can't tell you that."

I didn't say anything. Nick sighed. "He drowned."

"Drowned?" I whispered.

"He was hit over the head first."

"That would explain why there was no blood in the kitchen."

"It answers some questions and it raises others," he said.

I knew it would be pushing it to ask what he meant. I thanked him for calling and said good-bye.

I'd just come back from the staff room with a cup of coffee when my phone rang again. I leaned over to check the screen. It was Michelle.

"Hi, Sarah. Did Nick call you?" she asked.

"About five minutes ago," I said.

"So you know what the blood tests show."

"He told me about the traces of the drug they found."

"Rose was attacked and I dismissed what happened as just her being old," Michelle said. "I was wrong. I'm sorry."

"I appreciate that," I said. "Rose will, too."

"We're still investigating, and I won't be so quick to jump to conclusions."

"Then, as Gram would say, 'You learned something.'" I took a sip of my coffee. "And I don't want to sound like some public service announcement, but you weren't completely off base. Most strokes happen in people over sixty-five, which Rose is, and more women have strokes than men. You could have been right." It was easy to be magnanimous when I'd been proved right.

"I could have looked at all the possibilities, not just one."

"So you do that next time. C'mon, Michelle. You know there's going to be a next time with Rose and the rest of them."

She laughed then. "There probably will be."

"So," I said. "I know you can't give me any details about your investigation, but can you at least tell me if you think it will be wrapped up soon?"

There was silence and I thought she wasn't going to answer, but then she said, "Honestly, Sarah. I don't know."

There wasn't much more to say after that. I thanked her for calling and promised to be in touch if the Angels came up with anything. I went downstairs and found Rose out in the sunporch with Mr. P. I came up behind her and put my arms around her shoulders. "I talked to Nick," I said.

She turned her head and looked up at me. "And?"

"And there were traces of methohexital in your blood."

A triumphant smile spread across her face.

"So someone did drug Rosie?" Mr. P. said.

I nodded.

"We wouldn't have known that if you hadn't seen the needle mark on my neck," Rose said. She leaned her head against my shoulder for a moment before I let go.

"That was mostly luck," I said.

"Maybe," Mr. P. said. "You're also very observant, Sarah."

"I will admit I do like being vindicated," Rose said, "but I don't know how this information is going to help us."

I rested a hand on the table Mr. P. was using as a desk. "Nick said dentists often use the drug because it acts quickly and the effects only last for a short period of time."

"Leesa Cameron was a buyer for a chain of stores," Mr. P. said.

"No one has any connection to any dentist," Rose said.

I shook my head vigorously in frustration. "I feel like I'm missing something."

"So do I," she said.

I tapped the back of my head with three fingers. "There's something back here. I just can't pull it out."

"Give it time," Mr. P. said with a smile. "You know what they say about two heads being better than one."

I held up one hand and ticked off the fingers. "All right. But really, there's you, Rose, Liz, Charlotte and me. If two heads are better than one, what are five?"

"A basketball team," Rose said.

I put my arm around her shoulders and gave her a hug. "I have work to do," I said and started for the store.

"Love you, sweetie," she called after me.

"Just because you were vindicated doesn't mean you shouldn't keep having a regular checkup once a year." I stopped and turned back to look at her standing in the doorway.

"Don't you have to get back to work, dear?" she asked sweetly.

I pointed a finger at her. "This conversation is not over," I said.

She blew me a kiss and disappeared back into the sunporch.

It was a quiet morning at the shop, no bus tours and few tourists coming off the highway, probably because it was raining and people just wanted to get wherever they were going. Just before lunch I called Sam to see if I could get a second opinion on Mac's accordion. Liz had already threatened to show up at two a.m. with the other accordion he'd given to Avery and play Queen's "We Will Rock You" outside his bedroom window.

Mac had laughed and Liz had patted his cheek. "It's fricking cute how you think I'm kidding," she'd said.

Sam was in his office when I got to the pub. The door was open. He was sitting at his desk, his dark-framed glasses halfway down his nose.

"Knock, knock," I said.

Sam looked up and smiled. "Hi," he said. "That was fast."

"The shop's quiet," I said, pulling off my raincoat and draping it on the back of a chair. I set the bag with the accordion on the sofa.

Sam came around the desk and gave me a hug. "Where did you get an accordion anyway?" he asked.

"Mac," I said, "and actually it was two accordions." I told him the story of Mac helping Glenn move his uncle's couch and being offered the accordions or the growler of beer.

Sam laughed. "From what I know of Clayton's place, you could probably fill your store twice over, with enough stuff left for a good-size storage unit."

"I know," I said. "And it may come to that. I'm putting a proposal together for Glenn and his cousin for us to get the house a little more habitable."

"Good luck with that," Sam said. "Clayton has always been a bit of a pack rat.

He lifted the accordion out of the shopping bag I'd put it in. I leaned against his desk while he turned it over and examined the instrument from every angle. Finally he looked at me. "So what were you thinking?" he asked.

I shrugged. "Somewhere between four and five hundred."

Sam nodded. "I don't see why you won't get that."

I smiled at him. "Thanks."

"Do you have time for a sandwich?" he asked. "Applewood smoked bacon and fresh tomatoes."

"That does sound good," I said.

Sam pointed at the sofa. "Sit. I won't be long."

I sat. From the couch I could see Sam's photos from the early days of the pub and the band. My dad was in several of them. It always made me feel good to see them. He'd died when I was five, and both my mother and Gram had worked to keep my memories of him alive, but it was when I was with Sam that I seemed to feel the closest to him.

Sam came back with sandwiches and coffee for both of us. I groaned with happiness after the first bite of my sandwich. "What is this bread?" I said, my mouth half-full of food. "It's really good."

"Honey beer bread," Sam said, wiping a dab of mayonnaise from the corner of his mouth. "Glenn made it." His mouth twitched and he started to laugh. "I guess he had to settle for the beer since Mac took the accordions."

I laughed. "Well, that worked out well, because I'm not sure Mac can make bread, although Rose would probably be happy to give him lessons."

Sam's expression grew serious. "I heard the police found Jeff Cameron's body."

I nodded.

"Rumor has it his wife killed herself." He raised an eyebrow.

"Rumors are usually pretty accurate," I said.

Sam reached for his coffee. "I forgot to tell you when I saw you last week. I actually saw him—it would have been Monday—having some kind of heated conversation with someone."

"What do you mean by heated conversation?" I asked.

"Raised voices, mostly," he said. "Although I wasn't close enough to make out what was being said."

"Was this a male someone he was having the conversation with or a female someone?"

"Male." Sam leaned back and draped his free arm along the back of his chair. "My height, bit bigger build, hair cut close to his head." He frowned. "Why the questions?"

"No reason, really," I said.

"Rose isn't ready to let this go."

"Pretty much."

Sam let out a breath. "Just be careful, all right?"

I nodded. "I will. I promise."

The conversation turned to the bands Sam had lined up for the rest of the summer, and then I collected the accordion, gave him a hug and left. I hadn't said anything to Sam, but the description of the mystery man arguing with Jeff Cameron matched the photo of Mike Vega that Mr. P. had found online. As I drove back to the shop I wondered why anyone ever bothered to commit a crime in a small town like North Harbor. It seemed someone who knew someone who knew you was always watching.

We made up for the quiet morning with a busload of tourists in the afternoon on their way from Boston to Newfoundland who dripped all over the shop but spent enough that I didn't really mind. Just before we closed Rose came to find me. I was in the back, looking for a box of dishes.

"Two things," she said.

"Okay," I said, turning to face her. "What's number one?"

"Charlotte talked to Maddie. Maddie said that when Chloe's parents were out of town someone was staying with her. She has no idea who, but she saw someone getting into Chloe's car a couple of times. The person was wearing a hoodie with the hood over their face."

"Interesting."

Rose nodded. "I thought so."

"So what's number two?" I asked.

"I know why Chloe worked so hard to get the job with Jeff Cameron," she said, a self-congratulatory, cat-that-swallowed-the-canary expression on her face.

I pushed a stray strand of hair off my cheek. "It wasn't because they were having an affair, was it?"

"Heavens, no!" Rose made a dismissive gesture with one hand. "What happened is, I started thinking, what would make her so eager to have that particular job?"

"And?"

"Why do people do anything?" she asked. "Sex, money, power." She ticked them off on her fingers.

"You eliminated sex."

"I'm not saying Jeff Cameron wasn't an attractive man, at least physically, but he seemed a little long in the tooth for someone Chloe's age. And no one I talked to seemed to think she was interested in him in that way. In fact, she didn't seem to be interested in anyone. Up to the point that she took the semester off, all of her focus was on her studies."

I leaned against the workbench. "Okay, so sex is out. What about money?"

"Chloe turned down a job at the library that would have paid more."

"Really?" I said.

Rose nodded. "She had experience. She worked there during high school."

"That leaves power," I said. "What kind of power did Chloe Sanders get by working for Jeff Cameron?"

The smile returned to Rose's face. "I don't think she was looking to gain power. I think she was looking to use his, or to be more exact, his influence. Chloe wanted to transfer to the BA/MA program in international studies at Johns Hopkins.

I looked blankly at her.

"She needed a recommendation from someone with international business experience."

"Jeff."

Rose nodded. "Yes. And one of the professors on the acceptance committee worked at Helmark at one time. I think Chloe was researching the members of the committee and that's why she went to Jeff's lecture. When he mentioned he was going to hire an assistant for the summer, it must have seemed like the perfect opportunity to her. Remember, she did say it was her big chance."

"So how is that a motive for her to have killed him?"

"Because the deadline for all supporting documents is two days from now and the only reference they've received for Chloe came from one of her professors."

I swiped a hand over my neck. "From Dr. Durand."

Rose nodded.

"I can't figure out how she's tied up in all of this," I said.

"She does seem to be involved somehow, doesn't she?" Rose said.

"So you think what?" I asked. "That Jeff promised to give Chloe a recommendation and then reneged on that promise so she killed him or helped Leesa do it?" I raised a skeptical eyebrow.

"Chloe Sanders is a very competitive young woman."

"That doesn't surprise me. She was on the debate team Charlotte coached."

"And Charlotte admitted that Chloe wasn't always a good loser."

I rubbed my neck again. This case was becoming a giant pain in the neck. "It's a long way from being a poor loser to killing someone," I said.

Rose shrugged. "Not nearly as long as you might think." She bent down to pick up a lag bolt that was lying on the floor.

"How do you know all this?" I asked.

"Ardith Cramer." Rose straightened up and handed the large screw to me. I set it on the bench.

"Who's Ardith Cramer?"

"She was one of my best students. It turns out that she works in the registrar's office at Cahill College. Wasn't that convenient?"

"Very," I said. Between the three of them—Rose, Charlotte and Liz—it seemed they knew everyone in town. I knew from experience, it was not always a good thing. "We need to talk to Chloe again."

"Already in the works," Rose said. She reached over and patted my cheek. "Try to keep up, dear."

At the end of the day I sent everyone home and stayed behind to wipe up the footprint-covered floor.

"Can I help?" Mac asked.

I shook my head. "It's okay. I've got this." I looked at the floor. "It looks like we were giving tango lessons and put the footprints all over the floor for people to follow."

Mac squinted at the wide wooden boards. "It looks more like moonwalking than the tango."

"Does that mean you know how to tango?" I asked.

He smiled. "I might." He took the broom from my hands. "I'll sweep; you mop. It'll be faster."

We started at the far end of the store by the cash desk. I let Mac get a head start. "I didn't get a chance to ask you," he said. "What did Sam say about the accordion?"

"He agrees with me—we should be able to get four or five hundred dollars for it."

Mac grinned. "I really am glad I didn't take the growler of beer."

"Me, too," I said. I told him about Glenn's beer bread.

"Is that the same as making lemonade out of lemons?" he teased.

"Very funny," I said, "although I think you're right."

"Did you get the message I left on your desk?" Mac asked. "Nick called again."

I dunked the sponge mop in the bucket of hot water and oil soap, used the handle to squeeze out the excess and starting mopping along the baseboard. "I got it. Thanks," I said. "I called him back but I just got his voice mail. It's probably just about Thursday night. He's been meeting Jess and me at the jam."

"Are things okay with you two?" Mac looked up from his sweeping.

"Yes," I said. "Maybe." I shrugged. "I don't know. Rose isn't going to stop until she gets answers that satisfy her. Which means she's probably going to bang heads with Nick again."

"You think she's right?"

I scrubbed at a stubborn splotch of dirt on the floor. "Between you and me, yeah, I do. It's all just too neat, like a present tied up with a bow. Real life isn't like that. It's messy. You can't put all the pieces in a box and close the lid, to stretch the metaphor."

Mac lifted a chair to sweep underneath it. "So what's next?"

"Rose and Mr. P. are going to talk to Michael Vega tomorrow." I shook my head. "And I didn't tell you. When I was down at the pub Sam told me he saw Jeff Cameron arguing with a man a couple of days before Rose was attacked."

"Let me guess," Mac said. "It was Vega."

"The description matches him, which probably means it was him." I dunked the mop again. "You know what really bothers me?" I said. "Why did Leesa Cameron go along with Nicole giving her an alibi?"

"Because otherwise she didn't have one?"

I shook my head. "No. I mean what made her think Nicole wouldn't back out and tell the truth at some point? Jeff was Nicole's brother. I'm surprised Leesa didn't realize the alibi would eventually fall apart. No matter how mad I got at Liam, my first loyalty would always be to him because he's my brother."

"Not all siblings are like the two of you."

"What makes you say that?" I asked, keeping my tone casual.

For a moment Mac didn't speak; then he said, "I have a brother. We're not like you and Liam."

"I guess I'm lucky."

"So is Liam," he said. He made it to the stairs and leaned the broom against the railing. "I'm just going to get the dustpan. I think it's in the staff room." He headed up the steps two at a time.

So Mac had a brother. I thought about his apartment upstairs that didn't have a single photograph of anyone. As far as I knew, no one had visited in the more than eighteen months he'd been in town. What had happened in Mac's previous life? Maybe that was the real mystery.

Chapter 17

"Did you call Michael Vega?" I asked Rose as we walked out to the SUV Wednesday morning.

She shook her head and opened the door for Elvis, who meowed a thank-you and jumped onto the seat. "I think we should have the element of surprise on our side."

"What if he's not home?"

"He doesn't go in to work until twelve thirty on Wednesdays," she said. "I checked." She looked rather pleased with herself. "This is not my first rodeo, Sarah."

"I can see that, Little Buckaroo," I said.

Mr. P. was just coming along the sidewalk as we pulled into the parking lot. We waited by the car until he joined us.

"Good morning," he said, smiling at both of us and at Elvis. "Isn't this a beautiful day?"

"Yes, it is," Rose agreed, taking the arm he offered her.

"We could have picked you up," I said.

Mr. P. glanced back over his shoulder at me. "Thank you, my dear, but I wouldn't have been able to enjoy this blue sky and sunshine if you'd done that."

I unlocked the back door. Elvis headed purposefully through the workroom, followed by Rose. Mr. P. went into the sunporch. I looked at my watch. "Will about an hour from now work for you to go see Michael Vega?" I asked.

He set his messenger bag on the table they used as a desk. "Yes, it will," he said. He patted down the few wisps of hair that he had. "I appreciate you driving us." He hesitated. "I do have a driver's license."

"I thought you probably did," I said.

"I gave up my car a few years ago because it spent more time in its parking spot than it did on the road. I've thought about buying another one, but I don't want to end up becoming one of those old fools who doesn't know when it's time to stop driving."

I smiled at him. "Somehow I don't see that happening," I said. "But I'm happy to take you and Rose anywhere you need to go."

Mr. P. smiled back at me. "Thank you," he said, "for the taxi service and the vote of confidence.

I found Mac on his hands and knees with his head and shoulders in the storage space under the stairs. "Sarah, is that you?" he said, his voice partly muffled by his head being in the small closet.

"It's me. What are you looking for?"

"That box of vintage Pyrex casserole dishes, the red and yellow ones."

I closed my eyes and pictured the inside of the storage space. We had a list on the back of the door of what was inside, but not where it was. "Try to the right under what would be about the second step," I said.

Mac grunted, then began backing up, sliding a cardboard box out with him. I leaned over to check the writing on the top: *Pyrex dishes—red and yellow*, was written in Avery's angular printing. "Thank you," he said.

A dust bunny was stuck to the side of his head above his left ear. I brushed it away with my hand. "The dust bunnies are organizing in there," I said.

"I think they're more like dust elephants," Mac said, standing up and brushing more bits off his shirt.

Mr. P. came toward us, headed for the stairs with a round metal tin in his hands. "Good morning, Mac," he said.

Mac smiled at the older man. "Good morning." He craned his neck in the direction of the green-and-gold tin. "Did Rose make coffee cake?"

"No. I made date squares," Mr. P. said. "Would you like to try one?"

"Yes, I would," Mac said.

I leaned sideways into their line of sight. Mr. P. smiled. "Would you like one as well, Sarah?" he asked.

"Please," I said.

"And a cup of coffee, of course."

I nodded.

"Could I help?" Mac asked.

Mr. P. waved away the offer. "No, no. Finish what you were doing. I'll be right back." He headed up the stairs.

"What do you need the casserole dishes for?" I asked.

"Remember the guys who bought the armoire?" Mac said.

I nodded.

"They're hosting a wedding—a very small one—next weekend, and they were looking for more of these dishes, and possibly several wooden chairs."

"Chairs we have," I said, thinking there had to be a dozen outside in the garage.

"I thought I'd get Avery to bring in four or five and make sure they're dusted, just in case," he said.

"Fine with me."

Mac glanced over at the stairs. "Are you going with them to talk to the trainer?"

I nodded.

"What can I do?" he asked.

"Cross your fingers that we come up with some answers," I said as Mr. P. appeared at the top of the stairs carrying two mugs, followed by Rose with the date squares.

Mac and I had our coffee out at the workbench and went over the estimate I'd come up with for getting Clayton McNamara's house organized. The date squares were excellent and Mr. P. beamed when I told him so.

Just before nine thirty I went upstairs to get my purse and put on a bit of lipstick. Elvis was lying in the center of my desk, paws curled lazily in against his chest, half on the list of Web site orders that needed to be packed. "No, no, don't move on my account," I said. The cat's response was to roll on his side so he was covering almost the entire sheet of paper.

"You could take that down to Charlotte later," I said, tapping the one visible corner of the page.

"Mrr," he said, wrinkling his scarred black nose at me.

I got my keys and my purse and headed downstairs. Rose and Mr. P. were waiting by the back door.

Michael Vega and his wife lived in a two-story farmhouse-style home close to the downtown. The house had a small addition with a wide, shaded verandah and an attached barn. A carved gargoyle sat on the front corner of the verandah roof. Someone had a sense of humor, I thought.

Michael Vega answered the door. He was just above average height, an inch or so below six feet, I guessed. He had cropped dark hair, a day's worth of stubble on his face and the strong, muscled build of someone who worked out with weights, not the rangy body of a hard-core long-distance runner, I noted.

Mr. P. introduced himself, offering his private investigator's license as ID.

"Does this have anything to do with Leesa Cameron?" Vega asked.

"Yes, it does," Mr. P. said.

He nodded as though that had been the answer he was expecting. "Come in, please," he said.

We stepped into a living room with gleaming dark-wood floors and sunshine streaming through the windows. The space was neat without being fussy. Two sofas were at right angles to each other. A marble-topped table in the front window was covered with plants, and there was a stack of kids' picture books on the low coffee table.

A woman appeared in the doorway to the kitchen. She was curvy and petite, barefoot, with her dark hair piled on top of her head and paint on her black tank top. "Hello," she said, walking over to join what had to be her husband. She had a warm smile, and I couldn't see any tension between the two of them.

Michael introduced us. "This is my wife, Caroline," he said. She touched his shoulder as she perched on the arm of the closest couch.

"Please sit down," she said.

"They're here about Leesa Cameron," Michael said, making the introductions.

His wife nodded. "I thought so."

"Mrs. Cameron hired you to train her," Mr. P. said, getting right to the point.

Michael sat down on a black leather footstool that was placed in front of a wooden rocking chair with an upholstered seat and back. "Yes. I was training Leesa to run a half marathon as a surprise for her husband because Jeff was such an avid runner." He rubbed a hand over his neck. "I'm sorry. I'm having a hard time believing she killed him."

"Why did she hire you?" Rose asked. She gave him her best sweet little old lady smile. "I'm not doubting your skill as a trainer; it's just that the Camerons belonged to a gym. Why wouldn't she use one of their trainers?"

"I asked her that," he said. "She told me that she wanted to surprise her husband and he knew both the trainers at the gym. She felt if she went to either of them Jeff would find out and it would ruin the surprise."

"Did you think that was odd?" Mr. P. asked, frowning a little behind his wire-framed glasses.

Michael smiled. "I trained a woman once to run a full marathon—twenty-six point two miles. Her family didn't know what was going on until they got to the race, supposedly just to watch, and she peeled off her hoodie and sweatpants and showed them her number."

"Some people don't want the added pressure of their family's expectations when they're trying to get in shape or reach a goal," Caroline Vega said.

I studied Michael Vega. My instinct was that there was no way he'd been having an affair with Leesa Cameron. There was nothing evasive in his answers or his body language.

"When did you last speak to Leesa?" Mr. P. asked.

"We ran last Wednesday morning. It was a short run, though."

"Was she getting the miles in?" I asked.

Michael turned his attention to me. "Yes, she was. She wasn't a natural runner—you know she'd been a rower?"

I nodded.

"Her gait was a little awkward and she was still behind the time mileposts we'd set, but she was determined."

"I spoke to her Wednesday night," Caroline said. "She called looking for Michael. He was filling in, teaching fitness classes for a friend whose wife just had a baby, so he wasn't answering his cell phone."

"Do you have any idea what time she called?" Rose asked.

Caroline tucked one leg up underneath her. "I do. I was right there on that sofa watching *Gotta Dance*."

She grinned and ducked her head. "My guilty pleasure. The kids are with Michael's mom for the week and I've been painting quite late, so I fell asleep in front of the TV. The phone woke me up. The end credits were just rolling on the screen."

I pointed at the bold abstract canvas on the end wall of the room. "Is that your work?"

"Yes," she said, a smile spreading across her face.

"You're very talented," I said.

The painting, all shades of green and blue, had been drawing my attention since we'd stepped into the room.

"Yes, she is," Michael agreed, reaching out a hand to touch his wife's leg. It was impossible to miss the easy, loving rapport between the two of them.

"Did she leave any message?" Mr. P. asked.

Caroline shifted her gaze to him. "She wanted Michael to know she wasn't going to train anymore. She'd paid for the month but she wasn't looking for a refund. She said to tell Michael to keep the money because she was canceling on short notice."

I saw Mr. P. and Rose exchange glances. Nothing we were learning was confirming any of our theories.

"I don't know if this is any help," Caroline continued, "but it sounded like she was moving things. I got the sense that maybe she was packing. I know she was at home."

"Why do you say that?" Mr. P.'s forehead creased into a frown again.

"I could hear the foghorn in the background."

He shot a quick look in my direction. I had a feeling he was thinking what I was thinking. The Cameron cottage was on West Penobscot Bay. I had heard the foghorn when Michelle and I were at the house that evening. The unique curve of the coastline meant that stretch of shoreline was the only place the Deer Isle foghorn could be heard.

"I was going to call Michael when he had his break but I fell asleep again on the couch and wound up sleeping there until he came home." She smiled and rubbed her neck. "My neck is still kinked."

"Mr. Vega, did Leesa use any online training programs or tools?" Mr. P. asked. Nothing in his expression indicated that he knew about the BodiBudi Michael Vega had bought for Leesa.

Michael nodded. "She used a BodiBudi." He wrapped his thumb and index finger around his left wrist. "It's a silicone wristband. It has a computer chip and a digital readout." He stopped and his eyes flicked from side to side. Then he shook his head, the beginnings of a smile coming to his face. He looked at his wife. "They think I bought it for Leesa. As a gift. Because we were *involved*."

Caroline smiled and shifted to look at Mr. P. "Michael ordered that fitness tracker for Leesa, the same way he's ordered ones for, I'd say, fifteen other clients. None of whom he was involved with. We have four children, Mr. Peterson. There aren't enough hours in the day."

"Sixteen," her husband said, quietly.

She tipped her head in Michael's direction. "Sixteen other clients. They get a better price and Michael gets a small commission. Leesa paid in cash. I can show you the receipt."

"That won't be necessary," Mr. P. said with a smile of his own.

Caroline's expression turned serious then. "I know you're thinking that Leesa and Michael were having an affair, especially with all the secrecy Leesa insisted on." She smiled at her husband and held out her hand to him. He caught it and gave it a squeeze. "I know the wife is always the last to know, but I know my husband and they weren't."

Looking at the two of them, there was no way I didn't believe her. Liz had insisted no man could be quite as perfect as Michael Vega seemed to be. This was one time she was wrong.

Michael got to his feet and put his arms around his wife's shoulders. "Leesa didn't talk about, well, anything personal, but I saw how hard she was working, training for this half marathon. She was desperate to reconnect with her husband. I know what the police believe, what the evidence says. I just have a really hard time believing it." He let out a breath. "If she did kill Jeff—and that's a very big if—it had to be something that happened in the moment. I know a crime of passion is clichéd, but I don't see how it could have been anything else."

I remembered what Nick had told me about Jeff Cameron having been hit over the head and then drowned. There was nothing about that that said crime of passion. Nothing at all.

"There is one sort of odd thing that happened," Michael said.

"What do you mean?" Mr. P. said.

"It was a week ago Monday. I was on my way to The

Black Bear for takeout and Jeff Cameron bumped into me on the sidewalk. He made a big issue of it, as though I'd done it on purpose. I apologized a couple of times and managed to get past him."

"Do you think it's possible he knew you were spending time with his wife and thought there was something going on?" I asked.

"I suppose it's possible," Michael said. "But if that was the case, why didn't he say something straight out? Or punch me in the nose for that matter?" He shook his head. "It was just strange."

We thanked the Vegas and left.

"I believe them," Rose said once she was settled in the front passenger seat of the SUV.

"So do I," Mr. P. said from the backseat.

"What do you think about his story about seeing Jeff outside The Black Bear?" I said.

"If we didn't know Jeff was dead I'd be inclined to say he staged the whole thing to make it look like they'd had a confrontation. Which could be useful if one was going to fake one's death."

"But he is dead."

Mr. P. nodded. "Yes, there is that."

I nodded my agreement. "Now what?" I asked.

Rose reached for the ubiquitous tote bag at her feet. "I'd like to drop some cookies off to Nicole Cameron, if you don't mind. I expect there will be a service of some kind and people will probably be stopping by."

"I don't mind at all," I said.

I drove across town to Nicole Cameron's house and parked at the curb. A U-Haul van was parked in the driveway, wheels turned hard to the right. I'd just stepped out of the car when what looked like a large beach ball covered in paper-mâché and possibly coconut bounced into the street and caromed off the front fender. I caught it and looked around.

A woman was hurrying down the driveway across the street. "Sorry!" she called.

"Go on in without me," I said to Rose and Mr. P.

"We won't be very long," Rose said.

I walked across the street and handed the beach ball to the woman. "Thank you," she said. "I guess the out-of-control snowball really was out of control." She smiled. "I'm Deb." She gestured at the kids on the lawn, who once again seemed to be making another movie. "I'm the director's assistant, prop master, costume designer and lunch lady for this production." She had dark hair pulled back in a ponytail, warm brown eyes and a pair of retro tortoiseshell-frame glasses on her head.

"I'm Sarah," I said. I gestured at the beach ball. "Do I smell coconut?"

"It photographs like snow and if you get hungry you can eat it." She grinned.

"Weren't they doing some kind of creature-from-the-black-lagoon movie last week?" I asked.

She nodded. *"Sewer Pipe Swamp Thing."*

I laughed. "Very creative."

"That's all my daughter," Deb said, pointing to a fair-haired girl about ten or eleven years old who was positioning a boy I was guessing was supposed to be Bigfoot in his bath-mat costume. "She's the director and script writer. She got an old camera from her grandmother a couple of weeks ago and she's been making movies with it ever since."

The girl looked around, spotted her mother with the beach ball and ran over to us. "It went into the street again, Bayley," Deb said, pointing over her shoulder with one finger."

"Sorry," the child said, making a face.

"Say thank you to Sarah," her mother said, indicating me with a dip of her head. "She's the one who rescued it."

Bayley smiled at me. "Thank you for getting our ball," she said. She had none of the shyness with adults that I'd had when I was her age. "We're getting ants again," she said to her mom. "I think they're after the coconut. It's just like with the slime." She made a face.

"Baking soda and shaving cream," I said. "You can make some great fake snow with it."

Bayley's eyes widened. "Awesome," she said.

"By any chance do you know how to make slime?" Deb asked. "We used corn syrup and food coloring, which is why the ants, plus it didn't flow quite right."

"White glue and borax," I said.

"You must be a teacher."

I shook my head. "Former summer camp counselor, and I own Second Chance. It's a repurpose shop."

"Repurpose. That means you have old things." Bayley squinted in the sunshine.

"Yes," I said.

"Could we go, please?" she said to her mother. "I need stuff for my Godzilla movie."

"Make a list," her mother said. "I'll take you tomorrow." She held out a hand and her daughter high-fived her; then Bayley turned to me. "Would you like to see my movie?" she asked.

"I would," I said.

"Okay, stay right there." She bolted across the grass to get her camera. It was attached to a makeshift tripod, an empty soda bottle duct-taped to a stool.

Deb followed my gaze. "You don't by any chance have an inexpensive tripod at your store, do you?" she asked.

"I do," I said. "It's old but it's in decent shape."

"How much?" she asked.

"Ten dollars," I said, cutting the price I'd been planning on asking in half. I liked Bayley's energy and creativity.

Deb made a face and looked from the kids to the house. "There's no way I can get there today," she began.

I held up a hand. "Don't worry about it. I'll set it aside with your name on it."

"Thank you so much," she said.

Bayley came racing back across the lawn with her camera. I leaned over the view screen and watched *Sewer Pipe Swamp Thing*. It was funny and creative and I loved the way the child's eyes lit up when I laughed at the mom, aka Deb, putting the Swamp Thing in time-out for getting slime all over the kitchen floor. I caught sight of my car and Liz's in the background of one shot and Leesa Cameron's Audi in another. I had a feeling that someday I'd be watching one of Bayley's movies on the big screen and I'd be able to say that I'd indirectly been in one of her first films. I clapped at the end and she grinned happily.

"It was great," I told her. "If I come back in a couple of days, will you show me this one when it's done?"

"Sure," she said. She glanced in the direction of Bigfoot, whose costume was sliding sideways. "You should probably wait until Monday, though."

"Deal," I said. She scampered back over to her cast.

"You'll probably see us tomorrow," her mother said.

I nodded. I could see Rose and Mr. P. coming down Nicole Cameron's driveway. "It was good to meet you," I said.

Deb smiled. "You, too."

Mr. P. was quiet on the drive back to the shop, his head bent over his cell phone.

"Michael Vega wasn't having an affair with Leesa Cameron, was he?" I said.

"He wasn't," Mr. P. said from the backseat.

I glanced in the rearview mirror. He held up his phone. "I found photos of Mr. Vega on the gym's Facebook page teaching classes Wednesday night and leading a workshop all day Thursday and Friday."

"So who helped Leesa kill her husband?" I asked.

Beside me Rose sighed. "That's the sixty-four-thousand-dollar question, isn't it?" she said.

Chapter 18

"Maybe this is a case that can't be solved," I said.

"Alfred, would you like pork chops for dinner?" Rose said. "And maybe a spinach salad?"

"That sounds . . . very nice," Mr. P. said. He sounded a little puzzled by the sudden swerve the conversation had taken.

"Rose, are you ignoring me?" I asked. I shot a quick look in her direction.

"I'm sorry, dear," she said. "I thought that was obvious."

"It was," I said. "I'm just not clear *why* you're ignoring me."

"Because we're not walking away from this case."

I held my breath for a moment and then slowly let it out. "So what are we doing next?" I asked.

"I'm not sure."

I didn't need to take my eyes off the road to know she was sitting upright on the passenger seat, shoulders squared, chin out, a determined look in her eye that any student who had ever been in her class would know meant not to cross her.

"Okay, when you figure it out, keep me in the loop," I said.

It was about half an hour later, just as I was settling a very nice vintage Ibanez jazz bass into its hard-shell case for a customer, that Chloe Sanders walked into the shop. She was wearing a sundress the same shade of blue as the streak in her hair.

My customer headed for the door and I walked over to Chloe. She looked nervous, her right hand playing with the handle of the messenger bag she had over her shoulder. "Hi, Sarah," she said. "Is Mrs. Elliot here?"

"She's out in the workroom."

"Could I speak to her for a minute?"

"Of course," I said.

Avery was hanging several jean jackets Jess had up-cycled for us on a tall coatrack. "Avery, I'll be right back," I said.

She looked up, "Okay."

I took Chloe back to the workroom. Charlotte had the ironing board set up and was ironing a white lace tablecloth. She smiled and set down the iron when she saw her former student.

"Chloe, what are you doing here?" she asked.

"I'll let you talk," I said.

"Sarah, could you stay?" Chloe said. "I'd like you to hear what I came to tell Mrs. Elliot."

I nodded. "All right."

Charlotte came around the ironing board. "What did you come to tell me?"

Chloe cleared her throat. "When I was here before you said you were proud of me."

"I am," Charlotte said with a smile. "I know how hard you worked to get into college. You won a scholarship. I'm very proud."

"Mrs. Elliot, I lied to you."

I folded my arms across my midsection and stayed quiet, wondering what she was about to confess to.

Charlotte frowned. "What about?"

"About a lot of things." Chloe looked over at me. "You . . . you met Bella, Dr. Durand."

I nodded.

"We . . . were . . . a couple. I took last term off because I wanted to be with her and I couldn't do that if I was a student."

Suddenly a lot of things made sense, like who it was who had been staying with Chloe when her parents were out of town. "You're not together now?" I asked.

Chloe shook her head. "All the lying and the secret keeping: I couldn't do that anymore. I broke it off with her last night." She turned her attention back to Charlotte. "The thing is, the job here at Cahill was just a one-year appointment for Bella. In the fall she'll be teaching at Tauton University."

"In Maryland," Charlotte said.

Chloe nodded. "Bella and I wanted to stay together. I thought we could do that if I transferred to Johns Hopkins. I thought we could stop . . . sneaking around."

"You needed a reference from Jeff Cameron." I hadn't been sure if Rose had brought Charlotte up to date. Obviously she had.

Chloe nodded. "Yes." She ducked her head for a moment. "Which he figured out pretty quickly."

"He wouldn't write it for you," I said.

She turned to look at me. "Jeff kept giving me menial jobs like typing up address labels for him. He said he wanted to know how hard I was willing to work if I did get in the program." She let out a breath. "I finally realized he was never going to give me that reference. So last Wednesday I decided to quit. Quit. Not kill him. I was with Bella that night. We ordered pizza. You can check. She paid with her debit card."

"Why didn't you tell anyone you'd quit your job?" I asked.

"Because I didn't."

Charlotte and I exchanged a look. "I don't understand," she said slowly. "You said you decided to quit last Wednesday."

Chloe nodded. "I did. But before I could do that Jeff gave me this. She pulled an envelope out of her bag and handed it to Charlotte. Then she turned to me again. "Sarah, I don't know if this means anything, but Jeff had some brochures about Costa Rica in his briefcase. I asked him if he was going on vacation, and he laughed and said pretty soon his whole life was going to be a vacation."

I nodded. "Thanks."

Charlotte lifted the flap and pulled out several sheets of paper. She glanced at them quickly, then looked at me and nodded.

"I didn't kill Jeff," Chloe said. "Or help anyone else do it. I had no reason to."

Charlotte put the papers back in the envelope and

handed it to Chloe. "I believe you," she said. "Thank you for telling me the truth."

"I should have done it from the beginning."

Charlotte put both hands on Chloe's shoulders and smiled. "You did it now. That's enough."

I could tell from the smile that spread across the young woman's face that Charlotte's opinion meant a lot to her.

Charlotte walked Chloe out. I leaned against the workbench and thought about Jeff Cameron telling Chloe that his whole life was soon going to be a vacation. Had that been what got him killed?

The rest of the day was busy at the shop. I found the tripod and set it on the workbench with Deb's name on it. I made sure that both Mac and Charlotte knew why it was there in case I was busy when Bayley and her mother came in.

Late that afternoon I was in the workroom checking out the half dozen chairs Avery had brought in from the garage when Mac poked his head in from the store. "Sarah, Channing Caulfield is on the phone for you," he said.

He looked as baffled as I felt. "For me? Did he say what he wanted?" I asked.

Mac shook his head. "I could take a message."

I held up a hand. "No, it's okay. I'll talk to him. I'll take it up in my office."

As I headed upstairs I wondered why the former manager of the North Harbor Trust Company was calling me. Channing Caulfield had gone to school with Charlotte and had advised Liz on Emmerson Foundation business. He also had a soft spot for Liz.

I'd met the man in the spring after the Angels had gotten involved in the murder of a man named Ronan Quinn.

I remembered Avery saying Liz had been having dinner with Channing on Friday night. Did that have anything to do with today's phone call?

I dropped into my desk chair and reached for the phone. "Hello, Mr. Caulfield," I said.

"Hello, Sarah," he replied. "You don't need to be so formal. Please call me Channing."

I pictured the man. He was in his early seventies, about average height, but with the presence and confidence of a much larger man. He had silver hair combed back from his face, a ready smile and deep blue eyes.

"I called because Liz said to call you if I wasn't able to reach her."

"All right," I said. I didn't have a clue what he was talking about.

"She was right about the money," he continued. "It just took me a while to find the name the account was under."

"Liz usually is right," I said. It was the only thing I could think of.

"I thought it wasn't likely he'd use Jeff Cameron, but that was the first name I looked for. I checked California and Massachusetts, but I didn't come up with anything."

Okay, now things were starting to make sense, including why Liz had gone to dinner on Friday with the former bank manager.

"I didn't have any better luck with Jeff Hennessy,

either, but I hit pay dirt with Cameron Hennessy." I caught an edge of pride in his voice. "It turns out the money never left New Hampshire. The account is with an adviser in Manchester."

"You're sure it's the right person?" I asked.

"I'm certain," Channing said. "I e-mailed the photo Liz gave me to the adviser. It's the same man."

"Do you have any idea how much money we're talking about?" I reached for a pen and a pad of paper.

"I only have a ballpark figure, you understand," he said. "But I can safely say more than a million."

"Dollars?" I rasped. Jeff Cameron had a million dollars?

"Yes."

I tipped my head back and stared at the ceiling for a moment. "I don't understand. How did he get that kind of money?"

"That's actually quite an interesting story."

"I'd love to hear it," I said.

Channing Caulfield cleared his throat before he began. "In the late eighteen hundreds New Hampshire became a major manufacturer of textiles, and for many years the economy was booming in the state, but by the early 1930s the bottom had fallen out; mills were being built in the south, closer to the cotton fields."

"I remember some of that from school."

"That doesn't surprise me, Sarah," he said. "It's an important part of New Hampshire's history. Warfield Mills opened in 1871 and had managed to stay open despite the economic downturn. In 1935 they secured a contract from the federal government to produce the fabric for a series of high-altitude weather balloons. In

January of 1936 there was a fire at the main mill in New Ipswich. Thirty-seven workers suffered second- and third-degree burns. Nineteen died."

I swallowed hard. "That's horrible."

"Yes, it was," he said. "One of those thirty-seven workers injured was Catherine Hennessy's father."

"Jeff Cameron's great-grandfather." I couldn't think of the man by any other name.

"That's where the Cameron name comes from. Charles Cameron's wife, Alice, took her husband and their six children back to her family's farm in the northern part of the state. They stayed there until Charles died four years later. After that, they ended up in Connecticut, where Alice Cameron worked as a housekeeper to support the children. And eventually remarried. She either chose not to stay in touch with her family or perhaps they chose not to stay in touch with her."

"That's so sad," I said. I couldn't help thinking how different things had been for Catherine Hennessy when her father died than they had been for me. Gram, along with Rose, Charlotte and Liz, had wrapped their arms around Mom and me, literally as well as figuratively.

"I'm telling you all this so you'll understand the next part of the story," Channing said.

"I'm guessing it has something to do with the money?"

He cleared his throat again. "An investigation found negligence on the part of the factory's manager. A lawsuit was filed which took years, more than a decade, to work its way through the courts. Eventually the mill's owners settled. Each of the injured workers got twenty-five thousand dollars. I know it doesn't sound like much money by today's standards."

"But it was a lot of money at the time," I finished.

"Yes, it was," Channing said. "Charles Cameron wasn't the only one of the injured workers who had died by the time things were settled. In those cases the money was paid to the wives and children of the injured men."

I began to see how the details about Alice Cameron mattered to the story. "They couldn't find Alice Cameron or her children," I said.

"No, they couldn't," Channing said. "As incredible as it sounds, the money sat in a trust earning interest for more than sixty years."

"Twenty-five thousand dollars turned into more than a million."

"The magic of compound interest."

I set down my pen and ran a hand back through my hair. "So what happened?" I asked.

"Well, as far as I could ascertain, there was a new trustee in charge of the money and she decided to see if she could find any of Charles Cameron's children."

"She found Catherine Hennessy."

"Yes, she did," Channing said. "Catherine was the youngest of Alice and Charles's children. The other five were dead. All the money went to her."

"Do you know when this happened?" I exhaled slowly.

"Approximately four years ago."

"About a year before Catherine Hennessy died."

"Nine and a half months," he said.

"And when she died the money disappeared."

Channing made a sound of disapproval. "The account was transferred to another financial institution. That account was closed. Shortly after, a Cameron Hennessy opened his own investment account."

I looked at the notes I'd been scribbling on the pad in front of me. "How did he get away with it? What about his sister?"

"As far as I can determine, Catherine hadn't updated her will. And it's very likely that she hadn't told Jeff or his sister about the money."

"That doesn't make any sense," I said.

"You have to remember that Catherine was from a different generation, one that believed it built character not to have things handed to you."

"Jeff found out, somehow."

"I think that's very likely," Channing said. "Sarah, is any of this information going to be of any help to you? You do understand that most of what I've told you can't be used in a court of law?"

"Yes, I understand that," I said. I didn't want to know how he'd gotten his information any more than, most of the time, I wanted to know how Mr. P. got his. "It's still useful."

"Well, I'm glad I could be of help."

"You have been, Channing," I said. "Thank you. I know Liz will want to thank you personally." I was going to make her have dinner with the man again.

"My pleasure, Sarah," he said. "Please give Liz my regards."

"I will," I said before ending the call.

I sat at my desk for a couple of minutes, digesting

everything I'd just learned. I tried Liz, but both her home phone and cell went right to voice mail. Then I got a cup of coffee and went downstairs to share what I'd learned with Rose and Mr. P.

"If Jeff Cameron were still alive, I'd say it gave him a motive for disappearing and setting up his wife for his murder," I said when I'd finished telling them the story.

"It certainly gives his wife a motive for his murder," Mr. P. pointed out.

"And his sister for that matter."

Rose shook her head. "No. Nicole was home. Remember? She told us she was signed into the hospital computer doing some kind of online training."

I nodded. I did remember. I looked at Mr. P. "I'm guessing you checked."

He nodded. "She spent two and a half hours doing an interactive refresher on medication protocols."

Rose sighed softly.

"What is it?" I asked.

"I know it sounds foolish," she said, "especially because at first I was so certain Leesa had killed her husband, but I was hoping I was wrong."

"I know," I said. "So was I."

I went out to the garage and gave Mac a quick update on what I'd learned from Channing Caulfield.

"So what happens now?" he asked, wiping his hands on an old rag.

"There'll be an autopsy on Leesa Cameron, and unless it turns up something, the police will close the case. The only woman in Jeff Cameron's life aside from his wife and his sister was Chloe Sanders, and she has an alibi." I put my hands on my head and gave it a shake. "I don't want to think about this anymore right now," I said. "Show me what color you decided to use on the chair."

Mac showed me the deep cranberry red he'd chosen for the rocking chair and then we took another look at the two wicker chairs and agreed they would need a second coat of paint.

When I went back inside I found Avery at the workbench with her stack of postcards and a pile of mat board. "Do you know where your grandmother is?" I asked.

She looked up and gave me a blank look. "No."

"Is she picking you up?"

She shook her head. "I'm going over to Charlotte's to help her move some boxes in the garage, and then we're making pizza." She took the top mat off the pile, made a face at it and set it to one side. "Did you try her cell?"

"I did," I said. "I got her voice mail."

She looked at me again. "Yeah, she says she's been going to a bunch of meetings and then she doesn't answer her phone."

"You don't think she's telling the truth?"

Avery shrugged. "If she's going to a meeting, how come she never has any papers with her?" A sly grin spread across her face. "When she went for dinner with Mr. Caulfield I thought maybe they had a thing, you know?"

I did know, and there was no way there was any "thing" happening between Liz and Channing Caulfield. "I don't think so," I said, shaking my head.

"Yeah, Nonna said they'd be ice skating in hell before that happened."

I smiled. "I'll keep trying her."

Rose and Mr. P. drove home with me at the end of the day. I was in a crabby, unsettled mood. Something was niggling away in the back of my brain, something I had the feeling I'd missed from the morning. It was like having a line from a song running over and over in my head but being unable to identify the song.

And I still wanted to talk to Liz. Avery had said that her grandmother had been going to a lot of meetings. I thought about seeing Liz and Michelle together outside McNamara's. Was one of those meetings with Michelle?

When I unlocked the apartment door, Elvis immediately went for his cat tower, sprawling on the top platform as though he'd had an exhausting day. Part of me felt like doing the same thing. Instead I dropped my things, got a glass of orange juice from the fridge and tried Liz one more time. This time she answered.

"Hi," I said. "I've been trying to get you. Channing Caulfield called me this afternoon."

She made a sound of frustration on the other end of the phone. "I told him to call you if he couldn't get me and I forgot to tell you that. I'm sorry, kid. I was at a meeting."

"Do you have a few minutes right now? I'll come tell you what he said."

"I have all the time in the world and a half dozen of Glenn McNamara's lemon tarts."

"I'm on my way," I said. I stuffed my phone in my

pocket and grabbed my purse. "I'm going to Liz's house," I said to Elvis.

He lifted his head, made a "mrr" of acknowledgment and dropped it again.

Liz lived in a beautiful two-story house on a large lot in what she sometimes referred to as the la-di-da part of town. She'd made a pot of tea and set out the lemon tarts. We sat at the kitchen table and I told her what Channing had told me.

She used a knife to cut a tart in half. They were her favorite treat. "You're not serious?" she said. "The money sat unclaimed for more than sixty years?"

"I know it sounds crazy, but that's what he said." I swiped at a dab of lemon cream filling on my plate with one finger. "What I don't understand is why Catherine Hennessy didn't tell her grandchildren about the money. And I'm assuming she didn't just because we haven't found any evidence that she did."

Liz indicated the tray of tarts. "Have another one." She took a sip of her tea. "As far as not telling her family about the money, I understand that. I've told Avery and her cousin, Derek, that I'll pay their tuition when it's time for college, but they have to figure out how to pay for everything else, and if they're waiting around for me to die to get their hands on my money, they're going to be waiting a long time because it's all going to charity."

"You're tough," I said.

She shrugged. "It's been my experience that if people think they can get a free ride, they're a lot less likely to work for something."

"Why didn't you tell us why you were having din-

ner with Channing? Or that you were having dinner
with him?"

She reached for her tea, turning the cup slowly on
the saucer. "Because right after I invited him I decided
not to ask for his help. It felt as though I was using
him—dinner with me in exchange for information."
She gave me a wry smile. "It's an age-old transaction,
but it made me feel uncomfortable."

I'd known Liz all my life and she could still surprise
me. "So what happened?"

"Channing had heard about what had happened to
Rose. He offered to look into Jeff Cameron's background. I told him he didn't have to do that just
because I'd invited him to dinner. There was no quid
pro quo going on."

"And?"

"And he's a damn sneaky man." She couldn't keep
a smile from pulling at the corners of her mouth, so I
knew she wasn't really angry. "He said there definitely
was no quid pro quo because he'd arranged to take
care of the bill and since I hadn't paid for dinner I
didn't need to feel bad about accepting his offer of
help."

"I think he sounds like the perfect man for you," I
said, smirking at her.

Liz dipped her head in the direction of her plate. "I
would throw one of those at you if it weren't a waste
of a perfectly good lemon tart."

I laughed. "You're going to have dinner again with
him, aren't you?"

"Yes, Miss Smarty-pants, I am," she said. "And this
time I'll be buying dinner."

I got up, got the teapot and refilled our cups. "Was your meeting Emmerson Foundation business?" I asked.

Liz nodded, cut one of the tart halves on her plate into two pieces and ate one of them. "It took a little longer than I expected. Like I said, I meant to tell you that I'd told Channing he could call you, and it just slipped right out of my head."

I sat back down, added milk and sugar to my tea and leaned back in my chair, hands wrapped around the cup. "Avery said you've had a lot of meetings lately."

Liz wasn't one to prevaricate. "So it was you Friday, sitting in the line of traffic behind that moving van. I thought it was, but I wasn't sure."

"Why were you and Michelle together? And why keep it a secret?"

Liz's mouth twisted to one side for a moment, and then she sighed. "You know Michelle is convinced someone framed her father?"

I nodded. Like me, Michelle had been a summer kid in North Harbor. Then her dad had gotten a job as the director for the Sunshine Camp. The Emmerson Foundation, the charity started by Liz's grandparents, had bought the camp for kids with seriously ill parents. Rob Andrews had had the job less than a year when a routine audit showed there was money missing. He'd died in prison, less than three months after he'd been sentenced, from a fast-moving form of cancer that no one had known he had.

"She's been looking for any kind of evidence that might clear his name."

Liz nodded. "She asked for my help. She wants to take a closer look at the people on the board of the Sunshine Camp at the time."

I set my cup down. "So why the secrecy?"

She took a deep breath and let it out slowly. "She asked me not to tell you."

For a moment I just stared at her. "She asked you not to tell me? I don't understand."

Liz reached over and laid a hand on my arm. "She asked me not to tell you because John was one of the board members at that time."

My mouth actually fell open. "John? John Scott? Gram's John?"

"Yes," Liz said.

Gram's husband of a year, John Scott, had been a history professor before he retired. "I didn't know John had been on the board of the camp."

"It was a long time ago. Almost twenty years now," she said. "You know I introduced Isabel and John."

"Uh-huh."

"I don't think I ever told you that the reason I knew John was because he was one of Jack's grad students."

I shook my head. "I didn't know that." Jack Kiley was Liz's first husband.

"All through his teens he'd been a camp counselor. When we took over the Sunshine Camp he was just the kind of new blood I wanted on the board."

I leaned forward, one arm on the table. "There's no way John had anything to do with stealing money from the camp. You know him."

Liz nodded. "Yes, I do. Which is partly why I told Michelle I'd help her. There isn't going to be anything to implicate John because I know he had nothing to do with that money disappearing."

I studied her face for a moment. "Do you think Michelle could be right?" I asked. "Is it possible someone framed her father?"

"At this point, I don't know," Liz said. "And that's the other reason I said I'd help her—because I damn well want to find out."

I finished my tea and headed home. I told Liz that I'd talk to Michelle and tell her I knew what they were doing. I was hoping she'd let me help. I hadn't been the best friend I could have been when her father was convicted. Maybe now I could make up—at least a little—for that.

Chapter 19

I was still hungry when I got home. I made grilled cheese for supper, did a little work on the Web site and finally settled in with Elvis to watch *Gotta Dance*.

Drew Carey started with a recap of the previous week's show, and as I watched, it was as if all the little details from the past week finally slid into place in my mind.

"I'm stupid," I said to Elvis. He climbed onto my lap, walked his front paws up my chest and put his face close to mine. I had no idea whether it was supposed to be agreement or consolation. I kissed the top of his head and reached for the remote to mute the TV. Then I explained what I'd just realized to Elvis. The cat tipped his head to one side and listened, green eyes fixed on my face just as though he was weighing my reasoning.

"Should we go tell Rose and Mr. P.?" I asked.

He jumped down from the sofa and went to stand in front of the door. Before I could get up, someone knocked. When I got to the door, Mr. P. was standing there.

"I know who killed Jeff Cameron," he said.

"So do I," I said, wondering how he'd figured it out.

He smiled and inclined his head. "Ladies first, my dear."

"There were two episodes of *Gotta Dance* last Wednesday night. I think Leesa called the Vega house during the second one, *after* Michelle and I had been to see her. She wasn't at the cottage when Rose was assaulted, just like she always claimed."

Mr. P. nodded. "That makes sense."

"How did you figure it out?" I asked.

"Remote-access app."

"That doesn't mean anything to me."

He smiled. "That's all right, my dear. I'll explain." And he did in just two sentences. Then he gestured toward Rose's apartment. "Rosie's waiting."

I held up a finger. "Hang on a minute." I hurried to the bedroom for a moment, then came back. "I'm ready," I said. At my feet Elvis made a rumble of annoyance and squeezed past our legs.

Rose was waiting in the kitchen. I held out the glass jar of muscle rub I'd grabbed from the bedroom. "Smell this."

She took the container from me, unscrewed the top and bent her head over it. Then she looked up, comprehension spreading across her face.

"Did that make you think of those tea chests?" I asked.

"Yes, it did," she said.

"It's anise," I said. "The same thing you remember

from those chests." I took the jar from her. "I get this cream from a little place just around the corner from The Black Bear. I've been using it on my calf muscles after I run. It's wonderful for sore muscles. You know what this means? We can prove who killed Jeff Cameron."

Rose reached over to pat my cheek, a huge smile on her face. "Yes, we can," she said. "And this calls for pie."

I called Nicole Cameron in the morning. There were things she needed to know about her late sister-in-law before we did anything else. She said she'd be home all morning and I told her I'd stop by in about half an hour.

When I walked out to the SUV, Rose was in the front passenger seat and Mr. P. was sitting in the back. I opened the driver's door, folded my arms over my chest and said, "No."

Rose gave me a sweet and slightly condescending smile. "Sweetie, that didn't work when you were four. It's not going to work now."

"I just don't think it's a good idea to go talk to Nicole with an audience," I said.

"You're not going without us," Mr. P. said. "This is the last piece of the puzzle."

I stood there wondering how I could get both of them out of the vehicle.

"You might be able to wrestle one of us out of the car, but you can't take on both of us," Rose said as though she'd read my mind, which I was starting to think might be a legitimate possibility. She smoothed the purple and silver scarf at her neck, the one she'd gotten from rocker Steven Tyler at a concert years ago. "I'm wearing my lucky scarf. Don't fret, dear. Everything is going to be fine."

I tapped the corner of my right eye with one finger. "You see these wrinkles?" I said. "You're giving them to me."

Rose leaned across the seat and squinted at me. "I think you just need to wear a little more sunscreen," she said.

"I'll keep that in mind," I said darkly as I climbed in.

When we arrived at Nicole Cameron's house, Bayley and her friends across the street were working on what seemed to be a scene with the out-of-control beach ball/snowball. When Deb caught sight of us, she walked to the bottom of the driveway.

"I just need a minute to talk to Debra." Mr. P. tapped on my shoulder from the backseat. "I found a little piece of software that I think will work better with her security system. It's the program I was telling you about," he said.

Mr. P. and Mac were working on a new security system for the shop. They'd both laughed at my idea of the sound effect of a dog barking on a constant loop.

"Go ahead," I said. "Rose and I will go talk to Nicole. We won't be long." We started for the front door. Jeff Cameron's Jeep was parked in the driveway, wheels cut hard to the right.

Nicole had seen us and was waiting at the door in a flowered cotton skirt and a white tee. She led us into the living room, which was piled with boxes. A plate with a double-tipped cheese knife, half a pear and a chunk of cheddar sat on the coffee table. "I'm sorry for the mess," she said, gesturing at them. "The rental company is pressing me to get Jeff and Leesa's place cleared out."

"It's all right," I said. "You have a lot to deal with. We won't take much time."

"I'm going to Boston," she said. "I've already put in my resignation at the hospital. Jeff and Leesa's apartment will have to be emptied and there are a lot of things to handle for their estates."

"We understand," Rose said. "I'm sure there are a lot of reminders here of what happened."

Nicole nodded. "On the phone you said you had something for me."

I handed her the box with the two candlesticks. "Your brother bought these the day he . . . died. They're yours now."

"Thank you," she said. She turned the box over in her hands. "I still find it hard to believe Leesa did this. I thought she loved him."

"Did Leesa tell you she'd hired a personal trainer?" Rose asked.

I shot her a warning look.

Nicole frowned. "No. She didn't say anything to me. Why would she hire a trainer?"

"She wanted to run a half marathon," Rose said.

"Jeff could have trained her for that." Two frown lines appeared between her eyes. "Wait a minute. Are you saying you think this trainer could have killed my brother, not Leesa?"

Rose shook her head. "No, dear," she said. "You did."

Chapter 20

That wasn't how I had planned things.

Everything seemed to happen next in slow motion. I moved toward Nicole, and at the same time she snatched the knife off the plate on the coffee table and grabbed Rose, pressing the serrated knife edge to the older woman's neck. I came up short, one hand out in front of me in a stop motion.

"Don't do this," I said hoping she couldn't see my arm shaking. I shouldn't have let Rose and Mr. P. come with me. I should have taken a taxi. Or walked. Or tried to wrestle both of them out of the SUV.

"Back off," Nicole said. Her voice was flat and cold.

I took a step backward and then another one, keeping my eyes locked on Rose's face. She looked completely calm.

"I'm sorry, dear," she said, reaching up to gently pat the arm that was pinning her tight to her captor's body. "I shouldn't have blurted that out. It was rude."

I let my arm drop and tried to calculate whether I

could rush Nicole before she could stab that knife into Rose's neck. The math wasn't in my favor.

"Do you mind if I ask about your grandmother?" Rose said. "You said she raised you."

"Yes," Nicole said.

"She must have loved you very much to take on that kind of responsibility." She turned her head a little. "I have a grandson," she continued. "The light of my life, and if anything happened to his mother and father I'd do the same thing. I couldn't stand thinking about him being raised by strangers."

Nicole's eyes flicked away from my face for a moment. "That's what Nana said. She said we were family and family sticks together." Her face darkened and she tightened the arm around Rose's chest.

"Your brother left when she died."

I saw Nicole swallow hard. "I hate him," she said, her voice suddenly raspy.

Rose sighed softly. "What did he do?" she asked.

She really wanted to know, I realized. She wasn't stalling, trying to buy time. She really wanted to know what had driven Nicole Cameron to murder her brother and his wife.

"It doesn't matter now," Nicole said, so quietly I almost missed the words.

"It matters to you," Rose said.

We stood frozen in place for what seemed like a very long moment. Then Nicole spoke again. "I had to go on a course, away, just for a few days, and Jeff said he would be around. Nana was taking beta-blockers for an irregular heartbeat but she was fine. She could have lived for a long time."

"Oh, child," Rose whispered.

"The doctor said she thought Nana had forgotten to take her pills." A tear trailed down the younger woman's cheek and she swiped it away with her free hand. "She wouldn't have forgotten. There was nothing wrong with her memory." She pressed her lips together for a moment. When she spoke again her voice was stronger. "The day she died, Jeff said she gave him some money and told him to go out and enjoy his life. But . . . but I know she wouldn't have done that. She'd told me that it was time for Jeff to stand on his own two feet. And I knew she didn't have any money. I think . . . think he replaced her pills with something else."

"That's horrible," I said.

"It took me more than a year to settle everything," Nicole continued. "I had to borrow money to have a funeral. I had student loans. I couldn't keep the house. And I didn't even know where Jeff was." She was staring right at me, but it was as if she didn't even see me. "He didn't even show up for the funeral." Her mouth moved and she swallowed. "It wasn't until I was cleaning out the house that I found out about the money." She looked at me. "You know about the money, don't you?"

"Yes," I said.

"It was gone. Every penny of it."

"You'd been waiting a long time to get justice for your grandmother." Nothing in Rose's voice suggested she was in any kind of distress.

"I pretended I didn't suspect anything," Nicole said, and for the first time there was a hint of a smile on her face. "I pretended I was just happy to see Jeff when he came back. Nana always said patience is a virtue. When he told me he was planning on leaving Leesa, I knew it was time."

"You set her up." I shifted my weight from one foot to the other and managed to move a couple of inches closer to Rose.

"Do you have a dog?" Nicole asked.

I shook my head. "I have a cat. Elvis." It seemed to have been the right answer.

"Dogs love you no matter what you do," she said. "You kick them; you don't feed them. They still love you. Leesa was like that—all blind loyalty to someone who didn't deserve it."

"It was you in the pink hoodie," Rose said.

She nodded. "Yes."

"What did you use for the body? I know it actually wasn't your brother."

A hint of the smile again. "A first aid mannequin I borrowed from the hospital. I'm strong. It was easy to pull it across the floor."

"And easy for you to move Jeff," I said. "When you did kill him for real."

"You set me up to see the whole thing," Rose said.

Nicole shifted a little, leaning forward so she was in Rose's line of sight. I took advantage of her shift in attention to move a step closer to them.

"I'm sorry about that," she said. "Jeff told me the story about you and your friend's granddaughter and the cell phone. When he said he was having the candlesticks delivered—kind of a screw-you to Leesa—and was leaving her that night, I knew you showing up without a cell phone would help the plan. I told him not to hit you hard. I knew the methohexital would knock you out long enough for us to leave. I help out at a clinic once a month at a nursing home in Rockport. The dentist uses it with some of the seniors. I thought it was pretty smart of me to take some instead of something from the hospital. I didn't mean for you to get hurt."

"I know you didn't," Rose said.

It felt as though we were doing good cop/bad cop, with Rose in the role of good cop, except really she was just being herself.

"You came up with the plan to frame Leesa," I said. I moved my feet a couple of inches closer. If I could get near enough to them, I was hoping I could knock the knife away from Rose's neck.

"I told Jeff it would buy him some time and then in a few days he could get in touch with someone."

"Leesa really was with you the night of the so-called murder."

Nicole nodded, and it seemed to me she relaxed her grip on Rose just a little. "I put something in her coffee, and when she fell asleep I went over to the cottage."

"You signed in to the hospital's server from your laptop here and used a remote-access app on your phone to connect to the laptop." Mr. P. had explained the process to me.

Yes." Nicole nodded again.

"I don't understand," Rose said. "If you were setting up Leesa for your brother's murder, why did you give her an alibi?"

"Because it also gave you an alibi," I said, keeping

my eyes locked on Nicole's face. "In case anyone questioned whether or not it was actually you doing that refresher course."

"And I needed everyone to think he was alive so I could figure out where he'd stashed Nana's money. I needed to look around the cottage to see if I could find a clue," Nicole said. "But his body turned up sooner than I'd planned for, and somehow Leesa started putting the pieces together." She looked at me. "What was I supposed to do? I had to kill her."

Silence hung between us for a moment. Nicole spoke first. "How did you figure it out?"

"Leesa was training to run a half marathon to surprise your brother."

Nicole shook her head and gave me a wry smile. "She was always trying to do things to make him happy. He wasn't worth it."

"She called the trainer's house looking for him that night. His wife said it was during the show *Gotta Dance*, but there were two episodes for the show that night—one early and one late, at the show's regular time. She was half-asleep when the phone rang and she mixed up the times. When I realized she didn't know there had been two episodes of the show, I remembered you saying that you and Leesa were watching a rerun of *Murder Ink*."

"It wasn't on."

"No." I shifted my weight again and managed to edge forward a little more. Then from the corner of my eye I saw something move in the hallway beyond the living room, a flutter of something pale yellow. Mr. P.'s golf shirt. Good Lord, what was he doing?

All I could think was to keep talking, to keep Nicole Cameron's attention focused in my direction. I pointed at the front window. "The kids across the street were making a movie. In a couple of shots I could make out your sister-in-law's car in the driveway. *You* drove it over to your brother's house. The thing is, when you came back, you turned the front wheels hard to the right, the way you always do with your own."

"I didn't even notice," she said. "We lived on a hill when I first learned to drive. It's a habit I can't seem to break."

Directly behind Rose and Nicole, there was an opening to the hallway, right in my line of sight. Mr. P. appeared there carrying a large glass mixing bowl. He looked at the hand holding the knife to Rose's neck. Then he looked at me. He held up three fingers.

It was crazy and foolish and dangerous and a whole lot of other words. I gave what I hoped was an almost imperceptible nod. Mr. P. held up one finger.

"I'm sorry I had to kill her," Nicole said.

"We know that," Rose said.

"She figured it out. She said she smelled antiseptic on her hoodie and I was the only person she knew who smelled like that." Just the way I'd figured out that it was Jeff Cameron, not Leesa, who had attacked Rose because he smelled like the muscle rub, like licorice.

Mr. P. held up a second finger.

Nicole shook her head. She looked a little sad. "It was her or me and I picked me," she said. "And I'm picking myself now."

Mr. P. held up three fingers and launched himself

forward, raising the glass bowl in the air. At the same time I lunged at Nicole. I grabbed the hand holding the knife as the mixing bowl made contact with the side of her head.

She swayed and I yanked the knife free and threw it across the room. Nicole's eyes rolled back in her head and she crumpled to the floor. Mr. P. dropped the bowl and wrapped his arms around Rose.

Her scarf had fallen to the floor. I picked it up, hands shaking, knelt down and tied Nicole Cameron's hands together behind her back using pretty much every knot I knew. I checked to be sure she was breathing and had a pulse. She did.

I got to my feet. My knees were trembling. "Good aim," I said to Mr. P.

"You, too, my dear," he said.

"Are the police on their way?" I asked.

He nodded. "They should be. I told Debra to call them if I wasn't back in five minutes."

I put a hand on Rose's arm. "Are you all right?" I said.

"Of course I am," she said, her smile encompassing both Mr. P. and me. "I told you everything would work out."

Chapter 21

And just like that, it was over. Michelle arrived right behind the first squad car.

I was standing by the front door. She walked over to me. "Are you all okay?" she asked, searching my face.

I nodded. "We're fine." I cleared my throat. "Nicole Cameron killed her brother and faked his wife's suicide."

She looked around me into the living room. The mixing bowl was upside down on the floor. The box with the candlesticks was on its side on the coffee table. Nicole was sitting up, looking dazed, while a paramedic checked her head, her arms still bound with Steven Tyler's scarf.

Michelle's gaze came back to me. "So you decided to apprehend her with a mixing bowl, a set of candlesticks and a scarf?"

I laughed, partly because I was relieved that Rose was all right and partly because I realized how crazy this all must look to her. "I'm sorry," I said. "The candlesticks were just an excuse so I could come take a look at how Nicole parked her car. And then I was going to call you."

"Oh, well, that explains it all," Michelle said. She sighed. "Don't move. I'm going inside for a few minutes and talk to the first responding officer. Then I'm coming back out and you're going to start at the beginning and tell me everything."

I nodded.

It was lunchtime before we got back to the shop. We told everyone the short version of the story and Mr. P. was hailed as a hero, which in my book he was.

"We're not drinking because it's the middle of the workday," I said. "But I'm going up to put the kettle on so we can have a pot of tea and toast Alfred properly."

I put the kettle on and slumped against the counter, closing my eyes for a moment and rubbing my temples. I looked up to find Mac standing in the doorway.

"Are you really all right?" he asked, walking over to me.

I nodded. "I thought she was going to kill Rose, and then when I saw Mr. P. coming with that big glass bowl, I was afraid she'd turn around and see him and that would be it."

Mac smiled. "Alfred is pretty resourceful. And from what he just told me, he had some help." He looked at me for a long moment. Then he leaned down and kissed my left cheek. "Go get off your feet. I've got this," he said.

I nodded again without speaking and headed for the stairs.

It was Thursday night and the only real way to celebrate on a Thursday night in North Harbor, Maine, was at the jam. So that's what we did. Rose got up and danced with Sam to "Honky Tonk Woman," and as they like to say, the crowd went wild. Even Nick joined us. Sam had an extra guitar and managed to lure Nick onstage for "Me and Bobby McGee."

Everyone was on their feet, singing along with the chorus. Liz put her arm around my shoulders, tipped her head to one side and grinned at me.

"What are you grinning about?" I asked.

She made a sweeping gesture with one hand, taking in everyone from Rose, still dancing with Sam, to Jess beside me. "The fact that all of these people are your family." Then she turned, kissed my cheek and laughed. "And there's not a damn thing you can do about it!"

ABOUT THE AUTHOR

Sofie Ryan is a writer and mixed-media artist who loves to repurpose things in her life and her art. She is the author of *A Whisker of Trouble, Buy a Whisker* and *The Whole Cat and Caboodle* in the *New York Times* bestselling Second Chance Cat Mysteries. She also writes the *New York Times* bestselling Magical Cats Mysteries under the name Sofie Kelly. Visit her online at sofieryan.com.